The Direction of Language — Modern Symptomatology of Texts and Its Critique

Authored by Wu Shenggang

Translated by He Jianyu（贺剑瑜）

The Direction of Language: Modern Symptomatology of Texts and Its Critique
Authored by Wu Shenggang
Translated by He Jianyu（贺剑瑜）
Language: English
Word Count (for space of all pages): Approximately 251,000 words
Publisher: Chicago Academic Press
Number of Pages: 382
ISBN: 978-1-965890-87-5

Publishing	Chicago Academic Press
	5923 N Artesian Ave
	Chicago IL 60659
Email	contact@chicagoacademicpress.com
Website	http://chicagoacademicpress.com/
Book Size	6X9 inches
First Edition	November, 2025

CONTENT

Civilization and Degeneracy — On Issues Raised by Wei Wei's *Strangers* in the City

I

We must confront this reality: globalization deepens relentlessly. Simultaneously, China's development has forged an undeniable truth—the globalized world entwines with China's modernization. In other words, China's modernity and global integration have become inseparable counterparts, achieving increasing synchronicity. Meanwhile, China's small-town development strategy accelerates urbanization, hastening the transition from agrarian civilization to industrial civilization. China's modernization appears synonymous with urbanization. Within this context, the dominance of industrial and urban civilization has become an irreversible trend. As early as the 1980s, driven by rural labor surplus and lured by urban promises, masses of villagers flooded cities in pursuit of new livelihoods, giving rise to a distinct urban cohort: migrant workers. This marked merely an initial phase of urbanization. By the 1990s, a profound shift emerged: those surging into cities were no longer solely laborers from the fields. Intellectuals joined the gold rush to metropolises, while villagers gravitated toward towns, townsfolk toward cities, and residents of smaller cities toward major hubs. This nationwide "mass talent migration" birthed an urban white-collar working class. Indeed, China's urbanization narrative eerily mirrors the historical backdrop of globalization. Just as early industrialization in the West drew laborers from the developing countries, later followed by waves of intellectuals seeking new horizons in America-centric nations, we might conclude that the essence of urban civilization fundamentally compels displacement—a siren call that severs rural roots and sets adrift those who chase the metropolis' spectral allure.

But what of those who entered the cities? What did urban civilization truly mean for them? What toll did it exact upon their bodies, psyches, and souls? Wei Wei's Strangers in the City (published in People's Literature, Issue 10, 2004) traces the journey of Xu Zihui: "Three years in this vast city, and Zihui had changed jobs over a dozen times: copy shops, ad agencies, private bookstores, GRE crash course outlets… all small storefronts along back alleys, barely two or three bays wide. Inside, a hotplate for cooking, a foldable cot. Sometimes, Zihui slept right there at work." "Three years adrift, without fixed abode. She shuffled from the eastern districts to the west, her sole possession a large leather suitcase stuffed with bed sheets and clothes for all seasons. To float in this city demanded austerity. Winters found her in unheated rented rooms, feeding coal into a tiny stove for warmth, going to public bathhouses every few days. One brutal winter, temperatures plunged to minus twenty-odd degrees Celsius. Her stove sputtered out past midnight. Huddled under thin quilts, she and her roommates shivered violently, crammed onto a single bed. Outside, the wind howled. A wan light seeped through the window—Had it snowed? Was day breaking?"

To survive in the metropolis, one must master its rhythms and submit to urban civilization's demands. "She enrolled in a flurry of courses—English, bookkeeping, law self-study programs... all practical skills. A quiet hope flickered within Zihui. Though only a graduate of a secondary normal school, she refused to be diminished. Her plan: spend two or three years earning a college diploma, then a bachelor's degree. Surely then she'd secure respectable work. But in those two or three years, who could say? Perhaps she'd meet a young man, fall in love, marry, gain an apartment, a car. Perhaps emigrate abroad. Perhaps ascend to the heavens. Who could say?" Indeed, the metropolis dazzled: financial hubs, information nexuses, logistics centers; malls, luxury hotels, gated villas; extravagant nights of revelry, perfumed with song and dance. Yet its true siren call lay in the illusion of boundless opportunity—a place where ordinary lives could be magnified overnight. Where the poor might grasp instant fortune, watching wealth pouring in; where the obscure could ignite into sudden meteoric rise to fame, becoming household names. This was the authentic seduction.

Yet such opportunities rarely come easily. For some, they prove stingy, even harsh and cruel, leaving them teetering on the edge of the city. After all, the glittering metropolis operates as a colossal machine in constant high-speed operation. All clamor to board its tracks, but a moment's misstep risks being crushed by its gears. Consider Zihui: three years of struggling to survive in the city, relentlessly learning urban survival skills, adapting to metropolitan rhythms. Still, after changing jobs over a dozen times, she remained rootless, moving between eastern and western districts, perpetually stranded on the periphery. To endure here, they grasped at the most basic solution:

"For migrant women like Xiao Huang and Zihui, the only path to remain in this city was likely marriage. In other words, their relationship with the city was, fundamentally, determined by their relationships with men." Xiao Huang understood this calculus with brutal clarity: "From her first day in the city, she had focused on dealing with men. Her approach was pragmatic: first, no romance—love inevitably ends in separation; second, no physical entanglements unless absolutely necessary." Yet luck eluded her. "Her blind dates came and went in quick succession—men who rejected her, men she rejected." Zihui herself had ventured one romance: "But she sought not the man, but marriage itself. How to make him understand? She needed marriage as desperately as air or water!" Thus, she let down her guard and slept with a man. But the aftermath brought none of her expected outcome. The city spurned them. And the city's men did the same.

To be sure, in an era when material desires escalate while moral values depreciate, certain means of livelihood that violate common norms continue to lurk beneath the surface. Though metropolises shine with glory and dreams, filth and crime may fester in their forgotten corners. Particularly for women, when confronted with the predatory demands pervasive in a male-dominated world, using their bodies as resources often becomes a pathway to wealth and pleasure for some. This is no secret—not even a taboo subject. Zihui understood well that "in today's world, sleeping with someone is hardly a grave matter," and such transactions come effortlessly to young, attractive women.

Yet, in her view, she remained an educated woman with dignity as an educated person. She possessed self-respect, fundamental principles, and boundaries. She believed she could make a living without relying solely on her femininity; through diligent effort, she could surely secure respectable employment. Ultimately, after three years of relentless struggle and perseverance, she realized her dream: becoming an accountant at "a seemingly respectable" Sino-American trading firm, transforming into a veritable urban white-collar professional.

II

It must be said that Xu Zihui scraped and scrambled her way into securing a so-called "respectable job," giving her the right to settle in this city, thrive among the urban white-collar class, and shuttle constantly between upscale apartments, high-rise office buildings, Starbucks, Shidu Mall, and Ginza... Yet the crux lies here: precisely when she gained the qualifications and ability to enter the city's core sphere, an instinctive rejection of this metropolis welled up from the depths of her soul. *"When Zihui first found herself in such opulent surroundings... for some reason, she suddenly longed to return home—back to her small hometown of Ji'an. There lay green mountains and clear waters, where folkways remained pure and simple. That, she felt, was where she truly belonged."* Why this longing to return? Ultimately, Zihui was a product of small-town—even rural—civilization. She had never fully comprehended urban culture; when confronted with genuine integration into metropolitan life, she felt an involuntary inner resistance. If she managed to struggle on for three years, it was because those years of tumultuous striving allowed her, to some extent, to manifest traces of her authentic self. But once fate shifted and she could no longer express the true self, she could only return to where she came from.

Indeed, the incongruity between her and this city—between her and urban civilization—was palpable to Zihui, both externally and internally. First, she never truly understood why she had come to this metropolis. "She dimly realized that all these years, leaving her homeland and drifting through strange cities had served no concrete purpose—perhaps merely for the sake of leaving." Over the past two decades, China has been consumed by a mass migration craze. People hauled their families across provinces, yelling and bustling, migrating from native soil to foreign cities, then onward to yet another foreign land. Their faces flushed crimson with ideals and fervor, twisted beyond recognition. Peasants, factory workers, civil servants, petty intellectuals, university professors, the elderly, children—China had gone mad, each soul chasing pipe dreams.* Unwittingly, she too had been swept along by the current—whether by inner restlessness, yearning for the metropolis, or the latent drive to bridge disparities. Second, she had never genuinely grasped this city or its civilization. In her former understanding, metropolises were places of glamour, clamor, excess, romance, and passion. Yet upon entering this realm, she found that splendor and romance were not for everyone. For Xu Zihui, what she felt most acutely was isolation, neglect, and destitution.

She imagined the city would bring wealth, elevate status, and bestow dignity—but in reality, "she merely existed day after day: adrift, destitute and lowly, submissive. The poverty of a great city, in truth, proved even worse than in small towns..." Thirdly, the metropolis never truly welcomed her. Having drifted through this sprawling city for three years, Zihui diligently learned how to survive in the city, yet she remained rootless. Even as families reunited during the Spring Festival, she remained huddled in a dim corner of the city. Refusing to succumb to such desolation, "she forced herself and visited the Temple of Heaven fair. The pale sun hung in the sky, the cold unrelenting. Moving through the crowds, she was surrounded by strangers... After wandering aimlessly, she soon retreated." In a daze, she approached a courtyard dwelling in a hutong. "A young woman emerged, looking at her suspiciously." Before the gate could close, "Zihui suddenly started running wildly... She felt utterly crazed, burned with shame and fury." Nor did acceptance come when she secured her dream job. While apartment-hunting with Xiao Huang, Granny Li subjected them to relentless interrogation, finally, "still muttering: 'It's not that I distrust you outsiders, but the world's so treacherous nowadays. At my age, can I afford not to be cautious?'" After shutting the door, "Xiao Huang spat toward the hallway: 'That crone thinks we're in that line of work.'" Fourthly, her parents' strong distrust of urban civilization persistently eroded her resolve to settle in the metropolis. From the moment she left their small town, their hearts clutched at phantom terrors—for in their eyes, the city was not a place of opportunity. The gossip they heard confirmed their belief: urban survival demanded moral compromise, and even a girl as untainted as their daughter carried a 120% likelihood of corruption—their anxiety inflating probabilities beyond reason. "One evening, while on the phone with her mother, the sound of a broken liquor bottle erupted outside, followed by a man's drunken sobbing. Her mother tensed: 'Who's crying?'" "Zihui replied casually: 'A migrant worker next door had too much to drink.'" "Her mother's shrill cry pierced the line: 'You're living alongside migrant workers?!'" "After a choked pause, her mother sobbed: 'What are you doing there?... You're a teacher... We're a decent family.'" To the mother, her daughter had clearly been tainted by the city's corruption—a descent into moral decay. Henceforth, unexpected check-up calls came weekly. Once, when an old colleague visited, Zihui's laughter seeped into the call. "Her mother asked warily: 'Is someone with you?'" Zihui denied it, but "her mother's voice turned stern: 'Xu Zihui, you're lying. That was a man's voice... I've lived honorably my whole life—I won't have you throwing it away.'" "Everyone had grounds to doubt her, to interrogate her. She was an outsider, poor, and worse—she possessed a body. Her mother's implication hung thick in the air, all but articulated. Shame washed over Zihui." Fifthly, her hometown had become an inescapable physiological and psychological imprint. Though part of the modern younger generation, Zihui was deeply rooted in Ji'an. Its landscapes, customs, and rhythms had seeped into her, etching themselves into her marrow as defining traits of her identity. In her memory, Ji'an existed as a realm where—

Flagstone paths wound along stepped stone stairways; old houses stood with blue-gray brick walls and white plaster... all steeped in a classical Chinese painting's tranquility. Courtyards were shaded by camphor, locust, and banyan trees. Beyond the rear windows flowed crystal-clear streams—water pure enough to drink, to launder by, its murmurs echoing through the night. Ji'an, an ancient town in Jiangxi province, clung to its unadorned essence, where life unfolded in quiet rhythms, household after household, year upon year.

To put it plainly, Ji'an was a place of contradictions: poor yet wealthy; brimming with restless modernity yet cradling an otherworldly serenity. Its landscapes shifted from picturesque with clear waters and green mountains to barren mountains and treacherous waters; its folkways mingled raw simplicity with country shrewdness. She loved her hometown even as she resented it. One thing Zihui had to face: across all these years and miles, Ji'an had dwelled within her heart. In some profound sense, she had never left.

She was like a kite floating in the wind—soaring yet eternally bound by the tug of its tether. In essence, her hometown functioned as an emotional filter: all her agitation, anxiety, pain, and shame, even her fury, dissolved into tranquility, into nothingness, when soothed by Ji'an's scenery and rhythms.

III

The most striking revelation upon interpreting *Strangers in the City* crystallizes around the text's central revelation.

The fundamental tension in this work manifests through the concept of "alienness". Zihui's urban exile reflects not her personal failings, but rather the pathologies of the city itself. Revisiting our initial analytical framework: under the twin forces of globalization and modernization, the metropolis has ceased to embody humanity's aspirational—let alone poetically habitable—space. Its very functionality mutates; every facet of urban existence undergoes ontological distortion. Foremost, propelled by the historical march of market-driven modernization, metropolises have rapidly transformed into massive marketplaces. Within these spaces, logistics, information streams, capital flows, human tides, and sensory bombardments—intertwined with cutthroat competition, ruthless undercutting, bull markets, bear markets, overnight windfalls, and catastrophic bankruptcies—form the metropolis's sensitive nerve center. The market's fundamental role in resource allocation now extends far beyond material distribution; it infiltrates every urban domain. Every facet of the city, including its inhabitants, is chained to the market mechanisms. Human relationships are inevitably marketized; thus, gaining entry into this realm necessitates forging market-driven transactional bonds. Secondly, urban strata have undergone profound fragmentation. In market-driven metropolises, economic diversification manifests most intensely, spawning equally varied distribution models. We fully acknowledge the deterministic role of economic foundations: the rise of nouveau riche elites and impoverished groups stems directly from this multiplicity of economic structures and allocation mechanisms. The reshuffling of urban classes entails a radical redefinition of identity and status—effectively overturning and reconstructing the old urban order, inevitably fracturing the psychic fabric of its inhabitants. Thus, certain disorders or schisms in the urban spiritual order are comprehensible. Thirdly, the metropolis has forfeited its vanished purity. Chinese cities in the early 20th century were indeed realms of decadent neon-lit revelry. Post-1949, the nascent state engineered a radical purification, excising the soil of corruption, erecting a new order where *danwei* (note: Mao-era socioeconomic cells providing lifetime employment and controlling housing/healthcare, forming the bedrock of urban social organization) belonged to the state, individuals belonged to their danwei, and social identities ossified into fixed-class monoliths. Yet the post-1980 reforms shattered this planned economy, loosening the umbilical tether between individuals and danwei. Urban control faltered; floating populations surged inward, causing the urban fabric to expand rapidly. Concurrently, global integration accelerated the city's metastatic complexity. Fourthly, the metropolis now throbs with feverish acceleration—decibels rising, cacophony swelling, its *hothouse effect* (note: Metaphor for urban environments that amplify competitive pressure and sensory overload, eroding individual agency.) intensifying as social pressures cook human resilience.

Yet this mutated urban anatomy—its structures, processes, and rhythms—is precisely the “modern civilization” touted with relish by its inhabitants. Such dissonance inevitably provokes skepticism: Does the reality of China’s metropolises truly embody modernity’s essence or trajectory? This question haunts many within its vortex. Crucially, however, our inquiry must shift focus from the city’s form to its human consequences. Studies reveal a significant minority of urbanites suffer clinical depression, anxiety disorders, or adrenal fatigue syndrome; another survey identifies the 30-40 age bracket as the most pressure-crushed demographic within the urban workforce. This data holds diagnostic significance, piercing the veil of civilizational triumphalism. If urban dwellers are fundamentally products of metropolitan civilization, then the youth are its purest progeny, whether native-born or drawn by its siren call. When the life it offers becomes unbearable, it signals that metropolitan high-pressure exceeds human tolerance. More critically, it radically reconstitutes human existence: identities, statuses, and destinies mutate overnight. One may strike sudden wealth, owning homes and cars, ascending socially or even geographically, as Xu Zihui once dreamed. Equally possible is freefall into destitution, perched on the precipice of despair. Urban restructuring accelerates this *schismogenesis* (note: Anthropological term describing accelerated social polarization through feedback loops, here applied to urban class fragmentation), catapulting some into affluence while plunging others into the precariat. Confronting such life-changing moments, individuals must grapple with reality's gauntlet. Responses diverge: constructive resistance forges self-actualized beings; corrosive surrender breeds spectral existences. In the liminal space between humanity and specter, indeterminacy thrives—rendering the moral value of urban civilization fundamentally unquantifiable, and thus perpetually suspect.

Thus, we cannot dismiss the gnawing anxiety of Zihui's mother or Granny Li's interrogations as mere paranoia. Moreover, the metropolis now casts its elongated shadow upon towns and villages—Ji'an's commercial district mirrors the city's neon excess: "shops jostle shoulder-to-shoulder: hair salons, foot-massage parlors, saunas, karaoke clubs, even star-rated hotels and department stores. Enter this street, and every inch of the human body finds commodified solace. By nightfall, women of varied attire line the sidewalks." Is this civilization or decay? Their unease echoes far beyond two fretful women. For every migrant child in the city, there exists a family gripped by visceral dread, especially for daughters. Urban legends about young women proliferate, while the city's temptations shimmer with treacherous ambiguity. In the planned-economy era, urban entry meant securing a *Tiefanwan* (note: a state-guaranteed system of lifetime employment and social benefits emblematic of China's pre-reform industrial era)—a guaranteed ascent into respectability. Today's migrants must wield their survival arsenal to claw forward: accumulating capital, securing footholds. Yet the origins of their wealth face relentless scrutiny—were the means clean? The methods just? For women, such suspicions crystallize with cruel plausibility. Mention a young woman's urban livelihood, and minds conjure karaoke lounges, beauty spas, saunas—lexicons of the flesh. By implication, their banknotes bear invisible stains. Through the lens of traditional rural values, human actions and their moral weight eclipse material gain—"saving face trumps filling pockets" remains the sacred calculus. Thus, when Zihui returned home with conspicuous luggage, her parents' suspicions didn't abate; they metastasized. To them, her poverty would have signaled purity; her apparent prosperity reeked of corruption. They subjected her to a forensic inquisition: demanding a minute-by-minute account of three years, rifling through her suitcase to inspect each bra, panty, and negligee. These silken trophies—evidence of comfortable living and "vulgar" tastes—became evidence in their trial of fallen womanhood. Zihui's attempts at self-defense were thwarted; though she played the virtuous daughter, they whispered "prostitute" behind her back. Under their relentless barrage, even her selfhood fractured—she began doubting her own body's history, as if her flesh bore invisible ledgers of sin.

What, then, does the text ultimately articulate? If it speaks of urban civilization, that civilization carries within it a self-devouring corruption. Yet the line between progress and decay remains profoundly nebulous—a liminal haze that leaves Xu Zihui adrift in existential vertigo. Strangers in the City stands as a problem novel for the new millennium. Within its concise frame, it dissects the problems developing through Chinese society: market reforms liberated productive forces and rapid economic growth, but must civilizational "advancement" always demand tribute in dehumanization? Like the double-edged sword of capitalism itself, does every gain in material progress sever another thread of our human fabric? To reframe through Marx's lens: has alienation (Entfremdung), once diagnosed in 19th-century factories, now replicated itself in China's glittering metropolises? The novel offers no facile answers—its power lies in weaponizing these questions to pierce our complacency. Herein resides its significance: not as a sociological treatise, but as a powerful stimulus igniting critical consciousness.

Postmodern Poetics in Contemporary Chinese Literature — The Postmodern Metaphysics of Li Rui's *Ploughshare* (Li Hua)

Li Rui's short fiction *Ploughshare* (*October* Magazine, 2006 No.2), though a mere 6,000 words, condenses profound artistic and philosophical resonance. Its narrative simplicity belies conceptual density: Baosheng, a farmhand from China's vanishing countryside, frames through his monologue a searing allegory of modernity's violence. The core tableau unfolds at Beijing's Peach Blossom Golf Resort beneath the Yanshan Mountains: *"Weed-pullers crouch in single file, straw hats shielding bent heads. Each clutches a burlap sack, eyes scanning turf as hands dart down to uproot intruders. Under the blistering sun, their silhouettes crawl across manicured slopes—a procession of human snails grazing an emerald sea."* Juxtaposed against this labor spectacle stands a bronze statue: Old Manjin and Liuye frozen mid-plough beside a pine. Their presence is haunted by an artificial soundscape—recordings of Wurenping's water murmurs, wind sighs, cockcrows, dog-barks, cattle bells, forest whispers, children's laughter, and Manjin's field chants—all drowned by the roar of engineered waterfalls. The text's crucial revelation: how this facsimile of rural life vanishes instantaneously, exposing the void beneath modernity's stagecraft.

I. Primal Consciousness and Civilized Symbols

Golf originated in 15th-century Scotland, where shepherds used their herding sticks (crooks) to hit stones in informal competitions for distance and accuracy. This game gradually evolved into modern golf. The term "golf" derives from the Dutch word kolf (meaning "club"), later poeticized as symbolizing "a good life amidst green spaces and fresh air." Thus golf became a refined outdoor pastime, though its expensive equipment also earned it the label "the sport of nobles."

At its origin, golf existed merely as shepherds' unconscious pastime—a primal game whose motivation, chosen terrain, and form embodied unadulterated simplicity. Yet as it evolved into modern golf, the game accumulated layers of codified civilization—transforming into a purpose-driven activity meticulously bound by human-imposed order. Yet all civilized practices maintain a commemorative bond with primitive origins, using this connection to interpret civilization's essence. Golf achieves this through landscape replication: though modern balls and clubs bear no resemblance to stones and herding sticks, designers meticulously recreate pastoral environments to preserve the game's rustic spirit. The contradiction lies here: true wilderness cannot be relocated into civilized spaces. Given golf courses' vast land requirements and specific natural conditions—undulating terrain, water features, particular grass species—they inevitably become artificially crafted simulations, never authentic duplicates of the shepherds' stone-hitting games on Scotland's wind-swept moors.

Nonetheless, golf courses stand as defining symbols of humanity's drive to replicate civilization. Humanity sprang from nature's womb—indeed, humans remain woven into its fabric—yet since digging pit dwellings and kindling hearth fires, humanity has step by step widened the chasm between itself and the natural world, advancing toward civilization until human existence no longer harmonizes with nature; even when longing for wilderness awakens within humans, they appease this desire with artificially replicated nature, consoling themselves with illusions. Why does humanity simulate and duplicate nature? Ultimately, as a biological species, humans remain perpetually bound to nature through past, present, and future, their lifeblood pulsing with indelible primal consciousness—a primordial yearning for origins; but replicated wilderness and manufactured ecosystems, however convincing, are but symbolic constructs of civilization, never true nature. Golf courses exist as semiotic constructs—their signified simulates the shepherds' stone-striking game, promising immersion in pristine wilderness to rekindle primal joy; their signifier, however, delivers only a curated recreational commodity, a sterile cipher that gestures toward nature while remaining fundamentally algorithmic.

Symbolization has become integral to postmodern civilization. China currently inhabits a hybrid space where modernity and postmodernity coexist, yet core features of the latter emerge distinctly: alienation proliferates, reshaping human existence and sensibility; material abundance and incessant stimuli unleash insatiable desires, culminating in humanity's subjugation to objects; intellectual mediocrity and cognitive fragmentation breed collective unconsciousness—spiritual escapism, dormant souls, culture reduced to mass entertainment and vulgarity. Crucially, our lived world undergoes relentless symbolization. Technological advances, media saturation, instant communication, digital networks, and advertising inflation enable mass replication—transforming reality not merely into symbols but binary digits. When consumption, sensory experiences, or even physiological pleasures like gratification are sought, button-pressing and keystrokes suffice. Golf courses, though simulating nature, function as pure semiotic constructs. Players immersed in golf, unaware of its shepherd-origins, never associate it with crook-wielding herders striking stones. Thus, golf's *signifié* represents humanity's yearning for primal consciousness, while its *signifiant* manifests as a quintessential postmodern signifier.

II. Fabricated Realities and Genuine Illusions

Undeniably, the novel presents a viscerally authentic depiction. Whether depicting the weed-pullers on the lawn, the immaculate turf of the golf course, or the meticulously crafted scenery—"these slopes were engineered: 80% Kentucky bluegrass, 20% ryegrass sown at seven grams per square meter. Workers cleared trees, stripped topsoil, laid drainage pipes, then spread sand mixed with zeolite, peat, and fertilizer... Watering, seeding, rewatching—forty days of intensive cultivation forge this standardized green." Turf farming echoes agricultural rituals, prompting General Manager Chen to install bronze statues of Manjin and Liuye plowing beside pines atop the slope—"frozen mid-labour with oxen and ploughshare, seeding the earth beneath pines"—attempting to evoke nostalgia for agrarian authenticity. Yet growing turf diverges fundamentally from farming crops. Farmers cultivate life-sustaining grains through fluid, intuitive rhythms; turf technicians engineer ornamental grass via rigid protocols—a plant that grows wild in rural landscapes, demanding no such suffering. Had Manjin and Liuye understood this sculptor's intent, they would never have stood there in vacant stillness, doing a job that was not their own trade.

In truth, the golf course turf serves merely as staged backdrop, and the statues of Manjin and Liuye function as cultural signifiers, for authentic primordial ecology cannot be conjured through such curated fragments; though modern society remains deceived by semiotic saturation, this very deception fuels deepening existential yearning for unmediated wilderness. General Manager Chen—a former sent-down youth who labored in Wurenping—understands modernity's allure while intuiting primordial landscapes' psychic hold on human memory, thus endeavoring to transplant his remembered Wurenping into Peach Blossom Golf Resort. Returning personally with recording equipment, he digitally cloned Wurenping's ecology: "Twin pines stand shoulder-to-shoulder like fraternal pagodas, anchoring the lawn's left flank... hidden speakers erupt: water's rush, wind's sigh, cockcrow, dog-bark, basso moos and bronze chimes, forest's roar and fluted birdsong, children's laughter, Manjin's field chants—all cascade in ecologically dissonant yet hauntingly beautiful choruses." This technologically resurrected Wurenping achieves virtual indistinguishability from reality—even those who knew the original village might mistake this engineered nostalgia for true wilderness unless scrutinizing every slope, tree, and gesture with forensic intensity.

Naturally, Chen's semiotic reconstruction of Wurenping extends beyond mere replication; he caters to modernity's yearning for stylized emptiness, perfecting his symbolic universe. "Emerald oaks and maples cascade from ridge crests, their broad leaves punctuated by larches' somber spires. Beneath these arboreal giants sprawl thickets of tangled shrubs, yielding to dense grasses that surge downhill until halted by a granite escarpment—where a spring bursts through verdant waves to plunge as a nine-foot-wide, six-*zhang*-deep (note: Traditional Chinese length unit. 1zhang ≈3.3 meters) cataract. Sunlight ignites the torrent, shattering Peach Blossom Pool's jade stillness into mist-shrouded thunder... Beyond the pool, valley slopes unfurl like velvet carpets, where serpentine streams etch calligraphic curves through undulating fairways. Scattered along these aqueous veins, golden sand traps and silver lakes glint like jewelled inlays. This Taohua Stream, emerging from cloud-wreathed peaks, manifests as a dream conjured from the Yanshan Mountains' soul." Wurenping is grafted onto the golf resort; valleys and waterfalls are grafted onto Wurenping; all are grafted onto modern existence. Indisputably, the golf course, Wurenping, valleys, and cataracts form interlocking semiotic chains in Chen's curated cosmos of desire.

Whether as a symbolic system or an artificially constructed spectacle, all of this undeniably exists before modern individuals as tangible reality; yet this reality is fundamentally fabricated. When immersed within it, one confronts neither the authentic Wurenping nor the primordial valley and waterfall. "The moment the power fails, the waterfall vanishes, the river ceases to flow, and the myriad sounds emanating from the loudspeakers abruptly halt. As it stands now, all vitality dissipates, rendering the entire world artificial." Reality transmutes into illusion. The crux lies in its nature as a false authenticity: it transmits erroneous signals to consumers, inevitably eliciting counterfeit experiences. Consequently, it induces pervasive sensory confusion—an ambiguity between truth and fabrication, a fusion of the real and the illusory—that constitutes the postmodern condition of contemporary existence.

III. Postmodern Logic and Paradoxes of Reality

The work fabricates an authentic illusion, replicating a symbolic system—indeed, a disordered and erroneous one. Yet this illusion and symbolic framework remain vital to modern individuals. Foremost, multitudes consume it through modern civilizational practices, seeking lived experiences: "Beijing is not Wurenping; a golf club bears no resemblance to rural life. A membership card demands 300,000 yuan in fees. In Wurenping, to earn that sum, you'd need to cultivate two millennia's corn yield on one *mu* (approx. 0.067 hectares) of land, or two centuries' harvest across ten *mu*. Generations of relentless toil would scarcely suffice." Baosheng now comprehends: one cannot measure Beijing against the countryside, daylight against darkness, heaven against earth, much less dreams against tangible realities. Regardless of this experience's authenticity or its exorbitant cost, such symbolic stimulation and gratification appear indispensable—it has, in essence, become integral to contemporary existence. Fundamentally, however illusory this spectacle may be, we must regard it as real, for modernity necessitates it. It functions simultaneously as an object of consumption and an enterprise of wealth accumulation—a means of subsistence. Here, rigorous valuation proves unnecessary; closer scrutiny of its operative logic even less so. What persists must possess rationality: we cannot dismantle modern lived realities, thus we cannot alter the existential logic of symbolic systems. Consequently, when the impossible materializes, the tension between history and reality may fail to sustain correspondence or coherence.

In another sense, this fabricated spectacle and symbolic system function as vital subsistence resources. "The lawn serves as the facade of every golf course; its quality dictates the venue's reputation. People here depend on turf for their livelihood—thus, at Taohua Tan, we cultivate grass, not crops." Beyond Manager Chen, who naturally treats the golf course as a cash cow, peasants like Baosheng have abandoned food crop cultivation to tend golf course turf. Though performing identical agricultural labor through established practices, their yield transforms from tangible sustenance into semiotic commodity—symbolic turf sustaining artificial existence. The fundamental labor —

sustenance (food) — survival paradigm, representing authentic human existence, has mutated into labor — turf (symbol) — survival, epitomizing virtual reality. This compels modernity to discard authenticity for virtuality, signaling profound human metamorphosis—prompting essential inquiries: What drives modern humanity? What defines purposeful being? These questions permeate practical and spiritual realms, where conduct, praxis, and life purposes inextricably intertwine. Crucially, value assessments—whether applied to practical actions or spiritual pursuits—must derive from substantive authenticity, not virtual constructs, for they directly shape societal value orientation and decisively mold contemporary worldviews. Consequently, the inherent disorder of postmodern existence inevitably induces existential disorientation, rendering modern individuals' confusion regarding their purpose and actions fundamentally inescapable.

The title *Plowshare* carries profound symbolic resonance. Both the plowshare itself and Manjin, its operator, function merely as relics—artifacts devoid of utility on golf courses or within modern society. Their presence solely evokes nostalgia for traditional existence and primordial consciousness. As an agricultural tool sustaining Chinese civilization for millennia, the plowshare embodies ancestral survival, historical continuity, and agrarian heritage. Yet following modernity's advent—particularly mechanized farming—its significance has progressively diminished. Reduced to a historical signifier, its obsolescence demarcates the demise of traditional life. Though the land sustaining us endures and human existence persists, plowshare-tilling has vanished. Modern lifestyles have undergone fundamental transformation. When experiencing modernity through traditional sensibilities, or vice versa, we confront an irreconcilable rupture. Yet we inhabit this schism: reality generates profound disorientation. The plowshare remains tangible (it once guaranteed bountiful harvests); tradition feels familiar—yet modernity compels their relinquishment. Conversely, the turf is fabricated, the symbols virtual—yet we must enter and embrace them. This constitutes postmodernity's inescapable logic-reality paradox.

The author employs concise language to present Baosheng's perspective, unfolding through his observations and feelings. Baosheng's mind holds memories of the past and hopes for the future, experiences of hardship and dreams of illusions. Yet these thoughts remain fragmented: his present connects weakly to his past; Taohuatan shares little with Wurenping. Facing this fabricated reality and Manager Chen—who markets postmodern lifestyles—whether Baosheng can grasp his future remains uncertain.

All the Nights in the World: Death Narrative and Literary Value

Death constitutes an inevitable conclusion to human existence. Yet as a narrative resource in literature, death remains underutilized, for it invariably signifies misfortune, misery, sorrow, and despair—hardly suitable for bearing humanity's aesthetic ideals or embodying future hopes. Although death is a reality humans must confront, particularly during eras of violent social upheaval where it looms as both dire threat and commonplace occurrence, literary history seldom features death narratives. In peaceful times, such expressions grow scarcer; understandably, humanity has always hesitated to articulate death's obliteration of hope. Nevertheless, Chi Zijian's novella *All the Nights in the World* (Zhongshan, No. 3, 2005; winner of the Fourth Lu Xun Literary Award) intentionally engages death narrative, compelling us to appreciate its literary value.

I. Chi Zijian's Approach to Death Narrative

Undoubtedly, Chi Zijian possesses profound personal insight into death. Her husband's fatal car accident inflicted immense trauma, unleashing turbulent emotions that compelled her not only to confront mortality but to channel tremendous spiritual energy into narrating death.

Death narratives may adopt varied approaches. The simplest—often the least effective—involves naturalistic depictions of death scenes and bloodshed, evoking terror rather than aesthetic resonance. Chi Zijian, however, presents death merely as phenomenon and fact, focusing on its seismic impact upon human lives and psyches.

The story naturally begins with "my" grief. The magician was hit and killed by a *lame donkey* at the Fangzhouyuan crossing. From that moment, the once devoted couple was torn apart by death. Life changed instantly, like one of the magician's tricks. For "me," reality became emptiness—nothingness, an unavoidable journey. This life-changing event happened just because a donkey needed to pee. It shows that even death—life's most serious event—often has no grand design.

Death, as a pivotal human experience, manifests distinct impacts across life stages. The adage of humanity's three profound misfortunes—orphaned youth, widowed midlife, bereft old age—precisely captures death's uniquely devastating blows at different junctures. Widowhood makes "I" feel having "lost the world's most cherished gift." Yet death, having reshaped existence, cannot halt life itself; "I" must break free from its grip. The author charts the narrator's path forward: folkloric research at Sanshan Lake to "collect folk songs and ghost stories." This narrative design reveals death as one thread in life's tapestry, while folk perspectives on mortality—steeped in historical depth and primordial life significance—offer authentic enlightenment and transcendence.

The author enables "me" to gain deeper insights into death and its impact on the living through folkloric fieldwork. When heavy rain interrupted "my" trip to Sanshan Lake, "I" disembarked at Wutang. This coal-mining region also witnesses frequent deaths. Unexpectedly, mortality confronted "me" directly—so commonplace it barely surprises. The real issue lies in the hidden stories behind these deaths. The narrative involves multiple deaths: "my" husband, Jiang Bai, Chen Shaochun, the food stall owner's wife, Yunling's mother, plus unreported mining fatalities and ghost-story deaths.

Among all deaths, Jiang Bai's draws the keenest attention. His should have been a straightforward mining fatality—yet no trace of him was ever found, dead or alive. Wild rumors spread; his widow behaved bizarrely; even her dog searched for him relentlessly. His death became an insoluble puzzle. This very mystery forged Widow Jiang's unique understanding of mortality. It is "I"—the narrator—who uncovers the truth. Our shared grief and Widow Jiang's strangeness drove "me" to her home. On "a night cool as water," "I" stepped uninvited across her threshold. Yet two widows bound by tragedy felt no kinship—instead, she "shivered violently" at "my" intrusion. Only liquor lowered her guard. When "Widow Jiang passed out drunk," "I" took the brass key from her waist. Behind the "gloomy black padlock" lay a room of about eight square meters. No bed, no chairs—only white walls and tightly drawn white curtains. A dim bulb hung "like a withered pear," casting pallid light in the solemn space. Lifting the humming freezer lid revealed the secret:

A swirl of white frosty mist spiraled out like fog. As the vapor cleared, I beheld a truly hellish sight: a man with a severely disfigured face sat crouched inside, legs bent, arms crossed, head slightly bowed. On his knees rested a yellow miner's helmet, as if in deep contemplation. His blue cloth garments were coated with a thick layer of frost; snow and ice clung to his hair, resembling a figure seated at the foot of an iceberg. Without question, this was Jiang Bai. Finally, I understood why Widow Jiang became hysterical during power outages, why Jiang Sansheng gazed at the sky from rooftops. I also grasped why the promoted official in Wutang feared Widow Jiang: Jiang Bai's staged disappearance served as their ladder to promotion and ennoblement. By deliberately not designating him the tenth fatality, they evaded mandatory reporting of the accident—systematically downplaying its severity. No wonder Widow Jiang dreaded nights, drank herself into stupors, sought men to chastise her. With this frozen mountain ever present, she would never feel warmth. Her existence was condemned to a never-ending night.

The work narrates not death itself, but the stories behind it; death is tragic, yet greater tragedies exist beyond it. Jiang Bai's disappearance transcends mere mortality, just as Widow Jiang's agony exceeds spousal bereavement—concealing an absurdity that upends humanity itself.

The novel further depicts diverse deaths across multiple dimensions, each victim meeting distinct ends: Old Chen Shaochun perished when a picture frame crushed him while embellishing a peony painting for Niu Zhen's mother; the food stall owner's wife died under a veterinarian's care after desperately seeking treatment for dysentery; Yunling's mother succumbed to rabies from a casual scratch by her pet dog. Through these varied and frequent deaths, the author reveals death's indiscriminate nature—it spares no one, yet human resilience remains unbroken. What truly terrifies are the deliberate burdens imposed upon mortality. Liberation from such darkness has thus become humanity's collective aspiration.

Though the work does not deliberately depict death, the emotions evoked, the tonal palette, and the atmospheric density unmistakably convey death's gravity and its profound psychological impact. The novella remains steeped in dim, yellowish hues throughout—from the magician husband's demise in "the dimly lit night" to Wutang's chromatic essence: "Wutang's palette is ashen-yellow. All high-rises wear earthy yellow exteriors, while cottages crouch in gray." As "the light fades, this town resembles cold tea left overnight, exuding staleness." Even Wutang's street names—Green Clay Lane, Sunset Alley, Moonlit Tree Street—sound "bestowed by a weather-beaten yet romantic old scholar sitting under twilight." Notably, Revival Lane appears antiquated and dull. The narrator "I" mostly moves through nocturnal scenes, where moonlit vistas amplify her grief—tears and sorrow dissolve more readily into darkness.

The author's death narrative intertwines with folk songs, folktales, and ghost stories—a tradition deeply rooted in classical Chinese literature. Works like *Journey to the West*, *The Investiture of the Gods*, and particularly *Strange Tales from a Chinese Studio* epitomize this narrative legacy. Here lies a crucial metaphor: traditional storytelling divides existence into the world of the living (yangjian) and the realm of the dead (yinjian). The latter extends the former—death becomes life's continuation. In folk narratives, life and death, human and ghost, are but two states of being. Folkloric texts serve as potent testaments to life's indestructibility: death is merely a threshold where existence transforms. Mourning rituals—tears, wailing—become ceremonies celebrating this transition. Such storytelling satisfies the author's intellectual pursuit, achieving spiritual transcendence.

II. The Literary Value of Death Narratives

Death, as a literary subject, proves both unavoidable and inexhaustible—for literature, being the study of humanity, must reveal human existence in its multifaceted dimensions. While death marks the end of physical life, it does not constitute absolute termination. Humans, as dynamic beings, generate enduring spiritual and intellectual impacts that outlast biological cessation. This explains why Western religious philosophy interprets death as ascension to heaven, while Chinese tradition frames it as descent into the underworld—both ultimately affirming life's continuity. Herein lies the revelation: whether perceived or actual, life and death are dual states of being. Just as one's humanity manifests through biological existence, so too does it refract through mortality. Thus, literary depictions of death transcend futility.

More crucially, death profoundly impacts human existence, striking at the souls and psyches of the living. Human society persists through an unbroken chain of cause and effect—philosophically, death nurtures new life and progress. Yet for the living, death remains an unflinching mirror: when confronted with solemn scrutiny, it inevitably reflects existential dilemmas, whether universal or personal. Indeed, attitudes toward the deceased most fundamentally reveal one's humanity. Reactions to mortality vary wildly—fear, grief, composure, even cold calculation or hidden schemes. These divergent responses form a unique lens through which we examine the human soul.

Fundamentally, in human perception, the living and the dead, humans and spirits, constitute tangible and intangible realms. The tangible world is empirically verifiable, grounded in concrete evidence, while virtual domains like heaven or hell elude sensory proof—their perception demands spiritual devotion and moral purity. This very intangibility grants boundless narrative possibilities. In *All the Nights in the World*, Chi Zijian harnesses death's liminal nature. Anchored by her visceral grief, she claims authoritative interpretation of mortality, wielding death as both mirror to reality and gavel to the soul—achieving profound literary transcendence.

By transforming "my" husband—killed in a car crash—into a magician, the author casts a layer of magic over "my" existence. His conjuring arts once infused life with boundless joy, rendering his death an illusion—as if he had merely performed one final trick, vanishing momentarily from "my" sight. "I wonder if my magician hides behind the clouds, gazing at me tenderly as before. Do the sun and moon glow so radiantly because they've absorbed countless departed eyes? A wisp of cloud, light as goose down, reminds me of our happiest marital days." This blurring of reality and fantasy births infinite longing and bottomless grief. "My" magical perception, mirrored by the author's fantastical narration, becomes a spiritual demarcation of death—and ultimately, the aesthetic framework of the work itself.

The significance of death lies precisely in its capacity to evoke multilayered human responses. Folk conceptions of mortality embody these complex emotions, reflecting communal interpretations and value judgments. Within this expansive *cultural field* persists immense tension—a space where individual deaths are contextualized, and their ripples gradually stilled. Thus, the narrator's anguish over the magician's death finds catharsis through folkloric channels. In Wutang, ghost stories recounted by Granny Shi and the broom-selling girl articulate vernacular wisdom: death is stripped to its essence, revealing life's inherent suffering and moral clarity—*evil repaid with evil, good with good.* This folk philosophy, both pragmatic and transcendent, ultimately affirms ethical ideals. This elevates our understanding of death: while it inflicts profound wounds, and while evil deaths may be deserved, virtuous deaths need not be overly mourned—for they serve as revelations, awakening us to truths that command reverence even in the void. Old Chen Shaochun's mournful folk songs constitute precisely such ritual elegy for mortality. His ballads, all dirges locals call "funeral tunes," are deemed ill-omened by the living; yet for death itself, they form the purest rite. "I died once in my youth," Chen recounted. "A spooked horse-cart trampled me—I lay comatose for twenty days... When I awoke, haunting melodies lingered. Those notes could wrench tears from stone, and I've been enslaved by them since." In Wutang, only Widow Jiang and "I" truly attend his songs, for only those touched by death grasp their worth. "His voice conjures a moonrise in the shop—instant radiance. That tender sorrow flows like autumn moonlight on water, every strand brimming with longing. Within those aged-yet-youthful notes, I see my magician: tree-still by the door, watching wordlessly. No shaman's spell, yet the song lets me clutch his hand—and I weep." This is death transmuted into art—a symphony of mortality.

The novel, blending reality and illusion, narrates tales of death through grief—unfolding gently with the author's emotional cadence. After immersing in folk songs and ghost stories, after absorbing vernacular wisdom on mortality, "my" emotions and spirit undergo transcendence and purification. At Sanshan Lake, "I coated my face thick with mud by the Red Mud Springs, concealing all sorrow." In truth, having witnessed countless deaths and internalized folk perspectives on life's finitude, "I" emerge beyond grief—for death may represent life's supreme culmination. Though no magician's trick can reverse mortality, we must still pray for the departed's peaceful passage. Yunling, the boy, mourns his mother in a profoundly symbolic way. At his request, "I" join him on the fifteenth of July to release river lanterns at Qingliu. "According to Yunling," "I" narrate, "Qingliu is the clearest stream farthest from Sanshan Lake. His mother once told him that if someone goes missing, calling their name by this water will summon their spirit back." In this luminous world, souls are never truly lost. "Moonlit Qingliu meanders with murmuring currents—this narrow creek, no wider than a stride, resembles a zither string anchored to the earth. Plucking its notes are the breeze, moonlight, and a boy's hands." Yunling sets down his basket, brushes aside wild chrysanthemums, and retrieves two lanterns. Matchsticks flare; he passes me a lotus-shaped one. "...I study this lotus lantern meant for the magician... From my bag, I withdraw his razor case—its obsidian shell opening to reveal the silver blade... I tilt the tray, letting dust-fine stubble drift into the lantern... Calling his name, I lower it into the water. At first, it shudders in an eddy, as if bidding farewell, then glides downstream serenely... That night, no abandonment or grief remains—only heaven and earth perfectly joined. I know these lanterns will reach the Milky Way." Here, by these pristine waters, "I" perform the soul-summoning rite. The departed ascend, transfigured.

Yet the story lingers—its reverberations humming beyond the final note. Returning from Qingliu to my inn, half-reclined on the bed, "suddenly, I heard rustling from the box, windlike, as if whispers coiled inside... Startled, I waited. Soon, the sound resumed. When I lifted the lid, a butterfly—a sprite—spiraled out! Its cerulean wings fanned the air, circling me once before alighting silently on my ring finger, like a sapphire band slipped into place." This is Zhuangzi's butterfly (translator's note: Daoist paradox of existence) reborn, Liang-Zhu's metamorphosis (translator's note: iconic lovers' transcendence) reimagined. The author, wielding an aesthete's brush, renders emotion and spirituality utterly consummate. "This sublime, mythic gesture ritually completes the protagonist's forward-into-life-through-death journey."[1] Through prose at once lyrical, expansive, and eternal, she perfects the death narrative—elevating literature into boundless psychic realms.

① Ai Zhen. *Beard in the Moonlight.* Selected Fiction, no. 3, 2005.

Survival Memory, Folk Wisdom and Anti-Modernity — A Critique of Chi Zijian's "*The Last Quarter of the Moon*"

"*The Last Quarter of the Moon*" is the winner of the 7th *Mao Dun Literary Prize* (note: One of China's most prestigious literary awards, named after the renowned writer Mao Dun). The judging committee's award citation reads: "With her characteristically sincere and lucid heart, Chi Zijian enters the life world of the *Evenki people* (note: An ethnic group native to Siberia and Northern China, traditionally reindeer herders) , poetically recounting an ethnic minority's tenacious perseverance and cultural transformation through tender lyrical narration. This 'family saga'-style work can be regarded as the author's candid dialogue with the Evenki people, wherein she expresses the promotion of ideal human spirits—respecting life, revering nature, upholding faith, and distinguishing love from hate - that have been obscured by modernity. Chi Zijian's writing style is serene and graceful, with exquisite language. The novel possesses epic qualities and anthropological depth of thought, presenting distinctive style, profound artistic conception, and outstanding ideological and artistic merit—truly a masterpiece."

Indeed, Chi Zijian's works provide us with a distinctive reading experience. The author employs an unmarked, unscaled narrative perspective to recount the history of an ethnic group and a community—a history that not only grows increasingly distant from our contemporary reality but may fundamentally oppose modernity and resist realism. Precisely because of the complex historical, cultural and contemporary implications embedded within both the author and the work, "*The Last Quarter of Moon*" as a modern literary text deserves thorough examination to reveal its profound connotations and distinctive characteristics.

I. Survival Memory: Tracing Life Trajectories for Modern People

Human development shares commonalities, yet different ethnic groups exhibit distinct life trajectories. From a biological perspective, each individual possesses unique DNA, just as different ethnic groups have characteristic genomic patterns. While evolutionary changes may alter external physical features, the intrinsic imprints remain enduring and immutable. Culturally speaking, human existence and ways of life undergo tremendous transformations, with various communities and ethnic groups evolving alongside human development. Beyond essential biological evolution, changes in external living conditions and environments constitute crucial factors altering human existence. However, the transformations in different ethnic groups' lives follow their own inherent patterns—determined not only by distinct DNA and geographical environments, but more significantly by divergent lifestyle choices.①

---

① Wu Shenggang: "*Ecological Interpretation and Preservation of Culture*," Theory Horizon, no. 5, 2005.

The precise duration of human existence may elude definitive measurement, though recorded history provides clear demarcations. Yet for individuals whose lifespans rarely exceed a century, millennia of history stretch beyond comprehension. Human memory proves even more constrained—expecting vivid recollection of bygone ways of life becomes unreasonable, particularly when modern existence bombards consciousness with such overwhelming complexity that mental pathways clog, creating cognitive disruptions. This collective forgetfulness fixates humanity on the immediate present, rendering historical disregard a defining modern trait. Of course, for major civilizations, complete historical amnesia remains unlikely—their intact cultural systems, passed down through generations via written and other cultural forms, preserve historical consciousness. But smaller ethnic groups face historical loss precisely because their oral traditions, unanchored by writing, store history solely in living memory. When these memory chains break, entire histories risk vanishing forever.

The Evenki people, with a population of merely thirty thousand, are known as "the people who dwell in the great mountain forests." Most Evenki make their living as herders, while the remainder engage in farming. Yet their development has followed nearly the same historical patterns as other ethnic groups, leaving profound life trajectories imprinted across time and space. Though possessing their own spoken language, the Evenki never developed a writing system. Consequently, while they lack written historical records, their ethnic survival journey is deeply engraved in their collective consciousness and the very marrow of their being. Undoubtedly, this small-scale ethnic group has endured extraordinary hardships and circuitous struggles in their development. Yet Evenki history is also imbued with solemn grandeur, poignant beauty, and profound aesthetic elements that may well constitute an epic in both historical essence and literary significance.

Yet as humanity entered the 21st century, the hyper-speed development of modernity has propelled us increasingly further from history. "History becoming the past" has transformed from a slogan-like catchphrase into a stark reality. All people, including minority groups like the Evenki, are inevitably swept onto modernity's express train sooner or later. The growing separation from history, ancestral lands, and spiritual homelands has become an irreversible trend—much like potted plants, caged birds, or aquarium fish that must abandon their past to adapt to pristine, well-lit, comfortable environments. Complying with this modern trajectory, the Evenki have left behind their mountains, forests, and rivers. These "dwellers of the great mountain forests" no longer possess homes in the primitive, traditional sense. With transformed living environments come naturally altered lifestyles: the "Ulilen" communal dwellings and "Xilenzhu" conical tents have disappeared; reindeer, wild boars, elk, black bears, roe deer, and squirrels have vanished from their daily lives; entire clans have relocated to settlements like Jiliu Township. While these manufactured environments may offer comfort and stability, the Evenki's original way of existence has permanently vanished.

The natural elements that once permeated their lives—the bittersweet coexistence with nature, the passionate yet poignant cycles of reindeer herding, hunting, fishing under starlit skies and through windstorms - have all ceased operations. Admittedly, the new era necessitates protecting mountains, forests, rivers, wildlife, vegetation and ecosystems - this becoming a primary justification for the Evenki's displacement. Yet this protection stems precisely from ecological crises already underway, just as their exodus results from the collapse of their traditional survival chains. Regardless, the Evenki's departure has become irreversible, permanently altering their historical trajectory. Perhaps their lives will grow brighter, happier, and more secure henceforth—but at the cost of severing millennia-old bonds with the land that shaped their identity.

It is precisely through such historical transformations that the Evenki people's lives and history have gained comprehensive narrative potential. As an ethnic minority, the Evenki's traditional existence might have seemed too mundane to warrant extensive discussion—in our populous nation, the lives of merely tens of thousands could only claim uniqueness rather than universality. Whether framed as historical or contemporary narrative, their story alone might not have generated profound resonance or significant reflective space. Yet when the Evenki completely abandoned their ancestral lifestyle, irreversibly "shelving" their history, their past became worthy of remembrance and reimagining through modern perspectives. The substance of Evenki survival reveals extraordinary richness, authenticity, and poetic quality

-- this "authenticity" and "poeticism" embody an ethnic group's vital existence, leaving indelible imprints both on the land and in collective memory. Admittedly, within China's entangled pre-modern, modern and post-modern context, historical ruptures often induce collective amnesia. However, modernity's expanding cognitive voids and memory losses can paradoxically motivate vigorous efforts to reconstruct thought and rediscover memory. *The Last Quarter of the Moon* manifests precisely this possibility—diligently tracing life trajectories not just for contemporary Evenki, but for all modern people.

II. Folk Wisdom: The Unadorned Worldview and Way of Survival

The Evenki people have sustained themselves through their distinctive way of life. The work employs the perspective of a tribal chieftain's wife—the last of her kind spanning two centuries—to provide an eyewitness account of the Evenki's survival journey. Emerging from the depths of time, the Evenki have woven their existence around mountains, forests, rivers, reindeer herding, hunting, and fishing. Among these fundamental elements, the mountains, forests, and rivers constitute the poetic dwelling place of their world, while reindeer herding, hunting, and fishing form the core of their productive lifestyle. Without permanent settlements, the Evenki lived scattered across isolated, undulating woodlands—their nomadic Ulilen communities functioning as mobile villages, their Xilenzhu conical tents serving as temporary family shelters. This seemingly isolated living environment paradoxically fostered the Evenki's unique modes of communication and interaction. Through interpreting multifaceted connections within their ecosystem's symbolic systems, they developed a cultural system devoid of abstract textual interpretations—a tangible culture intrinsically intertwined with their very being.

Faith represents the Evenki people's ethereal belief system and their highest form of spiritual wisdom. They regard forests, mountains, water, and fire as sacred emblems of their identity, with divine forces serving as the guiding principles for resolving life's uncertainties and dilemmas. The forests and mountains have been intrinsic to the Evenki's existence since time immemorial, providing them with inexhaustible sustenance—reindeer, wild boars, elk, black bears, roe deer, squirrels, pheasants, wild mushrooms, and wild onions thrive in these woodlands, nourishing generations of Evenki. Their dwellings, the conical Xilenzhu tents, are constructed from pine poles arranged in circular formations, while their storage houses are built between two trimmed trees, reinforced with wooden planks and accessed by notched log ladders. Birch trees hold special significance for the Evenki, yielding not only birch sap, bark containers, gloves, and boots but also serving as the primary material for crafting canoes, Ulilen shelters, and Xilenzhu tents—making birch an indispensable part of their lives. Born and buried in the wilderness, the Evenki lay their deceased on sun-facing slopes, reflecting their profound reverence for the mountains and forests. These natural elements are not merely utilitarian but sacred symbols that shape their destiny and inspire their understanding of life. Water, though universally vital, holds exceptional meaning for the Evenki. Their survival depends entirely on nature's bounty—rivers and mountain springs are divine gifts, blessings that bind their lives to its flow. Fire, meanwhile, embodies the essence of Evenki vitality—an eternal flame symbolizing their unyielding spirit. As one chieftain's wife recounts: "My mother's wedding gift to me was a flame—the very fire I now tend. This fire was passed down from her father, my grandfather Nalgiye, when she married. She never let it die, not even in madness or migration." Beyond sustaining life, fire wards off evil and heralds communal hope. During celebrations, entire tribes gather around bonfires in song and dance, while every household safeguards an undying flame. The Evenki's awe of fire runs so deep that women are forbidden from stepping over it—a testament to its sacred role in their spiritual and cultural fabric.

The Evenki people's spiritual world centers around the *Malu deities*—twelve sacred totems that serve as vessels for interpreting life's mysteries and soothing existential anxieties. Shamans, as keepers of these divine symbols and wielders of supernatural power, mediate between the physical and spiritual realms. Living in near-perfect symbiosis with their ecosystem, the Evenki traditionally avoided intertribal conflicts, their existence unfolding in a state of primal harmony with nature. Yet nature's cyclical fury—seasonal extremes, violent storms, flash floods, and landslides—could abruptly disrupt this equilibrium, intertwining life and death, joy and sorrow, hope and despair with the natural world. Confronting such adversities, the Evenki developed a philosophy that attributes all uncertainties to nature's will. Born from and sustained by nature, they view death as nature's rightful reclaiming of life—a belief poignantly illustrated when Linke's fatal lightning strike is described as being "taken by thunder":

"Shaman Nidu worked through the night in that pine forest, selecting four trees standing at right angles to each other. He cut some wooden poles and laid them across the branches to make a final resting place for Linke. The platform was built very high, because as Shaman Nidu said, 'Linke was taken by the Thunder God. Since thunder comes from heaven, we must return him to the sky, so his grave must be closer to heaven.'"

The Evenki seem to share a natural connection with nature: "After the rain, a rainbow appeared in the sky... But as we watched, one rainbow suddenly faded and quickly disappeared. Although the other maintained its shape, its colors instantly became dull, as if dust had settled on it, turning it gray. The change in the rainbow made everyone's face pale, for all knew it was an ill omen. Mother returned early to the Xilenzhu tent... already mourning Father in advance." This may represent the Evenki's fate, but such fate is completely based on their profound connection with nature. Because humans possess spirit, and a people possess culture, they must find explanations for their existence and history that align with their understanding. The Evenki, based on their inseparable relationship with nature, see the mysteries of their existence as rooted in nature, developing a concept of life and death that moves with nature's rhythms - where death announces life, and life compensates for death.

"Nihao cried as she told us: 'When I left the camp, I knew that if I saved that child, I would lose one of my own.' When I asked why, she said: 'Heaven wanted that child. By keeping him here, my child must go in his place.'" In reality, the Evenki's Malu spirits represent the nature they depend on, so the effigies of the Malu spirits are all made from natural objects, reflecting the Evenki's respect and worship of nature.

Therefore, when the Evenki hunt bears, wild boars, elk, or even their domesticated reindeer, they perform sacrificial rituals before sharing the meat, demonstrating both piety toward the spirits and respect for the animals' lives. Their funeral practices for human life also follow the principle of being born from and returning to nature—through wind burials or sky burials—allowing human life to rest peacefully within nature's embrace.

This embodies authentic folk wisdom—a worldview and way of life fundamentally alien to modernity.[①] As the "Last Chieftain's Woman" of the Evenki people, she transcends being a mere cultural "USB drive." Witnessing her tribe's twilight, she actively inhabits their epistemology, becoming

---

① Wu Shenggang. *Narrative Characteristics, Aesthetic Principles, and Value of Popular Literature.* Journal of Xinyang Normal University, no. 4 (2011).

the living vessel of this survival ethos. Her narrative resonates as profound symbolism: her "lastness" certifies the Evenki's lived history—pure folk authenticity—starkly contrasting contemporary pseudo-folk and pseudo-history. Herein lies invaluable cultural capital, and ultimately, unparalleled literary potency.

III. Counter-Modernity: Abandonment and the New "Search"

Humanity has entered the 21st century, with all peoples eagerly advancing toward modernization. Human life has undergone—or is undergoing—qualitative transformations driven by political, economic, technological, cultural, and social forces. These forces reshape lives from multiple angles, ultimately remaking humanity itself. Modernization necessitates altering history and reality, creating distance from the past. Simultaneously, it seeks to comprehensively mold individuals, endowing them with modern sensibilities, consciousness, thought patterns, and inclinations—in short, instilling modernity. As Foucault contends, "Modernity is not merely the phenomenon of modernization, but rather 'an attitude': a mode of relating to contemporary reality; a voluntary choice made by particular peoples; finally, a way of thinking and feeling that simultaneously signals belonging and frames it as a task—much like the Greeks' notion of ethos."[①] This "attitude" demands adherence to specific ideas, approaches, and modes of engaging with contemporary reality—those deemed "modern" rather than "historical." The exclusivity of modern logic inevitably promotes modernity at history's expense, for the past is often seen as mere baggage.

The transformation of Evenki life has unfolded in tandem with China's modernization. When the new China institutionally defined interethnic relations and charted a collective future, the Evenki began migrating from mountains and forests—with Jiliu Township becoming their new ulileng (settlement). This shift embodies their voluntary choice to negotiate history and modernity, consciously embracing new paradigms.

When modernization becomes an irreversible tide for a nation—indeed, the entire world—human existence inevitably merges with its currents. Few can resist. The Evenki's entire lifeworld—their sensibilities, consciousness, thought patterns, and behaviors—stands in stark, irreconcilable contrast to modernity. The liminality between history and reality forces a choice: modernity now permeates both spiritual and material dimensions. It projects future visions while manufacturing new sensations, rationalities, ideologies, and psychologies—reshaping reality's very metrics. To embrace the past, history, or ancestral wisdom is to risk isolation from modernity—an isolation

① Yang Chunshi, *Modernity and Chinese Literary Trends*, SDX Joint Publishing Company, 2009, p. 1.

tantamount to marginalization or outright abandonment. This constitutes an existential paradox: crossing into modernity may signal history's end, a negation of collective memory. Such metamorphosis is agonizing—not merely through external ruptures (habitat, resources, subsistence) but through cognitive, psychological, and spiritual severance. It demands a holistic shedding, from physiology to psyche—a total negation. This is modernity's inexorable decree, pulling the Evenki onto tracks they never laid.

The "Last Chieftain's Woman" embodies Evenki history—a history forged in specific ecologies and temporalities. Severed from these unique spatiotemporal conditions, such history cannot persist. Thus, when her tribe migrated to Jiliu Township, she stubbornly remained in the ancestral forests. Her existence proves a paradox: while reality bends to human will and new lifeways, history remains immutable. The young traverse boundaries more easily, unburdened by historical weight; they embrace modernity's diversity without resistance. As the "last," she becomes a living suture between past and present—her symbolic and imaginative power eclipsing her literal significance. Through her, descendants periodically return to these woods, the Evenki remember, and the echo of their primal culture endures.

At its core, Evenki primal culture is counter-modern. Born of nature, sustained by nature, it perpetuates ancient hunting-gathering lifeways—a primordial state of being inextricably interwoven with the ecosystem. Though modern industrial goods have peripherally entered their lives, the essence of their ecological order remains unbroken: a centuries-old symbiosis governing relationships between the Evenki and their environment, internal social codes, and corresponding cognitive, psychological, and ethical structures. This order is fundamentally incommensurate with modernity. Modernity reshapes existence, declaring history's closure. While it brings material progress—instrumental rationality forging new survival logics—the Evenki drown in its waves. Each hammering surge leaves exhaustion, agitation, and void. Their bone-deep harmony with nature fractures. Thus, the "Last Chieftain's Woman" rejects this "reality," clinging stubbornly to her historical lifeworld until death. Yet this dissonance extends beyond her. Evenki youth who ventured beyond the forests—seduced by modernity's "abundance"—now numbedly mourn their lost heritage. Take Ilena: "Weary of the mountains, she'd return to the city with her paintings, only to retreat again, exhilarated, declaring cities unbearable—'Nothing but crowds, concrete, traffic, and dust.'... Eventually, she quit her job forever. 'I'm done with work, cities, and men,' she told me. 'Only reindeer, trees, rivers, the moon, and the wind never tire me.'"

Thus, the "Last Chieftain's Woman" searches—narrating Evenki stories, resurrecting lost histories. Ilena searches, her paintings straining to preserve vanishing lifeways. Xiban searches, carving Evenki scripts as eternal cultural imprints. Nihao, the last shaman of a tribe, searches to salvage all that defines Evenki existence. Yet all is futile. When the catastrophic 1989 wildfires engulfed the Greater Khingan Range—devouring their ancestral "homeland"—

history seemed to stage its final curtain call. "It was then Nihao donned her sacred robes, cap, and skirt for the last time, beating her spirit drum in a rain dance... Thunder and lightning erupted as she sang her final hymn—collapsing mid-verse into the torrential downpour." "Ilena could never forget Nihao's rain ritual," the narrator recalls. "She said that moment condensed a century of Evenki storms—so electrifying she had to paint it." Yet after two years laboring over this "monumental" canvas, Ilena walked into the Bieltz River with her brushes. Such searching merely delays the inevitable. History—in its irreconcilable clash with modernity—ultimately sacrifices itself. Like the Last Chieftain's Woman, the author recounts these "unremarkable" tales with aching tenderness, ensuring modernity's amnesia never fully prevails.

IV. The Paradox of Primordial/Classical Beauty vs. Modern Sensibilities

Though *The Last Quarter of the Moon* exhibits fragmentary, essayistic qualities in form and narrative, the text asserts an irreducible uniqueness—one that may whisper through the author's other works but finds its fullest incarnation here. This distinctiveness is fundamentally interwoven with the novel's substance, its mood, its stylistic signatures, and its storytelling ethos.

The Last Quarter of the Moon stands out for its rich natural imagery—azure skies, drifting clouds, the sun and moon, stars, snow, mountains, rivers, wind, and thunderstorms—all seamlessly interwoven with the Evenki people's existence. Living deep in the forests and mountains, the Evenki inhabit nature's embrace in its primal form, where these elements are not mere backdrop but the very fabric of their daily lives. Such intimacy with the natural world is unimaginable in modern urbanity. In ancient cultures and classical literature, celestial bodies, landscapes, and natural phenomena have long served as symbolic codes and aesthetic motifs. Consider Chinese myths: Kuafu chasing the sun, Chang'e fleeing to the moon, Yu the Great taming floods, the Foolish Old Man moving mountains, or Nüwa mending the heavens—alongside deities of wind and thunder. Classical poetry further elevated these images into lyrical expressions: "Picking chrysanthemums by the eastern fence, I gaze at the distant southern mountains." (Tao Yuanming) "Moonlight shines by my bed like frost. I look up to the bright moon, bow down, and think of home." (Li Bai) "East, the sun rises; west, rain falls—seeming heartless, yet full of tenderness." (Liu Yuxi) "The clear breeze over the river, the bright moon between mountains—heard as music, seen as beauty. Take it freely; it never runs dry." (Su Shi) These universal yet quintessentialnatural symbols have anchored Chinese cultural expression, offering vast interpretive possibilities. At their core, they reflect the symbiosis between agrarian civilization and nature-based economies. Humanity emerged from the cosmos, and before technological advancement, our dependence on nature was absolute. Nature dictated fate; it was our totality. People imbued natural phenomena with animistic vitality, believing in a spiritual resonance between the soul of the world and the human spirit.

The Last Quarter of the Moon presents natural imagery as the essence of Evenki culture. Their near-primal hunting lifestyle embodies a nomadic civilization deeply fused with nature—where natural elements become the codes and rhythms of Evenki life, shaping their aesthetic consciousness, thought patterns, and values. The author uses these revered natural symbols as narrative motifs, lyrically unveiling the true essence of Evenki nomadic culture while enriching its interpretive depth. Take the moon, an ancient image that seems to drift perpetually above the Evenki. The novel is filled with moonlit scenes—this distant, luminous jade disc stirs boundless imagination. Then there are the winds:

"At night, the shilenzhu (tent) carries whispers of the wind. Winter winds howl with beasts; summer winds hum with owls and frogs. Inside the shilenzhu, another wind exists—one woven with Father's breaths and Mother's murmurs, a wind created by Dalama and Linke."

Rivers, too, are lifelines for the Evenki. Yet the text speaks of a hidden river within women, accessible only to men who truly love them. For the Evenki, these elements are life—only when they see, hear, and feel them does their world feel real, their minds awaken. These natural symbols, steeped in primal cultural significance and classical beauty, gain profound aesthetic value when tied to Evenki history. Thus, this search for history becomes meaningful. The author relies not on narrative tricks but deep emotion, poetic language, and lyrical imagery, weaving these elements seamlessly into Evenki life—a life both rugged and refined, stirring our longing for the past.

Modern urban life pursues skyscrapers, bustling streets, shopping malls, restaurants, neon lights, and endless streams of pedestrians and vehicles. People are confined to apartments or swept along in this synthetic current, increasingly estranged from the azure sky, drifting clouds, sun, moon, and stars—let alone the mountains, rivers, forests, winds, and thunderstorms that once defined human existence. These natural elements now survive only as desiccated symbols in atrophied imaginations. As urbanites zealously adapt to metropolitan civilization, striving to merge with modernity's torrent, even our language and discourse struggle to evoke these primal images. The Evenki, too, having entered this system, find their transformed lifestyle unrecognizable from their ancestral traditions. Urban labor no longer engages with land, rivers, mountains, or forests, nor with hunted game, but with machines, technology, information, ideologies, and regulations—all interconnected through modern systems of logistics, data flows, capital, crowds, traffic, and noise. Though these anxiety-inducing concepts saturate daily life, they feel profoundly unreal, breeding subconscious existential void. Thus, moderns nostalgically recall nature's poetic and life-affirming symbols, artificially reconstructing them in urban spaces: rooftop gardens, indoor waterfalls, projected starry skies. Under modernity's influence, daily life undergoes wholesale aesthetic packaging. Yet this is not true nature but a semiotic construct, where "aestheticization" merely denotes superficial stylization incapable of generating profound beauty. Urban development cannot transplant authentic nature into concrete landscapes; it can only fabricate imitations to placate psychological yearning. These formalized simulacra offer transient spiritual relief, but prolonged exposure inevitably induces fatigue. Biologically and psychologically, humans crave real nature—timeless, poetic, and alive. Yet a tragic paradox persists: humanity can neither return to primal origins nor willingly embrace classical harmony, just as relocated Evenki cannot re-enter their forested homeland. This is the irreconcilable tension between historical essence and contemporary reality—where modernity's false constructs both mask and exacerbate our elemental loss.

The Value of Eco-Literature: A Perspective from *Avalanche in the Cloud*

I. The Realities of Literature

We have entered the 21st century—an era where modernization is not only accelerating but expanding in all directions. While it is difficult to comprehensively or precisely define the essence of this century, we can attempt to articulate some of its defining characteristics. It is not hard to imagine the staggering demands of nearly 7 billion people (as of 2009) carving an insatiable void into the planet. Though history's trajectory remains open to multiple possibilities, one thing is certain: the 21st century is anthropocentric—an age shaped by humanity's ever-growing desires and their relentless pursuit of fulfillment.

Faced with humanity's insatiable demands, what can the natural world offer—whether materially or spiritually? Amidst the clamor of mortal existence, how can humankind find tranquility or transcendence? While no life, whether gilded or humble, can rise entirely above material needs, yet, it ought to seek transcendence through the realm of the spirit. But if even the spiritual domain is industrialized and polluted by modernization, then self-redemption may become an impossibility.

As a vital dimension of the human spirit, literature serves as the psychological, emotional, and mnemonic record of human existence. Indeed, the history of literature unfolds in tandem with the evolution of civilization, faithfully mirroring humanity's raw and unvarnished developmental trajectory. Through the ages, literature has grown alongside humankind itself. Yet, with the advent of modernity, the deepening forces of modernization have spawned an inevitable offspring: globalization. This tidal wave of homogenization has swept into every corner of the world, forging an industrial chain of capital, resources, information, markets, monopolies, and competition that now dominates human living space. Just as industrialization has radically transformed daily life, modernization has profoundly altered literature's very essence. Contemporary culture increasingly lacks the serenity, harmony, and profundity of natural ecosystems. Modern man grows anxious amidst congested spaces, billowing smoke, and overwhelming noise, while industrialized culture—charred in the furnace of progress—leaves only existential bewilderment in its wake.

A survey of modern literature—particularly 20th-century works across cultures—reveals an overwhelming undercurrent of anxiety toward epochal transformations. From Tolstoy's *War and Peace* and Sholokhov's *And Quiet Flows the Don* to Boris Vasilyev's *The Dawns Here Are Quiet* and Romain Rolland's *Jean-Christophe*, these texts oscillate between visceral fear and moral condemnation of war, while simultaneously betraying profound unease toward technological rationality and industrial advancement. Chinese literature manifests parallel concerns. Mao Dun's *Midnight*, while primarily a lament for China's national industries suffocated under foreign hegemony, offers no optimism about industrialization's corrosion of human nature and ecological balance. Similarly, Jia Pingwa's *The Abandoned Capital* lays bare how modernization and urbanization precipitate spiritual decay and the erosion of the soul.

In the modern era, a shared lament has emerged: literature increasingly lacks profound emotional resonance, visceral power, and rich aesthetic sensibility. The root cause lies in literature's affliction with a distinctly modern malaise—the "disease of affluence." Its pathology reveals how, as literature grows ever more modern and postmodern in lockstep with societal modernization, monetary wealth and profit-driven industries have come to dominate human living space—inevitably encroaching upon literature's existential territory. The allure of capital proves nearly irresistible to both literature and its creators; the gravitation of literary production toward wealth and away from poverty has become inescapable. The most telling indicators of modernization's essence and reach are genres like industrial literature, urban literature, petty bourgeois literature (propertied-class literature), and the like. These branded literary forms largely confine their expressive horizons to modernization's epicenters—cities, metropolises, and the propertied elites who inhabit, evolve within, or parasitically thrive upon these urban landscapes. Such literature paradigmatically celebrates affluence, modernity, fashion, desire, seduction, and ruthless striving. While it may occasionally yield aesthetic fragments, the primal rhythms of human existence, innate contentment, and authentic lived experience have all but vanished. In essence, modernization has stripped humanity of its congenital grace, poise, and untrammeled spirit, while divorcing literature from its original symbiosis with both human nature and the natural world.

II. *Avalanche in the Cloud*: A Paradigm of Eco-Literature

Perhaps we cannot predict the future trajectory of human literature, yet our yearning for its untainted, original visage grows ever more irrepressible. It is precisely this fervent longing that drives our search for literature in its purest, most authentic form. Amidst an era where writers have become aristocratized and literature largely industrialized, it is heartening that works like Avalanche in the Cloud still strive resolutely toward the primal essence of both humanity and nature.

Avalanche in the Cloud (published in October magazine, Issue 1, 2006) presents a series of vignettes depicting the ecological interdependence of humans, animals, and natural vegetation on the Pamir Plateau. From the outset, the novel deliberately eschews intricate plotting, focusing instead on portraying the pristine, unadulterated natural ecology of the Pamirs – and the animals and humans whose lives are inextricably intertwined with this fragile ecosystem. The narrative follows Old Ma and Young Ma, two sheep traders, as they drive their flock through the mountains. This simple journey forms the skeletal plot of the work. Against the backdrop of the world-renowned Pamir Plateau – with its snow-capped peaks, barren deserts, and stony wastelands, but also its drifting clouds, meandering streams, and alpine pastures – the novel unfolds as a quiet meditation on coexistence.

Old Ma and Young Ma were making their way to the Karazuo Pasture near the snow line... Descending from the asphalt road at over 2,000 meters above sea level into the valley bottom, they wound their way through a hundred-odd kilometers of treacherous terrain. One moment they trudged through loose silt that swallowed their feet, dust clouds swirling about them; the next, they crossed vast, desolate stretches of gobi where gravel shimmered like molten gold. After traversing swampy meadows where flash floods might catch them unawares, detours around landslide debris could suddenly leave them stranded by glacial barriers.

Yet the murmuring waters of the Karazuo River, flowing alongside at a respectful distance with quiet forbearance, offered some small comfort to ease their spirits.

The rebellious river channel, having twisted and turned through mountain gorges, suddenly encountered this vast, open grassland and flung itself headlong into the expanse. In the span of a few breaths, the grasses grew thick and lush—stretching in patches, clusters, and mounds, arrayed like formations amid the web of waterways: oval, square, oblong, triangular, each shape unique as the river wove freely between them.

Wild ducks, geese, and cranes flew overhead. Sunlight fell in fragmented beams, rejected by the slick, icy slopes of the mountains. Where the water ran clear, tufts of cloud drifted upon its surface; where shadows pooled, the ripples shimmered in scattered flecks. The lingering wild geese ceased their drifting, bobbing like wooden toys upon the water—and for a moment, the river itself seemed to stop flowing.

The great meadow stretched before them, verdant and endless.

The work presents us with a vivid tableau of the Pamir Plateau's natural landscapes: the Muztagh Ata and Kongur Tagh mountain ranges, the Sanbeng Peaks, deep valleys, yak-grazing meadows, vast grasslands, the Karazuo River and its pastures, the arid gobi deserts, stony wastelands, alpine marshes, meandering streams, and vibrant wildflowers. Inhabiting these ecosystems are yaks, spirited horses, sheep, Bactrian camels, wild ducks, geese, golden eagles, marmots, and the elusive Tibetan wolves. Moving through these natural realms and interacting with its creatures are human figures like Nazilebek, Kurban, the radiant Meriiban, along with interloping characters such as Ahong, Old Ma, and Young Ma.

This is a realm far removed from modern material pursuits, a place seldom touched by outsiders. Here, nature has thrust the land skyward—a world of alpine cold, oxygen-thin air, perpetual snows, deep ravines, gravel-strewn deserts, and a near-primal ecosystem of unforgiving harshness. Within this landscape, figures like Nazilebek, Kurban, Meriiban, and Halenbu live in harmony with their yaks, spirited horses, sheep, Bactrian camels, wild ducks, geese, golden eagles, marmots, and Tibetan wolves, alongside the flora that sustains both animals and humans—all existing in accordance with nature's primordial rhythms. No tidal waves of globalization crash upon these shores; no industrial smog stains the horizon. What unfolds instead is an almost archaic pastoral tableau: the daily cycle of tending flocks at dawn and returning home at dusk, an echo of subsistence agriculture untouched by time.

Undoubtedly, the oxygen-scarce, inhospitable environment of the high-altitude Pamirs could never appeal to luxury-seeking modern urbanites. Only those as tenacious as yaks, camels, or Tibetan wolves—individuals like Nazilebek, Kurban, and the Meri Riban clan—can survive here, having forged a symbiotic ecological chain with this unforgiving landscape. Though the region boasts pristine whiteness, verdant hues, crystalline air, and unspoiled purity, it remains fated never to host dense human settlements. Like the sparse characters populating the novel's simple narrative, perhaps Providence scattered them here solely to serve as ecological counterweights—living elements maintaining the delicate equilibrium of this extreme ecosystem.

Thus, we behold the beauty of the Pamirs and sense a profound wonder—one that manifests in three dimensions.First is the marvel of natural ecology. At several thousand meters above sea level, every existence in the Pamirs is a miracle. Here, mountains and stones dominate the landscape—so ubiquitous that avoiding them is impossible. Yet these very mountains and rocks, as integral components of the Pamirs' ecosystem, possess their own extraordinary and unique qualities:

To the northwest of Karazuo, beyond the yak pastures some dozen li distant, stands the border mountain—commonly called Sanbeng Peak (Three-Collapse Mountain), though it's not particularly tall. In truth, within the Sarikol Range, eight or nine summits surpass it in height, their pinnacles vanishing into cloud banks for days on end. Though not lofty enough to boast the clichéd veils of mist, Sanbeng's summit often skewers a solitary dark cloud—a phenomenon that has long baffled locals. The strange tales and age-old legends surrounding it lie as thick as riverbed pebbles.

The snows of Sanbeng Peak are a marvel—a peculiar marvel at that, for they fall more frequently here than elsewhere, as if heaven itself had bestowed special favor upon this place. When not snowing, the blazing sun turns the mountain's porcelain-white summit, shaped like a traditional felt hat, into a dazzling spectacle. Viewed from Karazuo, the peak rises like a fan beneath its snowy cap, reminiscent of the spirit wall facing the entrance of a Beijing courtyard house—though with a distinct curvature. At first glance, one might mistake it for a colossal dam holding back mighty river waters...

To say Sanbeng Peak lies a dozen li from Karazuo is to speak of witnessing avalanches—hearing them. ... An avalanche cascades from heights of hundreds of meters, a deluge that blots out earth and sky in a shroud of white mist, swallowing the mountain whole. The great "V"-shaped gorge seems on the verge of being leveled, buried under meters of snow.

Yet the stones of the Pamirs are stranger still:

Iron-rusted boulders lining the riverbanks appear volcanic in origin, scoured smooth and round by centuries of plateau winds. Imagine them as congealed blood, and you stand perilously close to the heart of the earth itself. ... Occasionally, cliffs shed fragments that tumble recklessly, colliding and splintering mid-air. Gravel flies as if whipped upward by some unseen exhaust fan, while pebbles the size of sheep's knuckles pierce through waterside *quguli* leaves, drumming out a rhythmic dong-dong on their way down.

Certainly, the Pamirs also hold rivers and streams, grasslands, and unique flora like highland barley—precisely what reveals the plateau's ecological marvels. Ahong captured her observations thus: "Nature etches eternity into this land while celebrating each dawn's arrival. The eastern mountains' bones creak; western glaciers stretch skyward with the clouds; valley floods sprint on stone legs; and daybreak composes sonnets over the Pamirs' heaving chest." "Here, Earth's secrets are hoisted atop oxygen-starved peaks—held aloft by ridges that pierce the heavens."

The most extraordinary embodiment of animal resilience is found in *Qiong Maozi*—the legendary white yak. On the oxygen-starved Pamir Plateau, only creatures hardened by evolution's ruthless sieve can survive. Yaks, inherently cold-resistant and Herculean, are the very ships of the highlands. But Nazilebek's *Qiong Maozi* transcends even this standard. "The moment she was born—before Nazilebek could even take a proper look—she sprang to her feet. The pinkish hue of birth faded instantly, leaving her blindingly white, like a mound of solidified sunlight. The hairs on her swaying tail dried swiftly in the wind, fluffing up like a tethered snowball." "Years flashed by. That fluffy calf grew into a towering matriarch, her body uniformly muscular, her spine level with old Nazilebek's shoulders. Gone were her soft contours; she now resembled a slab of stone. Her head, neck, chest, and hindquarters—everything about her was massive. ... When in heat, she'd attract a procession of black bulls, mating with each in turn, never playing favorites." "To Nazilebek, she was no mere beast. What was she, then? Her voice carried the plateau's own timbre; her form mirrored the snow peaks; her eyes held the blue of Lake Kunchilega; her milk flowed like the Karazuo River; her udders outswelled a postpartum woman's hips; her hooves kicked up four obsidian stones. In this light, *Qiong Maozi* became a walking, breathing incarnation of the Pamirs itself."

Qiong Maozi was utterly wild—"once let out of the pen, she'd vanish without a trace." She roamed snow peaks and sheer cliffs, meadows and streams, always defiantly solitary, as if disdaining the company of her own kind. Yet this same creature possessed an almost human maternal instinct. After her wanderings, she would return unprompted—to nurse her calf and leave Nazilebek an extra half-bucket of milk. The two depended on each other for survival. In the evenings, the lonely old man would often visit her pen, sharing stories of the grasslands, the mountaintops, things seen and felt, past and present. "*Qiong Maozi* loved it, listening unblinking." Their bond transcended the mundane, reaching spiritual communion. She was not merely a nurturer to her calf but a lifeline for Nazilebek. When a blizzard stranded him in the Pamirs' labyrinthine gorges, *Qiong Maozi* shielded him with her body, pressing her warm udder to his lips, her milk sustaining him through the storm. Her maternal force even awakened Meriiban's barren womb—"Meriiban had believed herself infertile... yet after drinking *Qiong Maozi*'s milk, she bore the old man twin sons." Most astonishingly, she achieved symbiosis with the plateau wolves. After an earthquake spurred a surge in wolf pups, their desperate cries moved her to nurse them. Later, when the grown pack attacked Kurban's herd, *Qiong Maozi*'s sudden appearance and three thunderous bellows halted the assault. "They abandoned Kurban, reformed into a triangular phalanx, and escorted her in an 'S'-shaped procession toward the western pass."

Indeed, *Qiong Maozi* embodies the very soul of the highlands—a miracle wrought by nature's hand.

Yet the true marvel lies in the effortless harmony between humans and other species. Survival on the Pamir Plateau is a feat for any creature, but for humans—beings of higher consciousness who must consciously choose their dwelling places—it demands profound ecological attunement. The novel reveals a rare equilibrium between humanity and nature within this unforgiving landscape, suggesting we cannot dismiss the sentience of other species—a sentience that resonates with our own. Thus, Nazilebek and *Qiong Maozi*'s bond transcends the ordinary: humans can forge friendships not only with each other but with animals, bonds that may prove even more profound in their purity. And not just yaks—marmots, hares, golden eagles, even the plateau wolves can become companions in this high-altitude symbiosis.

In the narrative, the harmony between humans and nature is innate. The symbiotic relationships among the Pamir Plateau's people, animals, and flora have evolved over millennia within this unique ecosystem—one that is inherently exclusive. Any intrusion from outside inevitably disrupts its delicate balance. Though the Pamirs tower into the clouds—a frigid, oxygen-deprived realm rarely touched by humans—the tidal wave of modernization surges inexorably forward. Humanity's insatiable hunger for resources threatens to shatter this ancient equilibrium. Already, a film crew from the city employs modern technology to capture the plateau's pristine beauty, commodifying it for global consumption. Meanwhile, Old Ma and Young Ma have spent years trading the Pamirs' resources for trivialities: "jellybeans, lollipops, sewing kits, small mirrors, plastic combs, condoms, cigarettes." The story's tragic climax stems precisely from this unequal exchange and the ecosystem's violent rejection of foreign interference. A rift grows between Nazilebek and Kurban. In a fit of uncharacteristic rage, Nazilebek vents his frustration on *Qiong Maozi*. The yak, stunned and furious, abandons her usual gentleness—goring Kurban through the chest with her horns. Kurban perishes; *Qiong Maozi* vanishes. All that remains is "a pristine skeleton, left by the wolves to bleach on a sunlit slope."

III. The Value of Eco-Literature

Eco-literature, in essence, is a literary form that consciously articulates the relationship between humanity and the natural world. While ecological expression is not the sole foundation of literature's genesis and evolution, it undoubtedly constitutes a vital one. Literature's engagement with ecology is, at its core, an exploration of human existence itself. Science designates green as the color of life and labels unpolluted food as "green" precisely because green symbolizes natural ecosystems—the very environment that sustains us. From an ecological perspective, Earth belongs not to humans alone but to all species that inhabit it. We do not monopolize this planet; we share it. Humans and other organisms collectively form an interdependent system, where no single species exists in isolation. This system thrives on reciprocity: It is not that other beings need humans while humans need nothing in return; Nor is it that humans depend on other species while those species are self-sufficient. Each organism acts as a counterweight in this delicate equilibrium. The loss of any single "counterweight" destabilizes the entire system. Thus, humanity is but one component of Earth's ecological tapestry, just as other species are indispensable to our survival.

The assertion that "literature is the study of humanity" remains valid. But what, precisely, constitutes the human? This question demands reexamination. Marx posited that humans are the sum of their social relations—an observation concerning our societal attributes. Yet at our core, we remain natural beings. Beyond our capacity for thought, we differ little from other animals, even insects or simpler organisms. Thus, while humans possess social dimensions, we are ultimately governed by natural laws. Our biological imperatives align us irrevocably with other species, sharing comparable structural patterns and existential sequences. Nature generates beauty organically; human societies cultivate aesthetics. Though aesthetic appreciation arises from cognitive processes, its roots are undeniably ecological. Human thought, action, and value judgments invariably manifest a unity of purpose and natural law. Beauty, then, exists at the intersection of objective reality and subjective perception—particularly natural beauty, which persists independent of human observation. While humanity can create beauty, most beautiful forms (indeed their very essence) preexist our perception, obeying universal laws that encompass both nature and ourselves.

Aesthetic perception reflects an inherent harmony and order within nature, rooted in both humanity's kinship with the natural world and our own physiological structures. Consider the admiration for the curvilinear beauty of the female form, the prevalence of S-shaped contours in ancient Greek sculpture, or Hogarth's assertion that the serpentine line is the most aesthetically pleasing. "Curvature" may well be a universal state in the formation and transformation of all things—a principle vividly encapsulated in the ancient Chinese *Taiji* diagram (A classical Chinese symbol representing the interplay of *yin* and *yang*), which elegantly depicts the ceaseless dynamism of the cosmos. The astronomer Kepler famously believed in the "mystical mathematics" of the universe, even composing a musical piece based on planetary orbits. Modern science corroborates this curvature-centric worldview: Relativity reveals spacetime as warped; String theory posits subatomic particles as vibrating loops, not points; DNA, life's foundational molecule, adopts a coiled double-helix structure. Even musical beauty follows physiological logic. Nie Er's *March of the Volunteers* (National anthem of China) aligns precisely with the Golden Ratio—its structural brilliance mirroring life's innate rhythms. Remarkably, when scientists sonified DNA's base pairs (T, G, A, U) by assigning musical notes to each, the result was a breathtaking melody.[①]

Avalanche in the Cloud articulates an order intrinsic to both ecosystems and human existence. While the narrative centers on human lives, it refuses to cast humanity as the sole protagonist. If Nazilebek is a central figure, then *Qiong Maozi*—the white yak—is the undisputed lead. Yet the work devotes its richest prose to the Pamirs' natural world: *Qiong Maozi*, the plateau wolves, and the land itself become co-authors of a story about interdependence. The writer does not assume the identity of nature's sovereign to critique the natural ecosystem, but rather engages in equal dialogue and discourse with it from the standpoint and perspective of a needer and admirer. The work not only carefully contemplates the lives of highland people, but also pro-

① Wu Shenggang. *Ecological Expression and the Value of Literature*. Journal of Xinyang Normal University (Philosophy and Social Sciences Edition), no. 3, 2005.

foundly observes and savors the multiple vistas of the Pamirs' natural ecology. The author spares no ink in depicting the Pamir ecosystem and no mental effort in observing nature. Under the writer's pen, natural species are no less endowed with spirituality and thought than humans. Although the Pamir environment has its harsh aspects, the natural ecosystem shows no lack of tenderness and solicitude toward humanity. To read this novel is to hear echoes of *The Roof of the World*, that timeless ballad of the Tibetan Plateau. Its power lies in proving nature's capacity to stir the human soul, revealing how ecological narratives can move us as profoundly as any human drama.

Literature represents the artistic beauty created by humankind. Certain intrinsic affinities between artistic beauty and natural beauty have bridged the relationship between art and nature. Literature's expression of natural ecology essentially seeks beauty for art, while also reflecting the trend toward intrinsic harmony between artistic and natural beauty. Natural aesthetics constitutes humanity's earliest form of aesthetic appreciation. Through natural aesthetic activities, humans developed a sense of form, achieving the leap from sensory pleasure to psychological delight, thereby cultivating a spiritual appreciation of reality that transcends material utility. Natural aesthetics also represents the highest realm of aesthetic experience, capable of expanding and elevating the spiritual dimension of all aesthetic activities. In fostering harmonious coexistence between humans and nature, and in rebuilding the spiritual connection between them, natural aesthetics plays an irreplaceable role. It is far more than mere leisurely diversion—it is, first and foremost, a more immediate state of existence: the question of ecological beauty. Ecological beauty serves as the contemporary manifestation of natural aesthetics. It constitutes humanity's most fundamental natural living condition, an integral component of life's beauty, and simultaneously a noble form of spiritual life. Promoting the spirit of natural aesthetics aligns with the central cultural theme of our contemporary era.[①]

Therefore, ecological expression in literature is an essential necessity. First, it stems from the needs of literature's primary subject—human beings. Literature is the study of humanity, and humans possess both social and natural attributes. While literature's depiction of society reflects humanity's social nature, its portrayal of nature signifies a return to our biological essence. Indeed, whether viewed through the lens of social demands or physiological requirements, humans cannot exist apart from natural ecosystems—for we are natural beings, and society itself exists within the broader natural order. Second, it arises from literature's intrinsic demands. Literature seeks to create artistic beauty, yet such beauty does not originate solely from human endeavors. The natural world offers an inexhaustible wellspring of beauty—the most primal and fundamental form of aesthetic existence. Thus, when literature turns to nature for inspiration and selects natural elements as aesthetic subjects, it fulfills an indispensable requirement for artistic creation.

---

① Xue Fuxing. "*The Significance of Natural Aesthetics*." Journal of Shaanxi Normal University (Philosophy and Social Sciences Edition), no. 6, 2002.

Perspective of the TV Drama *Migrant Workers*

In 2005, China Central Television (CCTV-1) aired *Migrant Workers* during prime time, a drama with an ostensibly ordinary theme. However, the author contends that *Migrant Workers* is a work of profound realism and historical significance. Despite its seemingly commonplace subject matter, this series is poised to exert a substantial influence in the annals of Chinese television history.

I. The Perspective of *Migrant Workers*

The so-called perspective refers to one's position relative to others, the angle from which an issue is viewed, and the manner in which one engages with it. For artistic works, the creator's perspective is crucial to the work's success and its ability to evoke emotional resonance. The perspective of *Migrant Workers* thus serves as the starting point for our analysis. In the author's view, *Migrant Workers* adopts a standpoint firmly rooted in rural life, peasants, and migrant laborers—examining rural and urban spaces, as well as their inhabitants, through their lived experiences. Although the series employs the conventional third-person narrative mode typical of television dramas, the narrator's voice seamlessly merges with the second- and first-person perspectives of the characters ("you" and "I"). In effect, the storyteller's (and thus the creators') stance achieves complete alignment with that of the characters.

Since China's reform and opening-up, urbanization and modernization have advanced at an unprecedented pace. The rapid expansion of construction projects and their scale has led to a sharp increase in demand for labor. China's modernization trajectory closely resembles that of other nations—relying on cheap labor to accumulate capital for development. Given China's specific socioeconomic conditions, this role could only be fulfilled by the vast rural population. Thus, beginning in the 1980s, massive numbers of rural laborers migrated to urban areas for work, forming what we now call migrant workers—or more precisely, rural migrants. With their grueling labor, sweat-drenched toil, and meager wages, they have forged the miracle of China's urbanization and modernization. As Ju Shuangyuan remarks in *Migrant Workers*, "Every high-rise in the city is built by peasant hands." Gazing at these towering structures, one can't help but feel a sense of grandeur. Yet what follows this grandeur? The moment Ju steps down from a newly completed building, an overwhelming emptiness sets in. What have migrant workers truly gained from modernization? Beyond paltry wages, has their labor and worth ever been acknowledged? What of their living conditions? For far too long, these questions have failed to garner widespread societal attention. More troubling still is how certain segments of society—particularly urban dwellers—persist in looking down upon migrant workers with contempt, even demonizing them. Enduring backbreaking overtime labor, migrant workers inhabit makeshift shelters at construction sites—some even sleeping in the open—amid deplorable living conditions. Their already meager wages are routinely delayed or arbitrarily docked, leaving them virtually unprotected against exploitation. This systemic injustice ultimately compelled the Premier himself to intervene in wage disputes, catalyzing belated societal attention to migrant workers' plight.

Contemporary artistic productions in China do not lack representations of pressing social issues. Yet most gravitate toward sensational topics—anti-corruption campaigns, crime thrillers, imperial court intrigues, bourgeois lifestyles, romantic entanglements, eroticized narratives, and bodily aesthetics. By contrast, the "three rural issues" (agriculture, countryside, and peasantry) remain severely underrepresented. Who, then, will speak for rural China? Who will articulate—from the peasantry's own standpoint—their anguish, dilemmas, and systemic marginalization? The TV series adopts a documentary-style narrative trajectory, tracing the peasants' journey from their native loess lands to urban centers—capturing both their primal existence in rural ecosystems and their metamorphosis into migrant workers. This approach essentially becomes the workers' own epic of displacement. *Migrant Workers* achieves its narrative power precisely by adopting the workers' perspective to articulate their dilemmas, allowing audiences to penetrate the very heart of their lived experience—the dramaturgical core that elevates this work beyond mere storytelling.

II. The Contradictions in *Migrant Workers*

The television drama *Migrant Workers* is rife with contradictions, which form the very framework through which its central issues are articulated. Broadly speaking, these contradictions manifest primarily in the following dimensions:

(1) The Urban-Rural Contradiction

The tension between city and countryside constitutes the drama's most salient contradiction—a direct reflection of China's enduring societal fissures. Historically, urban development has been sustained by the rural sector's provision of cheap labor and undervalued commodities, yet the developmental gap persists unabated. While rural sacrifices forged urban prosperity, that very prosperity taunts peasants as an unattainable mirage. Their yearning for urban livelihoods clashes violently with the cities' contempt: metropolitan disdain manifests through overt discrimination, cultural denigration, and systemic exclusion, breeding profound resentment among the displaced. Thus, the rural-urban contradiction grows ever more pronounced. Ju Guangda, Ju Shuangyuan, and others like them feel keenly the poverty and helplessness of rural life. Driven by hopeful aspirations and the weight of familial responsibility, they come to the city hoping to earn some flexible income through sheer physical labor. Yet upon arrival, they discover that urban wages are hard-won—that the city is reluctant to accept them. Though they exhaust themselves working day and night, their pay remains pitifully meager, often delayed or arbitrarily docked. They must obtain temporary residence permits, lest authorities harass them. On the streets and public transport, they endure nothing but disdainful glances and condescending stares. Yet what the city truly demands from women like Li Ping is their youth and bodies—a transactional coexistence, never their authentic selves or dignified humanity. This brutal reality wounds Ju Guangda, Ju Shuangyuan, and Li Ping to the core: the divide between rural and urban proves absolute, their worlds segregated as irrevocably as the First and the Third.

(2) Contradictions Within Rural Society

Despite decades of reform, China's rural social structure remains rife with unresolved tensions. Migrant Workers unflinchingly exposes one particularly glaring contradiction: the fraught relationship between peasants and village committees—theoretically autonomous grassroots organizations that have effectively become de facto local governments. Legally designated as self-governing bodies with coordinating and service-oriented functions, these committees under the drama's village chief operate as coercive administrative organs: arbitrarily issuing edicts and inventing fees at will. This institutional distortion epitomizes how grassroots democracy becomes subverted by entrenched power structures. When villagers dared to disobey orders, the authorities would punish them through various means. For instance, when Ju

Guangda failed to pay village levies and fees on time, the village chief threatened to cut off his water supply. In daily life, villagers had to flatter and bribe the village chief—otherwise, they risked facing obstacles in every matter. Thus, atop the inherent hardships of peasant life loomed yet another barrier: the village committee.

(3) Contradictions in Ideology

In *Migrant Workers*, ideological clashes permeate every moment. These conflicts manifest not only as urban-rural divides but also as cognitive dissonance arising from rural transformation itself. In lived reality, such tensions interlock inextricably. Take, for instance, the clash between Ju's grandparents clinging stubbornly to their land and their sons and grandsons abandoning it to seek work in distant cities. Or the conflict between Ju Guangda's resigned acceptance of fate and Ju Shuangyuan's defiant refusal to bow to destiny. Consider, too, Li Ping and Pan Tao's pursuit of individuality and modernity, standing in sharp opposition to traditional rural women bound to domestic drudgery—bedside and stove. These ideological fractures form the very bedrock of the narrative's social critique.

(4) Interpersonal Contradictions

The conflicts between characters—sparked by love, kinship, and village ties—form the essential fabric through which the narrative unfolds. These tensions, rooted in intimate relationships, drive the story's emotional and structural momentum. The conflicts between Old Ju and his wife result in family matters always being decided by her will. In the strained relationship between Ju Guangda and Yanmei, Yanmei remains perpetually disadvantaged—enduring silently, treading carefully, never daring to overstep, until the unbearable pressure triggers her sudden fatal illness. Ju Shuangyuan and Li Ping progress from inseparable intimacy to irreconcilable differences, culminating in a painful separation. Meanwhile, the tensions between Guo Changyi and his wife persist throughout their marriage, deliberately downplayed to maintain the family for their son's sake. Li Ping and Pan Tao's rivalry, initially latent, emerges through contrasts in their wedding customs, then transforms into camaraderie through shared loneliness, only to shatter when Pan Tao's jealousy exposes Li Ping's past—precipitating the crisis in Li Ping and Ju Shuangyuan's marriage. These interpersonal conflicts collectively mirror the broader contradictions permeating contemporary rural society.

III. The Characters of *Migrant Workers*

The television drama *Migrant Workers* masterfully portrays a group of peasants—born of the loess soil, nourished by the rural land, and raised on its water. Yet, amid the tides of modern societal transformation, they also find themselves buffeted by the forces of modernization and globalization. The traditional agrarian lifestyle is ingrained in their very being, intimately familiar; yet the world beyond the countryside ceaselessly beckons, luring them to abandon the loess soil for the cities. Caught between an unseverable emotional tether to their homeland and the city's reluctant acceptance, they endure an existence defined by contradiction, confusion, and helplessness. Through these characters, we glimpse the raw reality of peasant survival—and perceive the very essence of the "three rural issues."

Li Ping is undoubtedly the character upon whom the creators lavished the most narrative care. At eighteen or nineteen, she arrived in the city carrying a rural girl's dreams of urban life and a young woman's romantic illusions. She first worked as a hotel waitress, gradually falling in love with the owner—only to be deceived: after taking advantage of her, he allowed his wife to publicly tear open her clothes and humiliate her, dealing Li Ping her first crushing blow. Later, she became involved with an educated man, only to be betrayed again. Repeatedly wounded, she grew filled with hatred toward men and despair toward life, leading to two years of self-destructive behavior during which she earned some money. Li Ping came to a bitter realization: "The city is a den of wolves and tigers—offer them sincerity, and you'll only end up as their prey." She vowed to find a rural man and return to the countryside for a tranquil life. And so, like waiting for Godot, she lingered near construction sites where migrant workers gathered, yearning for love—until she caught Ju Shuangyuan's attention and hastily married him, retreating to the village. Yet whether the countryside could truly become her final refuge remained a question even she couldn't answer with certainty. Indeed, after returning to the countryside, she desperately tried to conform—

to become the model rural wife, to live like other village women. Yet whenever exhaustion left her alone with her thoughts, waves of resentment and doubt inevitably surfaced. Li Ping's story epitomizes that of a generation of young migrant women. It must be said: she was once untainted, her mind brimming with romantic ideals, her heart full of hopeful yearning. Kind and sincere, she was brutalized by the city, forced to reassess urban life—and existence itself. This irrevocably condemned her to a psyche fractured by contradiction. Her union with Ju Shuangyuan may not have been rational, but it followed its own stubborn logic—the logic of her character. Returning to rural life, she endured its monotony—her grandmother's nagging, the constant criticisms, and all the mundanities of the countryside. This was not so much a surrender to urban or rural life, nor to circumstance, but rather a tactical retreat in her life's journey. Though the city left her feeling disillusioned—"filthy," as she herself admitted—she always knew, "I will return." And indeed, after her marriage to Ju Shuangyuan collapsed, she went back to the urban sprawl. Truth be told, even had their relationship endured, she would have inevitably found her way back to the city.

Ju Shuangyuan embodies integrity, resilience, courage, and ambition. Despite failing his college entrance exams after high school, he joins his father as a migrant worker—yet his education sets him apart from his peers, infusing his worldview with uncommon complexity. Though denied a gilded future, he refuses to capitulate to fate. Beneath his stoic exterior burns a rebellious defiance: he is convinced that raw determination and sweat alone can forge his own destiny. Thus, he labors with relentless drive, defiantly rejecting his father's admonitions—unwilling to tread the well-worn path of generational repetition. Even in marriage, he spurns rural conventions of matchmakers and parental decrees, insisting instead on an urban union that would shine with extraordinary brilliance. His father's furious opposition—culminating in a wedding boycott—meets only his cold indifference. He loved and hated fiercely. Though vaguely aware of Li Ping's past, he chose not to probe—even when her former lover sought him out to expose her "shameful" history, he retaliated without hesitation, delivering a brutal beating and a stern warning against further harassment. Yet Ju Shuangyuan harbored his own fatal flaw: face. Face before the villagers. While personally capable of accepting Li Ping's past, when rumors began circulating through the village, his tolerance shattered. In the end, it was this—not her history, but his inability to withstand the communal gaze—that doomed their marriage to anguish. Ju Shuangyuan's psyche epitomizes the inner world of contemporary rural youth—torn between inherited values and coercive modernity.

Ju Guangda, meanwhile, embodies the archetypal peasant-turned-migrant worker. Proud, obstinate, and at times calculatingly shrewd, he personifies the traditional rural patriarch—his very being a battleground where crumbling agricultural mores clash with urban survival pragmatics. Crushed by rural realities and familial burdens, Ju Guangda channels his helplessness into domestic tyranny—his sole coping mechanism being absolute household dominion. He dismisses his parents' advice when issues arise, and his wife and son's opinions never even enter his consideration. Not once has he genuinely listened to his wife's words, let alone considered her feelings—he has never truly valued his wife's feelings, nor even given them the slightest consideration. His approach to parenting relied solely on beatings and curses—to the point where not a single meaningful conversation ever passed between father and son. His default epithets for his wife and child were "that damned woman" and "worthless brat." Crushed by life's relentlessness, he resigned himself to fate, powerless to change his circumstances. His migration to the city aimed merely at providing some meager improvement to the family's desperate situation.

Yan Mei epitomizes the traditional rural woman—industrious, kind, docile, timid, and excessively cautious. Every facet of rural norms, traditions, and customs is deeply ingrained in her. She dedicates herself to serving her father-in-law, mother-in-law, husband, and son, seldom considering her own needs. Though her husband shows her neither care nor attention, she endures in silence, resigned to her fate without the slightest resistance. When an opportunity arises to work as a housemaid, she hesitates—first doubting her own capability, then agonizing over seeking permission from her in-laws and husband. Never does she dare make a decision for herself. When Guo Changyi expressed his affection and spoke to her from the heart, she was seized by overwhelming panic. She abruptly quit her city job—where she had earned her own income—and retreated to her monotonous domestic life, locking away her emotions. Yet when the harvest season arrived, a time demanding both physical labor and emotional support, her husband remained absent. It was Guo Changyi who steadied her as she teetered on the brink of collapse. In his kindness, she recognized genuine male compassion—something she had never known—and in an unguarded moment, they crossed the line together. Yet when she came to her senses, she was crushed under the weight of her own guilt—a suffocating shame that ultimately drove her to death. Yan Mei's fate is undeniably tragic, the inevitable culmination of both her conditioned psyche and the relentless grip of rural tradition.

Pan Tao epitomizes the modern rural young woman—romantic yet impractical, yearning for urban sophistication but lacking the worldly experience to grasp it. Though drawn to novelty and urban trends, she neither truly understands them nor possesses the daring to pursue them, let alone the perseverance to achieve them through hard work. From the moment Li Ping arrived at Xiema Village, Pan Tao secretly competed with her—comparing their clothes, possessions, and demeanor—yet she could never match Li Ping's innate grace. What drew her to Li Ping was precisely what she herself would never possess, and so her envy festered, unresolvable. Though Li Ping confided in her, baring her past with raw honesty, Pan Tao succumbed to that quintessential rural vice—gossiping. Whether intentionally or not, she let slip Li Ping's secrets to her mother-in-law, effectively broadcasting them to the entire village. This directly precipitated the collapse of Li Ping's marriage. And as Pan Tao herself became pregnant, gave birth, and gradually aligned with her mother-in-law's worldview, she was destined to dissolve, without a trace, into the faceless ranks of ordinary rural women.

IV. The Artistic Merits of *Migrant Workers*

The artistic distinctiveness of *Migrant Workers* lies at the heart of its emotional resonance. Unlike conventional TV dramas, it forgoes grandiose narratives and meticulous plotting, opting instead for a fluid, prose-like storytelling that unfolds with effortless grace. The rural world of Xiema Village and its migrant laborers is rendered not as a staged drama, but as an organic extension of nature itself—where the earth and its rhythms dictate life's cadence. The countryside and its people exist in symbiosis with the natural order: the land awakens, flourishes, and withers with the sun's rise and fall, the stars' slow pivot, the relentless turn of seasons. And just as the crops obey these cycles, so too do the people—trailing behind time's footsteps, scavenging what meager sustenance they can. Though societal progress has long shattered the ancient agrarian rhythms of work at sunrise, rest at sunset, rural life still moves in reluctant harmony with nature. This is why the countryside remains, at its core, a place of quietude—where existence unfolds without grand upheavals. Even as the people of Xiema Village migrate into bustling cities, they remain peripheral figures, a marginalized underclass. They must adapt to the urban order, for the city will never adapt to them. More often, it is the city that harasses them—never could they dare provoke it. Their minds and bodies are chained to the clock, laboring dawn to dusk before collapsing into makeshift shacks, only to repeat the cycle anew. Life here is simple, its stories unadorned—no grand narrative architecture is needed. Yet within this simplicity lies complexity; within monotony, vitality pulses. The series' aesthetic austerity mirrors its subject matter with unflinching fidelity. The series culminates in upheaval—Yan Mei's abrupt death and the collapse of Ju Shuangyuan and Li Ping's marriage—a tragic finale that delivers profound existential shockwaves. Yet this rupture emerges not as narrative contrivance, but as the organic culmination of the story's internal logic: an ending that is at once devastating and inevitable, perfectly consonant with the work's unflinching realist aesthetic.

Another defining artistic feature of *Migrant Workers* is its use of sketch-like portraiture within its prose-style narrative—a technique that etches characters with striking clarity through minimalist strokes. The series employs cinematic close-ups to amplify Ju Guangda's existential paralysis—capturing his vacant facial tics and aimless, hands-clasped wanderings in repetitive frames. Ju Shuangyuan's stubborn fortitude manifests through sculptural stillness: his sun-blackened face, muscles locked in tension, and wide, unblinking eyes that seem to petrify time itself. For Li Ping's psychological turmoil, the camera freezes her in silent tableaux—slack-jawed stares, immobilized silhouettes—then fractures these with muttered soliloquies, exposing the fault lines of her melancholy, distrust, and despair. This approach masterfully amplifies the distinctiveness of character portrayal, allowing each figure to emerge with heightened individuality.

In conclusion, *Migrant Workers* constructs a polyphonic portrait of peasant and migrant life, immersing us in their world through layered contradictions that expose rural China's raw realities. By anchoring itself in an unflinching ideological stance, the work spotlights the nation's agonizing "three rural issues" (agriculture, countryside, peasantry). Crucially, it transcends mere economic/political critique—sounding a cultural alarm that demands we confront how rural existence is symbolically annihilated in modernity's narrative. At its core, the "three rural issues" stem from the economic and political marginalization of rural communities—but equally critical is the erosion of their discursive power, a silencing that perpetuates their systemic exclusion. Within China's contemporary cultural sphere, proletarian narratives and subaltern voices remain fragmented and muted. In this context, *Migrant Workers* constitutes a radical discursive intervention: an attempt to reclaim narrative agency for those whom history has rendered invisible.

The Distance Between Lived Experience and Literary Narrative — An Analysis of the Text *Candy*

The novelette *Candy* by Henan-based writer Shao Li (originally published in *Writer*, No. 8, 2012) is undoubtedly the author's most emotionally concentrated work. Dubbed by critics as "autobiographical," this text channels the writer's entire emotional reservoir precisely because its narrative likely stems from firsthand lived experience. Yet when such raw personal truth enters a literary work—or rather, undergoes transformation into fiction—critical questions arise: What narrative modes might emerge from this process? How does it shape the textual flesh and blood? What potential impact might it exert on the fabric of the text itself? *Candy* stands as a paradigmatic case for examining these very issues.

I. Lived Presence and Literary Narration

The novel is entirely framed through the perspective of an "I" who narrates from a position of immediate presence, recounting the story of their own family or lineage. From the very beginning, the text establishes its self-referential nature: "I love May… Most importantly, it was in May, amid a season of golden flowers blanketing the ground, that I gave birth to a daughter. … My daughter is the greatest prize of my life, my finest creation." The narrator begins with the source of their deepest joy and pride—their daughter—before abruptly introducing the story of Su Tianming and Jin Di, which intrudes upon the narrative like an artificial barrier, almost as if to remind the reader of the constructed nature of fiction. Yet the true narrative remains rooted in the "I"—their domestic life, experiences, emotions, and lingering attachments. The very fabric of the text confirms that this is an account narrated from a position of lived presence. The "I" here is simultaneously the author, the narrator, and—indisputably—a protagonist within the work, for the narrative includes not only descriptions of the "I" but also clearly delineated traces of the "I"'s actions. More crucially, every character in the story exists in relation to the "I", and every event stems from the "I"'s lived experience. Within the author's narrative and emotional confessional, figures like Yaoyao, Jingchuan, Father, Mother, Father-in-law, and Mother-in-law form the chain that structures the story—they are the foundational elements of its narration. Whether recounting Yaoyao and Jingchuan or the parents and in-laws, these are ultimately the "I"'s stories, for these characters are all relational extensions of the "I". This manifests the hallmark of zero-distance narration—a storytelling mode where the narrator's presence permeates every layer of the text.

Indeed, literary works are composed of both the fictional and the real—yet even within the "real," there exists a distinction between artistic truth and lived truth. To examine the interplay of fiction and reality in literature, one cannot merely catalog characters, motifs, or symbols deployed in the text. A holistic assessment must consider: the author's narrative tone, the trajectory of emotional undercurrents, the psychological plausibility of characters' actions, and other implicit layers of meaning. *Candy*, as a first-person narrative, exemplifies this complexity. Generally speaking, first-person narration in fiction operates in two primary modes: one establishes a purely observational and expressive lens, where the "I" is a fictional construct; the other anchors the "I" as an actual participant within the story's events. *Candy* unmistakably belongs to the latter category. This is evident from the author's emotional investment and the narrative's palpable authenticity, which allows readers to viscerally perceive its lived reality. There is no doubt that Shao Li is a writer of profound emotional intensity—even emotional dependency—a distinctive strength that particularly characterizes many female authors. In reality, every individual possesses their own life experiences and authentic personal history, all of which may serve as reference points and raw material for literary creation. Likewise, every writer draws from their own lived encounters and sensibilities, which undeniably form the most immediate wellspring of creative impetus. The author of *Candy* experienced certain upheavals in life—or rather, lived through a kind of storied reality—and these disruptions profoundly impacted her existence, reshaping her perception of the world and life itself, while also purging and transforming her inner emotional and spiritual landscape. For a writer, such lived experience and raw emotional truth often become the catalyst for creative outbursts. However, literary creation is never mere documentation of life, especially in narrative fiction, where the essential elements lie in the depth and cohesion of characters, plot, and storyline. This demands that lived experience, personal stories, and raw truths undergo a necessary process of fermentation—only then can the writer distill, reimagine, and ultimately transmute them into literary narrative.

In my view, *Candy* is a genuine outpouring of the author's deepest emotions. "All great works are written with the flesh and blood of their creators. The spiritual essence of characters must carry the pulse of the writer's own lifeblood; the vicissitudes of their fates must bear the spray of the writer's tears."[①] Shao Li's writing brims with raw, unfiltered love for her family and kin. Precisely because of this profound attachment, when unforeseen turmoil struck her domestic world—a realm that had never before occupied her literary focus—it became a visceral confusion, an obstacle on life's journey, and ultimately a puzzle demanding literary resolution. As a government official's wife, the author had maintained a complete family life and emotional stability—a normal existence that required no particular introspection—until her husband's sudden fall from grace. This rupture in domestic harmony forced the narrator to reexamine and reexperience life anew. The central question becomes: How does such personal trauma manifest within the literary work? The plot of *Candy* is deceptively simple: The narrator's husband, a civil servant, encounters unexpected political disgrace. This shock leaves the protagonist reeling, utterly disoriented. Neither friends' concern nor relatives' comfort can calm her turmoil. When her daughter—away at school—calls during a violent thunderstorm, the narrator impulsively rushes out, hails a taxi, and

① As cited in *Editor's Manuscript Notes*, Selected Fiction Monthly, No. 9, 2012.

boards a crowded train. "In that moment, only one conviction possessed me: Find my daughter, the sole family member I could still face. I needed to be with her." Yet this constitutes merely the narrative framework of the novel—at most, the skeletal plotline. Indeed, when confronting a literary conflict like "an official's downfall," readers naturally anticipate richer dramatic development: political intrigues, moral dilemmas, or institutional exposés. The author, however, makes a deliberate narrative pivot here. Rather than mining this tension for conventional drama, she deliberately shelves the political thread, dissipates the crisis atmosphere, and redirects her focus inward. What emerges is a different kind of storytelling—one of quiet introspection rather than public spectacle.

The narrative of *Candy* can be divided into three types: first, the present-tense story including Jingchuan's incident, the narrator's literary activities, Yaoyao's storyline, and their interactions; second, past-tense stories comprising the narrator's personal experiences and the histories of her parents and in-laws, all carrying biographical authenticity; third, fictional narratives, namely the interspersed story of Su Tianming and Jin Di woven into the author's main narration. The present-tense narratives form the core thread of the work, containing the most plot-driven life episodes and conflicts. Here, the author could have easily expanded the story around pivotal moments—particularly "my" perspective and the incident involving Jingchuan—to create a broader, more dramatic arc with heightened twists and turns. Yet the author deliberately shifts focus and simplifies the narrative, a clear strategic choice. We recognize that "an official's downfall" is inherently sensational—a socially explosive event. Its prolonged repercussions, until the final societal outcome is settled, send shockwaves with far-reaching consequences. At the family level, however, the impact is nothing short of devastating. Without delving into whether the author could fully navigate such complex events or how they might be evaluated within the narrative, the sheer devastation inflicted upon family and emotional bonds tests the limits of human endurance. By containing the spread of this narrative thread—preventing Jingchuan's incident from dominating the story—the author demonstrates subtle intentionality: As both the first-person narrator and direct stakeholder entangled with Jingchuan and the events themselves, the "I" struggles to comprehend their unfolding or deliver unequivocal moral judgments. A zero-distance narration confronting these events head-on would pose profound creative challenges. This narrative restraint ultimately streamlines the story's complexity while enhancing textual control.

The past-tense narratives represent both the author's diverted plot threads and the untold backstories behind the main events. As a narrative work, *Candy* requires constructed storytelling to embody its textual essence—here, the author deliberately chooses to recount these background stories: the narrator's father as a "career revolutionary" and "local chief official," her mother as a "professional working woman" and their marital dynamics; her father-in-law (Jingchuan's father) as an "old-school intellectual bureaucrat" and his wife's story; as well as her grandmother Shang's life, among others. Yet these remain cursory sketches—the author merely outlines characters and events without detailed characterization, much less fully developed portraits. Through the author's narration, we only glimpse the rough outlines of these characters—their full richness never materializes in the text. Strictly speaking, the past-tense stories in Candy bear little connection to the initial plot threads; they are, in essence, non-essential narratives. The author's decision to abandon what could have developed into climactic storytelling in favor of these muted, unembellished accounts itself becomes a new narrative strand. Objectively speaking, once Jingchuan's incident serves its purpose as the story's catalyst, it inherently resists further development: The narrator "I"—being both author and protagonist—can neither resolve the crisis, nor foresee its trajectory, nor bring herself to speculate about outcomes. For the present "I," this remains an unsolvable equation. Such a life-altering catastrophe forces upon the narrator existential questions: What is the meaning of life and lived experience? What does calamity signify? Thus, the author sets aside the Jingchuan incident and immerses herself in stories that grapple with this fundamental question. Human life constitutes a fragment of history—to contemplate existence, one must enter history's stream. The father, mother, in-laws, grandparents—each embodies a distinct historical narrative. By returning to these ancestral histories, the author's purpose transcends mere storytelling: she positions personal catastrophe within history's vast current, examining trauma through history's expansive lens to dilute its immediate sting. This constitutes an act of psychological and spiritual alchemy—transmuting present suffering through historical perspective. As the text poignantly states: "Life accumulates countless grievances, yet upon closer examination, who among us isn't carrying their own heartbreak?" History serves as both mirror and compass—the lived experiences of fathers, mothers, in-laws, grandparents form tangible reference points. No catastrophe proves insurmountable, for life brims with quiet tenderness, lingering warmth, and aftertastes of grace sufficient to dissolve all tribulations, transforming existence into something honeyed and radiant.

The fictional subplot ultimately carries little substantive meaning—at most, it serves as a narrative foil, subtly hinting at alternative possibilities behind Jingchuan's downfall. Given *Candy*'s sensitive subject matter, the author likely grappled with a fundamental creative dilemma: how to transmute raw life experience into literary narrative. More precisely, how to articulate the "I"'s deeply personal ordeal through appropriate aesthetic means, when the experience itself remains fraught with contradictions and even "unspeakable secrets." Yet this very trauma also serves as the work's irresistible creative impetus—an urgent catharsis that demands expression. Thus, despite the text's exhaustive narration, readers still sense lingering restraint, as if confronting words trapped behind glass. After all, such intimate experiences demand necessary space for reflection and filtration—raw life cannot flood directly into the work. It must be said that the author demonstrates remarkable skill in narrative craftsmanship. Though the Jingchuan incident could be framed as a family crisis, it is fundamentally a political and social event. Such an incident invites multilayered judgments—political, legal, moral, and ethical. Outsiders may freely dissect it, but for the protagonist, who is directly entangled, even literary expression grapples with dual constraints: the subjective and the objective. So what truly precipitated Jingchuan's downfall? The author avoids direct exposition, instead engineering the stories of Su Tianming and Jin Di with deliberate artifice. Yet even these tales remain fragmentary—mere vignettes echoing other narrative threads, their elisions and pauses betraying the author's careful calibration of revelation and concealment. Though subtle, these fictional shards refract light onto Jingchuan and the narrator, offering a rare prism through which to interpret the central scandal. Herein lies the value of Su and Jin's narratives: they are allegorical keys to truths too volatile for direct handling.

The three narrative strands we encounter remain skeletal outlines—the author provides distilled narration rather than fully fleshed-out events, resulting in an impression of stories without plots. These deliberately understated recollections serve as textual groundwork, their muted tones carefully preparing the emotional and philosophical substrate for the work's ultimate revelations.

II. Narration: Subjective or Objective?

We can ascertain that *Candy* employs a familial narrative—more precisely, a narrative of the my own family and lineage. Family narratives inherently bear a stronger connection to the narrator. While seasoned writers carefully calibrate their narrative resources and techniques—considering their own positionality and distance from events—factors like personal stakes, emotional ties, and psychological bonds inevitably influence one's psyche, hidden sensitivities, and self-regard. Thus, a tension persists between third-person detachment and first-person confession, a struggle over narrative control and disclosure. This duality not only reflects the author's sociological lens but also underscores her moral stance and value judgments. "Literature invariably engages with three fundamental dimensions: the writer's sociological grounding, the social substance within the work itself, and literature's societal impact."① Indeed, familial life constitutes a form of social existence—one equally amenable to sociological scrutiny. The crux lies in how externally observed social reality and lived social reality impart radically different impressions, inevitably shaping divergent evaluative standpoints. Generally, outsiders maintain relative objectivity and rationality, while insiders operate with inherent subjectivity and emotionality. Literary narration, though a specialized mode of processing social experience, remains tethered to universal cognitive patterns. As both participant and narrator, the author must navigate fundamental questions: How should the "I" position itself toward familial events? What temporal, psychological, and emotional distance should be maintained from both the incidents and those involved? These determinations directly shape the narrative's texture and form. Evidently, the

① René Wellek & Austin Warren, *Theory of Literature* (trans. Liu Xiangyu et al.), Jiangsu Education Publishing House, 2005, p. 102.

author adopts what she deems the optimal approach—one that allows the "I" to disentangle the intricate web of characters, events, emotions, and moral logic.

The "I" functions as both the author's constructed first-person narrative device and an existentially significant character within the story—indeed, the "I" serves as the pivotal axis around which both plot and narration revolve. The narrative focuses exclusively on the past and present experiences of "I"'s immediate family and lineage, deliberately excluding broader social contexts beyond this intimate circle. Rather than following a linear, birth-to-present chronology of family life, the story erupts into being through sudden domestic rupture—Jingchuan's (the husband's) political downfall serving as its catalytic genesis. Strictly speaking, this "I" might have remained storyless. Even if we concede that writers often possess richly textured personal histories, literary works routinely transplant, fictionalize, and redirect such raw material. In *Candy*, Jingchuan embodies the my tripartite bond—shared interests, emotional ties, and collective happiness. His downfall directly threatens the family's stability and domestic equilibrium, rupturing its fragile emotional balance. As Jingchuan's most intimately connected counterpart—his wife—the "I" cannot possibly remain detached. In lived reality, core family members naturally dominate domestic narratives; likewise in literature, family stories cannot be authentically enacted by outsiders. The "I", being both primary witness and central actor, inherently claims narrative protagonism.

More crucially, without this "I", the very ontological grounding of other characters would collapse—their existence in the story derives meaning solely through relation to the narrating self. In *Candy*, the author maintains my identity as a writer while further eliminating any fictional pretense, thereby expanding the narrative and lyrical space for this voice. The "I" exists simultaneously as writer, wife, mother, daughter, and daughter-in-law—the family's sudden destabilization forces this multifaceted protagonist to the forefront, tasked with continuing existing family narratives while forging new ones, and more crucially, with healing the household's wounds and maintaining its precarious balance. Here, the writerly identity becomes irrelevant; what matters is how the "I" fulfills the obligations and responsibilities of wife, mother, daughter, and daughter-in-law, embodying these familial roles in their purest form. The narrative reconstructs other characters, events, and details entirely through my actions, recollections, and supplementary accounts - if we were to translate this narration into cinematic terms, my perspective would unquestionably dominate every frame. Thus, although the author makes no deliberate effort to sculpt my image, the very fact that all stories originate from and flow through this narrator inevitably amplifies my significance. Moreover, since every element is filtered through my perspective, the narration becomes profoundly subjective and emotionally charged.

Jingchuan serves as the narrative catalyst - my husband, a man entrenched in bureaucratic circles. Through my narration, he emerges as a talented, strong-willed official who aspired to make meaningful contributions, only to suffer an untimely downfall at the peak of his ambitions, like “a hero cut down before fulfilling his mission.” His sudden disgrace precipitates the collapse of our family’s stable world, delivering a profound physical and psychological shock that reverberates through the entire clan, ultimately unveiling the complex backstories surrounding me, Jingchuan, and our respective families. In truth, the text dedicates surprisingly few passages to Jingchuan—were this a play or film, he would scarcely qualify as a supporting character. Yet his importance is monumental: he is the emotional linchpin for both my psyche and all characters in my orbit, the neural center of the entire narrative. Without Jingchuan, neither the story’s events nor my profound lyrical outpourings could exist. Yaoyao, as the child binding me and Jingchuan in our nuclear family, remains constrained by her student’s limited worldview—perhaps naive, certainly immature, even childish in her perceptions. When the family crisis struck, my first instinct was to protect Yaoyao, shielding the child from harm. Yet in this turmoil, she unexpectedly revealed remarkable maturity and resilience, becoming the emotional anchor for both my crumbling self and our disintegrating household. That Yaoyao could transform into such a pillar of support speaks to both narrative necessity and profound psychological sustenance—a dual function that sustains the story’s emotional architecture while providing vital spiritual ballast. Yaoyao’s youth liberates her from the weight of family history and the entrenched mental frameworks of older generations. Unburdened, she alone can break through the psychological barriers erected by this crisis - becoming both my personal beacon and the embodiment of our family's future possibilities. Her very existence represents hope distilled: untainted by generational baggage, uncompromised by cyclical trauma.

As for the related figures—father, mother, father-in-law, mother-in-law, even grandfathers and grandmothers—they serve as essential narrative elements, symbolic representations within my storytelling, and vessels for lyrical expression. The author deliberately confines all characters to the immediate and extended family circle, thus defining this as a pure domestic narrative. Although this family maintains extensive and profound connections with society at large, and although Jingchuan himself was deeply immersed in the worldly affairs of officialdom—his experiences inherently rich with social implications—the author deliberately excises and filters out these broader contexts. Only those belonging to my familial orbit are summoned forth, their stories distilled to their essential, domestic resonance. How many characters populate this family? How many stories lie within its walls? We can well imagine. The author's deliberate narrative construction stems from an essential truth: each family member serves as a lyrical vessel, perfectly suited to channel the author's emotional needs. As the critical principle reminds us: "Only when we comprehend a novelist's artistic methods, and can concretely—not abstractly—articulate how the fictional world relates to its social reality, does our analysis gain true significance."①

① René Wellek & Austin Warren, *Theory of Literature* (trans. Liu Xiangyu et al.), Jiangsu

III. Textual Form: Personal Lyricism or Public Narrative?

We may tentatively categorize Candy as the writer's personal narrative. As a creative endeavor, literature inherently constitutes individualized expression—a form of private storytelling in one sense. Yet more fundamentally, literary works articulate universal human experiences and collective emotions, ultimately destined for public circulation as consumable narratives, thereby transforming into communal discourse and cultural artifacts. *Candy* is classified as personal narrative precisely because its content remains inextricably bound to the author's own lived experience—indeed, it essentially chronicles the writer's private world. While lacking convoluted plot twists, the work compensates with extraordinary emotional and intellectual depth, where feelings and ideas ultimately eclipse storytelling mechanics—this constitutes its distinctive literary signature.

The work's intellectual essence manifests in its meditation on life and family. The author deliberately transcends the initially established plotlines, transitioning into fluid, arrhythmic narration that meticulously recounts the lifetimes of my father, mother, in-laws, and grandparents. Here, the true intent is never mere storytelling, but rather existential examination—each bi-

Education Publishing House, 2005, p. 112.

ography becomes a case study in human endurance. Take my father: a lifelong revolutionary who held regional leadership with unyielding integrity, only to face solitary old age marked by uncharacteristic compromise with his children. Or my mother—industrious, frugal, unadorned—"a thorough revolutionary who devoted 80% of her energy to work, 10% to my father, leaving the mere remnants for her children." The father-in-law, a scholar from a once-prosperous family, sought refuge with his betrothed's household when his family fortunes collapsed—living thereafter in undistinguished comfort, free from worldly concerns, finding solace in simple pleasures. His wife, fiercely determined, existed solely for husband and children: "Her husband was her heaven, even if merely symbolic. So long as that heaven didn't collapse, her world remained whole—she was, above all, wife and mother." Then there was Grandmother Shang, daughter of a landowning family, who "lived a life of vegetarian piety", whose "eyes reflected all creation yet held no human presence", who "found joy in but two pursuits: planting trees and chanting sutras"—existing with Daoist transparency and imperturbable serenity. Though bound by blood, each relative embodies distinct lived experiences and philosophies—every life forged its own path, every existence justified its own logic. Within these seemingly simple biographies dwell profound complexities, yet whether facing adversity or fortune, all met their circumstances with unflinching equanimity, steadfastly transforming ordinary existence into something honeyed and poetic. Life brims with fractures, families with shadows, yet the household remains our fundamental habitat—where neither personal calamities nor domestic misfortunes constitute sufficient cause to abandon life's journey or shatter familial bonds. For the narrator, Jingchuan's downfall violently disrupted domestic order and stability. Confronting this crisis demanded transcending the incident itself—liberating oneself from the trauma to rediscover life's fundamental truths: existence isn't perpetual comfort, nor is daily living endless sunshine. Misfortune and pain constitute but one modality of being; life overflows with greater beauties worthy of pursuit and contemplation. Guided by this very conviction, the author redirects the narrative trajectory to excavate family history and ancestral legacies. Through this process, my turbulent emotions gradually settle—the initial agitation and resentment cool into measured reflection, ultimately crystallizing into a rational historical perspective. On this macro level, wounds prove ultimately healable; the act of living, and living well, retains irreducible meaning.

Candy's most luminous quality lies in its emotional abundance and depth. Undoubtedly, my love for family and kin is absolute—my entire emotional being resides within this social unit. Any disruption to this repository of affection sends seismic tremors through my psyche, which explains why Jingchuan's downfall so violently destabilized my emotional equilibrium, unleashing years of pent-up feelings. His crisis became both catalyst and vessel for my lyrical outpouring. Readers will unmistakably perceive that this work transcends mere storytelling to become pure emotional articulation. The "I" in this work expresses a tapestry of intimate affections—familial, domestic, and ethical—with emotionality serving as the golden thread woven through every passage. My love for Jingchuan resonates particularly deeply: "He was a teenage poet who once held some sway among university literati." "Our romance began at seventeen, blossomed into marriage at twenty-one, and has remained unshaken by major emotional ruptures." Though both families initially opposed our union, though "we spent over a decade living apart," our bond endured—a mutual adoration and profound interdependence where, as the saying goes, "a man's half is woman, just as woman's half is man." Though mundane as still water, Jingchuan's crisis resurrects every shimmering moment of our love—each memory now luminous with retroactive preciousness. Yaoyao stands as our joint masterpiece, my most treasured creation, and my emotional anchor amidst the storm. While maternal love is universal, my devotion to her borders on narcissistic obsession: "I gave birth to her in a season of golden blossoms blanketing the earth. As she grew, I would summon friends with unapologetic pride just to witness her existence." "Look," I'd proclaim, "my daughter!" I cared not if they called me narcissistic—while I'd never boast about my novels, I could rightfully flaunt this perfect creation. When friends saw her, their awestruck praise confirmed it: this was mastercraft. ... She is life's greatest prize, my finest work. Thus her health, growth, future loves—all became inextricable concerns. Even Jingchuan's final plea after his downfall was primal: "Take care of our girl." "I" loved my father deeply, yet carried profound guilt toward him. "After retirement, we sent him to Shenzhen with my youngest sister, justifying it as better for his health—never letting him return home...In his final years, he became utterly pliant before us, demanding nothing, his gaze as meek as a lamb's. I knew what he desired, yet denied him even the chance to speak, arbitrarily silencing him." "Father drank lifelong and smoked three packs daily. I'd threaten him—'This will kill you.' My mother, who had managed him for decades, pleaded: 'Can't he at least smoke less?' I refused. Terrified of my disapproval, he quit entirely."The family crisis and its attendant pain magnified love's preciousness—yet toward my father, I'd doled out such meager affection. "From my earliest memory, he funded my pocket money," yet my reciprocation paled wretchedly in comparison, leaving irreversible regret that claws at my conscience. It is precisely by plunging into this torrent of familial love that the author's soul undergoes catharsis, emerging with crystalline understanding of life's value, existence's purpose, and being's essence.

As a woman writer, Shao Li demonstrates particular mastery in rendering and channeling emotions. Thus, *Candy* might be more accurately classified as a lyrical novel than a conventional novelette. While emotion is universally acknowledged as literature's vital core, this work achieves extraordinary affective density—every sentence saturated with the author's passions and moods. Even structurally, the text reveals its essence: rejecting chronological or spatial logic, it flows entirely according to emotional currents, making feeling its foundational architecture. Consequently, the narrative unfolds with a gentle, organic rhythm, devoid of tightly-woven plotlines typical of fiction. The author "moves freely between reality and fiction, using language to artistically redress life's deficiencies while offering imaginative solace for its wounds"[①]. We may fully interpret Candy as channeling familial experiences into lyrical meditation—these personal epiphanies, though intimate, achieve universal resonance.

① As cited in *Editor's Manuscript Notes*, Selected Fiction Monthly, No. 9, 2012.

On the Personalized Characterization of Shao Li's Literary Narrative

Shao Li stands as one of the most inventive female writers within the contemporary Central Plains literary circle. Her gendered identity imbues her works with distinct feminine attributes. Notably, her creative approach frequently employs a female perspective to mold the masculine world, while subtly maintaining an intrinsic permeability between these gendered realms. The writer appears to construct a harmonious universe through her gynocentric cultural cognition. Shao's literary narratives are saturated with intense lyricism, which operates as a parallel mode of expression alongside her storytelling. Together, these elements coalesce into the singular signature of her narrative style.

I. Feminine Perspective: The Foundational Mode of Experiencing Life

Gender consciousness manifests as both an expression of sexual identity and a feature of cultural cognition. As a woman writer, Shao Li' s works inherently embody feminine cultural cognition—not as deliberate feminist posturing, but as an organic mode of perceiving and experiencing life. "Shao Li is no 'feminist'; she asserts no confrontational gendered stance. Yet within complex social landscapes and quotidian gender dynamics, her fiction inevitably manifests a feminine perspective—one intrinsically interwoven with personal experience and lived understanding."①

① Li Qun (ed.), *Studies on Shao Li, Qiao Ye, and Ji Wenjun*, Henan University Press,

As a writer, Shao Li is profoundly intuitive, possessing that heightened sensitivity peculiar to women's perception of the world and lived experience. She consciously embraces her feminine identity, aspiring to embody womanhood in its entirety—to be a whole woman, a dutiful daughter, a devoted wife and mother. "My domestic circumstances are rather fortunate," she reflects. "My husband is my childhood sweetheart, our bond remains strong, and by conventional standards, life has treated me kindly—a respectable career, a good marriage. For a woman, this might be seen as the ultimate fulfillment, as if further yearning would be ungrateful. Perhaps I too have acquiesced to fate—beyond my work, there was only tending to husband and child. When my daughter began piano lessons at seven, I devoted every ounce of energy outside my career to her."① This constitutes a crucial self-positioning that fundamentally shapes her worldview.

The dichotomy of masculine fortitude and feminine gentleness reflects physiological distinctions. Psychological research confirms women's heightened olfactory sensitivity, psychological granularity, and perseverative cognition. Shao Li's feminine perspective embodies a robust, holistic womanhood. As a woman, she inhabits all conventional feminine roles with equanimity—grappling with life's tribulations, viscerally experiencing earthly joys and adversities, accumulating quintessential feminine wisdom. Yet as a

---

2015, p. 45.

① Li Qun (ed.), *Studies on Shao Li, Qiao Ye, and Ji Wenjun*, Henan University Press, 2015, p. 39.

writer, she transcends ordinary womanhood through refined perceptivity: her world-sensing achieves microscopic precision, her life-observation attains penetrative profundity. Thus, her feminine consciousness lacks coerciveness or exclusivity. Within Shao Li's conceptual framework, gender composition follows natural logic—she perceives no primordial chasm between masculinity and femininity. Each gender occupies its ordained position in the world's architecture: men need not dominate women, nor women resist men. Patriarchy may prove illusory in lived experience, while feminism/feminist ideology finds no epistemological foothold in her philosophy. She demonstrates not only empathetic understanding toward women, but also a capacity for masculine perspectival immersion—perceiving the world through the dialectical framework of gender dyadism. Yet her perception transcends masculine ruggedness and reductionism, just as it surpasses certain women's preoccupation with superficialities. Instead, she employs holographic feminine receptivity to life's tactile minutiae, wielding a woman writer's penetrative gaze to capture existence's vital essence and illuminate the fundamental nature of human duality.

Shao Li declares: "My abiding love for life remains the perennial wellspring of joy."[①] This devotion stems, first, from her embrace of life's tumultuous currents through the lens of an emotionally whole woman. Moreover,

---

① Li Qun (ed.), *Studies on Shao Li, Qiao Ye, and Ji Wenjun*, Henan University Press, 2015, p. 40.

she perceives our society as fundamentally sound—where both realized and potential narratives unfold within rational bounds, leaving no warrant for groundless hatred or unwarranted abandonment. Despite life's inevitable misfortunes, contradictions, and perplexities, Shao Li's creative work remains rooted in ardor and oriented toward gratitude. Thus, her writings consistently radiate warmth. As she observes, "I believe my works carry a certain luminosity—take Candy for instance. Though it portrays pain, loss, and misunderstanding, you'll find no hatred, no resentment or indignation."[①] "If one insists on reducing life's meaning to tattered rags, or trampling beauty into worthlessness—isn't that its own brand of affectation and hypocrisy?"[②] Thus, her works embody authenticity and scrupulousness. With visceral engagement, she renders life's tapestry; with empathic insight, she narrates each character's journey. Nearly all critics have viscerally resonated with the emotional veracity in Shao Li's works—an intensity seemingly achievable only by women writers, and a profundity attainable only by one who, like Shao Li, embraces existence with such wholehearted fervor.

① Ibid., p. 32.

② Ibid., p. 39.

II. The Masculine Sphere: Architectural Core of Narrative

As a standard-bearer of literary realism, Shao Li champions lived experience without societal antagonism or critical impulse—her imperative being unmediated articulation of existence. Her narratives dissect stratified social realities, excavating latent contradictions, existential quandaries, and relational complexities to faithfully reconstruct the raw textures of common lives: their joys, sweetness, bitterness, and disquietudes. Stationed at life's vital crossroads, she panoramically surveys the human theater, capturing quotidian trajectories and epiphanic instants of both genders. Though a woman writer, she deliberately avoids constructing a gynocentric distortion—eschewing subjective or dogmatic feminist posturing to maintain anthropological equilibrium. A comprehensive survey of Shao Li's oeuvre reveals her deliberate construction of the masculine sphere through a distinctly feminine lens—perhaps reflecting her perception of ontological authenticity. Within life's theater, men predominantly occupy the proscenium; in Shao's immediate orbit, masculine narratives evidently resonate with particular profundity, impelling their artistic transmutation.

In *The Quality of My Life*, Wang Qilong emerges as the author's meticulously sculpted protagonist. A quintessential farmer's son—born, educated, and raised rurally before ultimately escaping agrarian confines through university admission—this earthy provincial lad embodies dogged diligence as existential default. Yet his trajectory confirms life's cruel paradox: though study and labor remain one's sovereign duties, destiny refuses to bow to individual will. Thus unfolds his odyssey of institutional caprice: college entrance preferences mysteriously altered; post-graduation assignments revoking campus retention, exiling him to his rural origins; agricultural bureau postings abruptly redirected to agrotechnical schools. When Wang Qilong resigned himself to this purgatorial existence, cosmic irony intervened—administrative redistricting catapulted him via the headmaster's whim to Xinyuan Agricultural Bureau. This karmic detour launched his bureaucratic metamorphosis: from office director to deputy bureau chief, county magistrate, Party secretary, and ultimately mayor—each promotion burnishing the rustic youth into a statesman of improbable polish. The early Wang Qilong, rooted in societal substrata and burdened by ignoble status, often found himself at mercy of capricious fate. Yet the author plants deliberate narrative seeds—his bones carry aristocratic marrow, his veins thrum with patrician blood. His grandmother, daughter of a Nanjing merchant-prince during the city's gilded six-dynasty era, became a refugee in the Central Plains after Japanese troops massacred the city. Though his father shattered her expectations, she invested her hopes in the boy. Raised under her tutelage, he absorbed her rigorous cultivation—a spiritual askesis designed to transcend rural vulgarity, ultimately propelling him toward the metropolitan world of her lost past. Having entered officialdom, Wang Qilong appears to have shed his former self, emerging as a man of pronounced agency. In his later years, save for the lingering frustration and resignation stemming from his marital ties to Xu Caixia (a vestige of his past existence), he navigates life with piscine ease and unshakable confidence. A consummate practitioner of interpersonal and bureaucratic arts, his ascent—from deputy director of the Agricultural Bureau to county magistrate, then Party secretary and ultimately mayor—unfolds with hydraulic inevitability. Not a trace remains of his erstwhile timidity and vulgarity. This transformation can't help but strike us as a fundamental rupture in the continuum of Wang's character and conduct. Wang Qilong epitomizes the triumphant male archetype—both socially and bureaucratically. Through him, we glimpse the author's sociological acuity and the ideals encrypted within this characterization. In our hypercompetitive era, where men perpetually spearhead the charge (particularly in officialdom), success proves elusive for women—and paradoxically more arduous for men. This constitutes Shao Li's essential thesis: her narrative traces a commoner's odyssey of struggle and self-actualization, while exposing the buried strata beneath sanctioned triumphs.

In *The Quality of My Life*, Jing Chuan and Su Tianming similarly inhabit the bureaucratic sphere. Though Jing operates primarily as a background presence in the narrative architecture, his structural significance proves indispensable. Su Tianming, meanwhile, functions as Jing's photographic negative, serving as the author's dotted line—a strategic, half-visible thread guiding readers through the story's political labyrinth. Jing Chuan emerges as a competent, strong-willed official with reformist aspirations. Like many bureaucrats, he ascended smoothly through the ranks after university—no scion of political aristocracy, yet achieving preternaturally early promotion to regional leadership. His career trajectory epitomizes bureaucratic fortune...until catastrophic collapse at the zenith of his ambitions. This tragic denouement—contrasting sharply with Wang Qilong's narrative—provokes the author's ontological interrogation of officialdom's vicissitudes, tracing two generations' cyclical rises and falls (including the narrator's father) through the merciless gyres of political destiny. Herein lies life's unvarnished truth. The political arena, predominantly male-dominated, presents a Janus-faced reality: the glittering allure of success counterpoised by its undercurrent of bitterness and tragedy. An official's destiny never unfolds in isolation—it interlaces irrevocably with familial orbits, ultimately refracting broader sociocultural and ethical constellations. Herein perhaps lies the author's narrative impetus. Jing Chuan's joys and sorrows resonate inextricably with his family's—the masculine sphere encompasses the feminine, mirroring society's intricate tapestry. This interplay transcends mere power dynamics, revealing fundamental human and social truths. Thus, the bureaucratic arena is no exclusive male dominion. It becomes a crucible testing human resilience and fate, entangling the complexities of human nature itself. Neither cynical disdain nor blind reverence suffices—only clear-eyed reckoning with its paradoxes.

In *The Fortieth Circle*, characters like Niu Dazhuizi and Qi Guanglu—alongside Liu Wanfu from *The Case of Liu Wanfu*—epitomize society's substrata. Even Police Station Director Zha Weidong remains a grassroots officer. These ordinary men, akin to Wang Qilong in their struggles, confront adversity while shouldering familial burdens with masculine fortitude. Yet unlike Wang or Jing Chuan—who orchestrate grand designs through institutional authority—they wage solitary battles as individuals. They constitute an essential stratum of the masculine cosmos within Shao Li's literary universe. Niu Dazhuizi epitomizes the get-rich-quick archetype of China's early reform era—a chef whose culinary virtuosity propelled him to seize the moment when enterprise contracting began. While others hesitated, he "slapped his thighs" and signed a five-year contract, embodying the Darwinian ethos of "the bold feast while the timid starve." His restaurant, spearheaded by the signature "Yuan-style noodles" and anchored in regional Henan-Anhui-Hubei cuisine, soon thrived spectacularly. Almost overnight, he transformed—donning Western suits and cruising in sedans—a quintessential nouveau riche ascension (*The Fortieth Circle*). Just as his restaurant peaked, the contract expired—ownership transferred, his golden luck severed. "Those managerial years inflated Dazhuizi's ambitions yet atrophied his skills; his hands could no longer grip cleavers nor ladles." Now toting a briefcase, he morphed into a full-fledged wheeler-dealer. While his business ventures' success remains dubious, he "certainly dined well daily, chauffeured about with entourages, the very picture of fleeting glory" (*The Fortieth Circle*). Such was the limited metamorphosis available to a cook amid societal upheaval. Qi Guanglu, a laid-off factory worker turned disabled after a forklift crushed his leg, became a government-subsidized meat vendor. Initially scraping by, his fortunes turned when Niu Dazhuizi mentored him in meat-arranging techniques—a skill amplified by street market renovations that transformed his stall into prime real estate. Yet harboring no grand ambitions beyond securing Niu's daughter Guangrong as his wife, he sought only to sustainably operate his butcher shop and provide for his family. That modest dream shattered when ex-officer Zhang Hetian's machinations not only destroyed his business but framed the couple with fabricated charges, landing them in prison. Niu Guangrong's desperate attempts to save Qi Guanglu first cost her unborn child, then her life in a fatal leap. Driven to rage, Qi ambushed Zhang Hetian's brother-in-law—Police Chief Zha Weidong—with his butcher knife, sealing his fate as a murderer. Liu Wanfu epitomizes the perpetually overlooked peasant class. As a rural patriarch, his familial burdens weighed heavier. Mining coal to survive, he cheated death in a shaft collapse; later, a truck crash nearly claimed him until a police commissioner's intervention. His odyssey—village to city and back—finally led to orchard stewardship, pursuing modest prosperity and hard-won peace. Yet the true descent began when local bully Liu Qi—exploiting a prior feud—systematically tormented the family: publicly harassing his wife, sabotaging his construction materials business, and ultimately violating his daughter. When Liu Qi again invaded their orchard to assault both women, Liu Wanfu seized his cleaver in righteous fury. Liu Qi and his accomplices died on the spot. Knowing the ancient code of "a life for a life," Liu surrendered voluntarily—only to receive a life sentence. "Three deaths and three rebirths"—this phrase encapsulates the peasant's odyssey of existential vicissitudes. Though a civil servant, Zha Weidong remained entrenched in society's substrata. Born into poverty, his post-university assignment as a detective showcased his investigative brilliance—decorated and promoted to police chief through sheer meritocratic striving. Zha Weidong's death at Qi Guanglu's blade may have been unwarranted, yet his role as both Zhang Hetian's brother-in-law and the police station chief—a focal point of public grievances—implicates him inextricably. Given that Qi's wife Guangrong died in custody at his station, and his officers detained the couple, Zha's tragic end becomes tragically logical. Herein lies China's social Gordian knot: where law and morality promise clarity, they instead reveal an irreducible entanglement of power, kinship, and systemic failure.

Shao Li's portrayal of male characters presents a microcosm of Chinese masculinity. While we cannot exhaustively catalog every male character in her works, figures like Wang Qilong, Jing Chuan, Su Tianming, Niu Dazhuizi, Qi Guanglu, Liu Wanfu, and Zha Weidong—interwoven with officials, laborers, peasants, intellectuals, and private entrepreneurs—they collectively constitute a polyphonic masculine universe. If women hold up half the sky, men arguably form its structural foundation. In both traditional and contemporary Chinese consciousness, men are mythologized as indispensable pillars—the collapse of male stability spells familial ruin, especially in physical labor contexts. This perception extends to society at large, where masculinity functions as a load-bearing structure. With unflinching clarity, Shao Li's narratives expose the fissures in these supposed pillars, revealing the complex social textures woven from performative masculinity and unspoken fragility. In her narratives, men strive as societal pillars—sheltering families yet enduring greater hardships, weathering fiercer physical and psychological storms. Their increased vulnerability makes their stories more epic, more tragic. Ultimately, their sagas mirror society itself. This explains why Shao Li, as a woman writer, trains her gaze so intently on masculinity.

III. Gender Dialectics: The Value Architecture of Narrative

While constructing her masculine sphere, Shao Li simultaneously sustains feminine narratives. Her male world never exists in isolation, but rather as an inextricably gendered tapestry—warp and weft eternally interlaced. Her masculine and feminine spheres coexist without hierarchy or antagonism—a true synthesis of being. As daughter, wife, mother, and career woman, Shao Li possesses intimate knowledge of feminine existence, yet equally profound insight into masculine realities. She conceptualizes men and women as fundamental social elements in dynamic relation, through which life's meaning emerges. This vision finds crystallization in her twin novels—*The Quality of My Life* and *The Quality of My Survival*—interrogating human (gender-neutral) modes of existence and their intrinsic value.

Wang Qilong's existence remains perpetually intertwined with feminine presence—indeed, women constitute the very impetus for his growth, struggles, and triumphs. During childhood, he dwelt entirely beneath his grandmother's wings. From infancy, she enveloped him in her embrace; they ate and slept together as she sought to mold this grandson according to her own ideals. Henceforth, she dictated his every move, investing in him the family's aspirations. Under her dominion, he moved with circumspection, never daring to contravene her will—studying what she decreed, obeying without question. His childhood diverged radically from others'. In essence, the grandmother functioned as his existential double. The admiration Wang Qilong received from rural classmate Li Xiang likely marked his adolescence's psychological idyll—an indispensable gender awakening. Yet his university peer Feng Jia's rejection harshly revealed the urban-rural historical divide. The woman truly enmeshed in his existence, however, was Xu Caixia. Their entanglement originated in her dysfunctional marriage's craving for normalcy, while Wang's attraction stemmed equally from her calculated seduction and his own sexual awakening. Their eventual union bred profound dissonance: while physical possession ignited complex passions, all else withered into ennui. Perhaps constrained by political, social, ethical, and cultural forces, Wang Qilong never discards Xu Caixia, instead channeling his frustrations into relentless work—this very sublimation ironically becoming his "secret" to success. Characters like Huang Xiaofeng, Dai Xiaotao, and Li

Qingping function as symbolic foils: the ex-lover, the spa attendant, the college girl strategically placed before the matrimonially-weary Wang, testing his masculine resolve while attempting to compensate for his gendered existential lacks. In truth, Wang Qilong's life had solidified—this void proved irreparable. Xu Caixia was both his historical anchor and inescapable reality. The author then strategically introduces Annie into his orbit: a cultured, sophisticated modern woman from an elite family, whose haughty demeanor crumbled unexpectedly before Wang's conquest. Though narratively abrupt, this device blatantly amplifies Wang's masculine potency. Their intellectual rapport and effortless harmony delight him. To facilitate Annie's entry, the author terminates Xu Caixia via vehicular fatality—a seemingly logical yet ultimately reductive narrative maneuver, for life's true logic demands historical continuity. Ultimately, Annie and Wang part ways amid profound regret. Yet regardless of outcomes, these women remain constitutive to Wang's existence. "As masculine becoming's referential framework, the novel meticulously chronicles the key women shaping Wang Qilong's trajectory...Each actively molds his successful masculinity, serving as indispensable Other-mirrors throughout his development."①

① Lv Dongliang. "*In Search of Modes to Articulate Existential Being: On Shao Li's Novelistic Art*." Journal of Xinyang Normal University (Philosophy and Social Sciences Edition), no. 2, 2014.

Jing Chuan's relationships exhibit remarkable harmony. In *The Quality of My Survival*, his relationship with his wife— "I" traces back to their childhood sweetheart days. A university poet—embodying that era's masculine charm—he later became a high-ranking official. "I" am a writer—a person of intellect and refined taste. Our marriage epitomizes perfect harmony and mutual understanding. "Jingchuan and I fell in love at seventeen or eighteen, married at twenty-one, and have enjoyed a fulfilling marriage without major emotional breakdowns." "I love May...most importantly because in May, when golden flowers blanket the earth, I gave birth to a daughter. As she grew, I would proudly summon friends to admire her. 'Look,' I'd say, 'my daughter!' I didn't fear being called narcissistic—while I couldn't boast about my novels, I had every right to showcase my perfectly conceived child. My friends would sincerely marvel: 'This is truly exquisite work.'... My daughter is life's greatest award, my finest creation." (*The Quality of My Survival*) Their daughter Yaoyao is undoubtedly the crystallization of their love, and the trio of "I," Jingchuan, and Yaoyao formed a happy family. Life was originally a serene and harmonious picture, until Jingchuan's incident mercilessly tore it apart. The triangular structure of "I," Jingchuan, and Yaoyao was shattered, and the natural interdependence between men and women in life was lost. Without the support of Jingchuan, the woman had to stand up in life. "I" and Jingchuan's first thought was to protect their daughter: "At that time, I had only one belief—to find my daughter, the only family I could see, and to stay with her" (The Quality of My Survival). In the male consciousness, women are the most vulnerable to life's upheavals, hence men instinctively prioritize protecting them. Yet women too can grow resilient through adversity, bearing life's burdens in their own way. Neither "I" nor daughter Yaoyai collapsed under the strain—proving far less fragile than imagined. Here we witness how men and women form an integral whole, with gender serving as the very adhesive that binds life's unity.

Though Niu Dazhuizi was a nouveau riche profiteer, he held no sway at home with women. His wife, chronically ill yet tyrannical, forced him into constant retreat. Even with his daughter, he could neither scold nor strike—instead, she joined her mother in tormenting him. After his wife's death, he married an out-of-town magazine peddler, plunging the household into chaos: "Guangrong and her stepmother clashed like gamecocks—pecking and clawing without respite" (*The Fortieth Circle*). Later, after Dazhuizi was dismissed as restaurant manager and Guangrong suffered severe injuries in her new marriage, the household dynamics shifted. "These events unexpectedly mellowed Dazhuizi's new wife—her demeanor toward Guangrong softened, no longer as spiteful. When seeing Guangrong overwhelmed or in need, she'd proactively assist." With the restaurant defunct, his wife resumed her old trade: "peddling newspapers, magazines, and office supplies, earning steady monthly income." Paradoxically, domestic harmony emerged (*The Fortieth Circle*). The narrative reveals how daily conflicts and setbacks necessitate mutual understanding, tolerance, and support between genders. Qi Guanglu colluded with Niu Dazhuizi to forcibly marry Guangrong through a fait accompli. Though Guangrong had previous romantic entanglements and sustained severe injuries, Qi remained enchanted by her "delicate, fair-skinned beauty." Even after discovering Guangrong "lying naked in bed" with her stepbrother, Qi avoided outright confrontation—his sole demand being that she bear him a son. This forbearance gradually transformed Guangrong. She actively assisted Qi's meat business, their lives gaining vitality as genuine affection blossomed. When framed later, Guangrong prioritized protecting Qi, ultimately leaping to her death to free him; Qi, in turn, became a murderer to avenge her. While portraying an extreme form of love, the work exposes the devastating costs—to both family and society—of shattered bonds and ruptured harmony.

In The Case of Liu Wanfu, the protagonist's homicide ultimately stemmed from defending his family, protecting women, and upholding dignity. Though Liu Qi's notorious village tyranny provoked widespread outrage, it wasn't the trigger. What drove Liu Wanfu to kill was Liu Qi's repeated sexual violations against his daughter and harassment of his wife—crossing the ultimate line of tolerance. Despite his wife and daughter urging forbearance for the family's safety, Liu Wanfu—as a man who cherished his family, possessed humanity, courage, dignity, and responsibility—could endure no further. "Literary narrative constitutes a distinctive mode of engaging with social realities, yet remains aligned with fundamental cognitive patterns."① The story's inevitable conclusion sees Liu eliminating Liu Qi through primal justice—complex legal avenues having ceased to be narratively viable. Thus, women embody a mode of existence for men, just as men do for women. In a world composed of both genders, each lives for the other. Shao Li's works suggest that human flourishing requires gender symbiosis—only through such harmony can families thrive, societies stabilize, and positive energies proliferate.

IV. Lyricism: Narrative's Parallel Expression

Adopting a feminine perspective for storytelling inherently involves balancing objectivity. In Shao Li's works, the author undoubtedly narrates the tales of men and women from her own lived experience. While the female viewpoint offers uniqueness, it naturally carries limitations. Ideally, one would maximize its distinctiveness while transcending its constraints—a perfect scenario. Yet such paradoxes prove inherently unresolvable.

Shao Li's literary narratives distinctly amplify feminine subjectivity. Whether in character portrayal or storytelling, they overflow with the author's emotional richness, mirroring her psyche. Most female characters in Shao's works fiercely guard their emotional autonomy—a clear reflection of

① Wu Shenggang. "*The Distance Between Lived Experience and Literary Narrative: An Analysis of Candy.*" Journal of Xinyang Normal University (Philosophy and Social Sciences Edition), no. 2, 2014.

the author's gendered consciousness. In Shao's universe, women should positively inhabit male lives, possessing careers, families, love, dignity. They become the primary vessels for Shao's deepest affections. In *The Quality of My Life*, the grandmother and Annie represent the author's most cherished female archetypes. The grandmother embodies a transcendental feminine spirit—her youthful tryst having altered her destiny, she seeks redemption through molding Wang Qilong, determined to restore aristocratic living through him. This reflects a woman's steadfast devotion to her beliefs, infused with the author's own psyche. Meanwhile, Annie—a willful "iron lady"—defies expectations by gravitating toward Wang, a narrative choice driven by authorial sensibilities. Here, the subconscious pull of the "scholar-beauty" trope emerges: an accomplished mayor naturally attracts refined companions, deliberately contrasting Xu Caixia's domestic mundanity. Indeed, the grandmother and Annie represent female archetypes meticulously crafted from the author's ideals, each shaping Wang Qilong's persona at different stages. This schema mirrors Shao Li's psychological and emotional logic. Thus, her narratives flow less from plot or character development than from the author's own affective currents—her unreserved infusion of lived wisdom and raw sentiment into characters renders the storytelling process essentially "emotionally adrift". Minghui in *Minghui's Christmas* similarly functions as the author's emotional "mirror". Proud and self-assured in her rural life yet defeated, she seeks urban status and dignity. The narrative traces her journey—when fleeting tenderness, bought with physical and emotional currency, briefly convinces her of dignity's attainment. Yet this illusory existence demands her ultimate sacrifice as the illusion shatters. To my reading,

Shao Li's distinct lyricism stems precisely from this unimpeded emotional flow, explaining her fiction's pronounced prose-poetic qualities. "Shao Li's fiction typically avoids overly convoluted plots or sensational narratives." Her works reveal characters and events through emotional exposition: "Narratively, Shao maintains remarkable composure—she never amplifies evil or erotic elements, exercising restrained, even repressed storytelling that renders her works pristine yet tension-filled."① Shao tells stories rather than presenting them as cinematic story-streams, resulting in measured pacing and deliberate fragmentation—all manifestations of formidable authorial control. In *The Quality of My Survival*, characters and plot unfold according to the narrator's meandering thoughts and emotions. The author adopts a discursive style—shifting between husband, daughter, parents, even grandparents—with flashbacks that defy conventional storytelling. Through the narrator's cyclical recollections, Shao conveys nuanced experiences, "striving to articulate both the difficulty and necessity of mutual understanding between people." "While we cannot simplistically equate the female protagonists with the author's externalized psyche, we keenly sense her overwhelming control over narrative progression, female characterization, and psychological revelation."② Balancing emotional restraint with narrative development proves inherently challenging.

① Li Qun (ed.), *Studies on Shao Li, Qiao Ye, and Ji Wenjun*, Henan University Press, 2015, p. 53.

② Lv Dongliang. "*In Search of Modes to Articulate Existential Being: On Shao Li's Novelistic Art.*" Journal of Xinyang Normal University (Philosophy and Social Sciences Edition), no. 2, 2014.

While Shao Li's masculine world reflects contemporary China's "political realities," her narrative approach rejects conventional bureaucratic fiction tropes—be it corruption/anti-corruption or power struggles. Instead, she portrays their lives and psyches with empathetic compassion. This understanding fuels her emotional investment in these characters. Works like *The Quality of My Life*, *The Quality of My Survival*, and her "Temporary Posting Series" engage with bureaucratic life. Whether depicting Jingchuan, Wang Qilong, county Party secretaries, or Police Chief Zha Weidong, Shao neither glorifies their virtues nor coldly exposes their flaws. She instead renders China's bureaucratic and social ecosystems with nuanced elasticity—a realist narrative stance underpinned by humanist values. Moreover, Shao Li's works conspicuously avoid severe gender conflicts, reflecting her intrinsic belief in gender harmony. While masculine narratives often adopt rigid paradigms—legendary exploits, extraordinary deeds, chivalric righteousness—Shao, as a woman writer, persistently filters her storytelling through a distinctly feminine understanding of life and masculinity, maintaining narrative fluidity. This authorial posture aligns perfectly with her literary ethos: "My fiction prioritizes thought and emotion...My novels are fundamentally mine—this constitutes my artistic creed."[①] Consequently, Shao's narratives resonate with uncommon emotional potency.

① Li Qun (ed.), *Studies on Shao Li, Qiao Ye, and Ji Wenjun*, Henan University Press, 2015, p. 33.

Er Yuehe's Mode of Historical Narration

Er Yuehe's *Great Emperor Kangxi*, *Emperor Yongzheng*, and *Emperor Qianlong*—a trilogy of historical novels centered on Qing monarchs—transformed the landscape of contemporary Chinese historical fiction. Grounded in his personal interpretation and grasp of history, he adopted the perspective of the general populace, employing a folkloric mode of thought to blend literature's didactic and entertainment functions. In doing so, he forged his own historical narrative, manifesting a distinctive style and unique value. The Qing Emperor series garnered not only fervent readership but also critical acclaim within literary circles, with *Emperor Yongzheng* even shortlisted for the Mao Dun Literature Prize. Consequently, Er Yuehe emerged as one of contemporary China's most widely disseminated and influential authors. His position within modern Chinese literature remains singular.

I. Conforming to and Departing from History

It must be acknowledged that Er Yuehe's historical narrative aligns closely with orthodox historiography—a direct reflection of his historical outlook. From childhood, he harbored a deep fascination with history, driven by an insatiable curiosity and an urge to probe its depths. His preference for history was shaped by familial influence and upbringing. Both of his parents were veterans of the Communist Revolution, their arduous and circuitous struggles embodying the broader trajectory of China's revolutionary history. His mother, in particular, stood out as one of the few female police commissioners during the advance into the Funiu Mountains. In Er Yuehe's eyes, she was "a figure possessing the desolate, austere grandeur of a lone wild goose traversing the boundless desert"—"I worshipped her as a hero."① Thus, he also carried within him a hero complex, and since heroes are invariably buried within history, he felt compelled to seek and unearth them from its vanished depths. Thus, he immersed himself in extensive historical texts: The *Twenty-Four Histories*, Fan Wenlan's Concise Compendium of Chinese History, Ren Jiyu's *Concise History of Chinese Philosophy*, as well as *Comprehensive Mirror for Aid in Government, Sequel to the Comprehensive Mirror, Book of Hidden Wisdom, Sequel to the Book of Hidden Wisdom*, among similar works. As he remarked, "I read relatively more of this category—books heavy with historical material."② This cultivated within him a relatively objective understanding of history. On one hand, he marveled at the strategic brilliance of the "Emperor for the Ages" Kangxi in navigating both external and internal conflicts, admired Yongzheng's diligence, rigor, and dedication to governance, and appreciated Qianlong's effortless grace and the flourishing prosperity of his era. On the other hand, he lamented the decline and decay of the late Qing dynasty. Compelled to articulate his historical insights, he found literature to be, without question, the most vivid, dynamic, and richly expressive medium.

① Lu Zhao, *Face to Face with "The Emperor's Uncle" Er Yuehe*, Henan Literature and Art Publishing House, 2011, p.27.

② *The Struggle* (Interview with Er Yuehe), CCTV, March 23, 2010.

Of course, the true challenge of literary narration lies in balancing historical authenticity with artistic license. "When addressing 'historical authenticity'—the most contentious yet malleable issue in historical fiction—Er Yuehe adopts the same rigorous caution as orthodox historians. In depicting pivotal historical events and figures, he strictly adheres to 'official historiography,' prioritizing textual evidence and empirical verification. His principle is 'no assertion without documentation.'"① For instance, *Great Emperor Kangxi* depicts the intellectual duel with the Oboi faction, the suppression of the Revolt of the Three Feudatories and Yang Qilong's "Zhu San Taizi" uprising, the recovery of Taiwan in the east, and the campaign against Galdan in the west. *Emperor Yongzheng* portrays the Succession Struggle of the Nine Princes, the clearance of fiscal deficits, the implementation of the *tan ding ru mu* land tax system, the policy of mandatory civil service for scholars and commoners alike, the bureaucratic reforms in the southwest (*gai tu gui liu*), and the appropriation of *huo hao* surcharges for public use—all pivotal political, economic, military, and cultural events documented in Qing historiography. These form the core narrative framework of the Emperor Series. The true narrative dynamism lies precisely in major historical events—the greatest dramatic tension is inherently embedded within history's own logic.

① Zhang Shuheng & Xu Wanchun, "The Dilemma and Choice Between Poetry and History: On the Aesthetic Features of Er Yuehe's 'Emperor Series'," Journal of Henan University (Social Sciences Edition), no. 3, 2001.

Er Yuehe possessed a profound grasp of this historical logic. His works invariably traverse the depths of history, allowing readers to witness its undulating rhythms through literature and perceive history's authentic visage. This achievement stems from his conscientious integration with, and adherence to, orthodox historiography.

However, Er Yuehe's fidelity to history and adherence to its inherent logic in literary narration never devolved into rigid, uncritical replication of historical events that might reduce historical fiction to mere historiography. Rather, working within historical causality and specific contexts, he deployed literature's imaginative richness to expand historical figures and events—particularly those tersely recorded in annals yet pregnant with dramatic potential and narrative possibility. Through meticulous elaboration and concretization, he transformed them into intricately plotted stories and vividly realized characters, ultimately crafting a comprehensive historical narrative. For instance, historically verifiable yet sparsely documented figures like Xiong Cilü, Zhang Tingyu, Wu Sidao, Fang Bao, and Cao Xueqin—all substantively portrayed in the Emperor Series—exemplify this approach. Official records offer only fragmentary glimpses of their lives, but through meticulous historical research, Er Yuehe uncovered their latent narrative potential. Whether in Kangxi's, Yongzheng's, or Qianlong's reign, history was never shaped by solitary actors, but through dynamic interplay between monarchs and their ministers, advisors, and inner court circles. Crucially, both politics and historiography were invariably co-authored by rulers and the literati—which explains why the most gripping and intricate narratives invariably orbit these relationships. Figures like Xiong Cilü (Kangxi's tutor), Zhang Tingyu (Yongzheng's chief minister), Wu Sidao (strategist), Fang Bao (Qianlong's confidant), and Cao Xueqin (whose family ties crossed three reigns) existed at this combustible intersection of throne and scholarship. The stories latent in their courtly interactions are, quite literally, the stuff of historical fiction. Er Yuehe harnessed his artistic imagination to full effect, returning to historical settings to reconstruct authentic circumstances and trajectories of historical figures. He bridged narrative gaps left unconnected by official historiography, thereby manifesting literature's unique capacities for richness and concretization. In his works, figures like Xiong Cilü, Zhang Tingyu, Wu Sidao, and Fang Bao emerge as principal characters, their intricate, multifaceted relationships with emperors and the imperial court forming the crucible for countless narratives. Without the author's successful "resurrection" of these historical personas, the storytelling would lose its essential vitality and plausibility. Remaining faithful to major historical trajectories and events is not merely an obligatory adherence to historicity in historical fiction, but also a prerequisite for its richness and profundity. Although literary narration cannot substitute for specialized historical scholarship, historical literature must nevertheless observe history's fundamental logic and essence.

This is a demand imposed by both history and literature themselves. Historical fiction must never disregard history, offer arbitrary interpretations, indulge in willful distortions, much less contravene history outright.

Moreover, Er Yuehe incorporated entirely fictional characters and events into his historical narrative—a creative act fully justified by historical and literary logic, serving the needs of plot development and character interaction. As we recognize, any historical period comprises the lived experiences of countless individuals. Historians inevitably filter and omit vast quantities of people and events in their selective recordings, including many figures and incidents brimming with literary potential. From a purely literary standpoint, history stripped of these rich human elements would risk appearing hollow and incomplete. Thus, Er Yuehe salvaged numerous such overlooked historical fragments, weaving them into his narratives to compensate for this inherent thinness in conventional historical accounts. Take for instance Wu Ciyou (a purely fictional name punning on "no such friend") and Gao Shiqi—two entirely invented "eccentric scholars" embodying the archetypal erudite literatus. The former represents the composed, dignified type while the latter epitomizes the unconstrained, bohemian variety, together exemplifying contrasting models of imperial scholars who enjoyed exceptional imperial favor. While these figures never existed historically, their presence remains plausible within Yongzheng's court context. Emperors and princes routinely maintained coteries of proteges, and Yongzheng's personal fascination with Buddhism and Daoism made him particularly receptive to extraordinary talents. Such individuals likely influenced political machinations in ways orthodox historiography deliberately omitted. By incorporating these narrative supplements, Er Yuehe achieved fuller character portrayals, enriched historical storytelling with greater narrative appeal, and ensured the plots unfolded with complete verisimilitude and adherence to lived experience.

II. Conforming to and Transcending the World

The "Emperor Series" historical novels depict the socio-historical life of the Qing dynasty. History typically develops according to its own inherent rhythms—while there may be sudden rapids and treacherous shoals along the way, its ordinary course remains largely placid and uneventful. Consequently, day-to-day history and mundane social existence are not necessarily filled with dramatic, suspenseful narratives. Yet literary storytelling demands emblematic characters and compelling plots, creating an apparent paradox. Should an author strictly adhere to history's natural state and original contours, even roughly following its inherent tempo, the narrative risks becoming insipid and devoid of dramatic tension. This challenge proves particularly acute for the Kangxi-Yongzheng-Qianlong triumvirate—the zenith of Qing power—when major upheavals and disruptions were relatively scarce. Crafting intricate, captivating stories within this historical framework was therefore no simple feat.

In his *Emperor Series*, Er Yuehe masterfully balanced the relationship between historical authenticity and literary narration. The author fully recognized that neither historians nor literary writers can exhaustively document all aspects of history—they must inevitably select what is essential and serviceable to their purposes. The distinction lies in their approaches: historians profess to record major historical events and figures with objective detachment, while literary writers openly acknowledge their subjective, emotional, and empathetic engagement in portraying historical life—including its events and personalities. Crucially, literary representation transcends the mechanical, simplistic chronicling of historical texts; it vividly, imaginatively, and concretely reconstructs and revivifies historical existence, often capturing even the most minute details. Thus, in his works, Er Yuehe meticulously reconstructs the social life of the Kangxi-Yongzheng-Qianlong era, striving to authentically reflect that period's societal panorama. A prime example emerges in *Emperor Yongzheng: The Succession Struggle of the Nine Princes*, where Wu Sidao's return visit to Yangzhou's Slender West Lake is rendered with exquisite detail: "To tour Jiangnan without visiting Yangzhou would be incomplete; to experience Yangzhou without crossing Rainbow Bridge would be unthinkable. This landmark faces the lake while adjoining the river, with 'Spring Dawn on Long Dyke' to its west and 'Lotus Breeze from Puji' to its east. Here stand Rainbow Bridge Pavilion, Daybreak Tower, Zephyr Hall, Sea Cloud Shrine... North of the bridge sits an unusually named temple—'Rainbow Bridge Earth Spirit Shrine'—whose annual New Year sacrificial fair locals colloquially dub the 'Wealth-God Blessing Festival.'" The author further elaborates on the vibrant spectacle of Yangzhou's February temple fair—a teeming tableau of street vendors, acrobatic performers, fortune-tellers, and devout pilgrims—breathing palpable life into the city's historical atmosphere. Another revealing moment occurs when Dai Zhuo settles his meal payment: *"He fished out a silver ingot from his robe and tossed it over. The waiter caught it—a 'True Perfect Circle' piece weighing a full five taels, its central vein running clear through, the honeycomb texture of its casting still frosted with silver dust. This was authentic 98%-pure Taizhou minted silver, prompting an instant bloom of smiles." Such passages attest to the author's encyclopedic grasp of Qing-era social minutiae. In Emperor Qianlong: Phoenix Pavilion Under Clouded Skies, a scene captures Qianlong incognito with Liu Yong and Heshen strolling past jade emporiums near the Temple of the Jade Emperor. Heshen engages a curio dealer in exhaustive discourse on forgery techniques for antiques and calligraphy—from authentication methods to storytelling performances—rendering each moment viscerally immersive. Beyond this, the work demonstrates encyclopedic command of historical-cultural domains: medical chess strategies, poetic drama conventions, *máyī* physiognomy, character-divination, celestial geography, Buddhist sutras and Daoist canon, extraordinary talents, and courtly protocols. As noted, "The author constructs a historical 'discourse field' through period customs, vernacular, and sartorial codes."[①] All this stems from the author's profound mastery of Qing-dynasty historical life. As Er Yuehe himself observed: "When I read Qing-era diaries documenting the price of tofu per catty or wheat yield per acre—what significance could such minutiae hold? Yet now these have become historical materials more substantive and valuable than official chronicles."[②] Such details remain inaccessible in conventional historiography. The author's rigorous pursuit of minutiae serves a singular purpose: to anchor the narrative in the lived reality of Qing society.

Yet literature's purpose lies in storytelling—in presenting the most captivating tales of human experience, allowing readers to understand and contemplate life's complexities and uncertainties through intricate, vivid narratives that reveal its fundamental truths. This requires concentrating life's most dramatic moments rather than mechanically piecing together its mundane, fragmented, and rhythmless aspects. In the Emperor Series, Er Yuehe extracts the essence from historical life by politicizing history, typifying daily existence, transforming historical progression into pivotal events, imposing narrative rhythm on transitional moments, and embedding historical figures within intricate webs of conflict—in short, distilling everything into the perilous struggles of politics and power. In *Great Emperor Kangxi*, the young

① Pan Feng, "*History, Humanity, and Modernity: Reading Er Yuehe's Historical Novel Emperor Yongzheng*". Chinese Language Teaching and Research, no. 6, 1999.

② Er Yuehe, "*Correspondence with Professor Lu Shuyuan*" *in Selected Works of Er Yuehe.* Zhengzhou: Henan Literature and Art Publishing House, 1999, p239.

Kangxi's confrontations with Oboi culminate in the emperor's strategic capture of his adversary—each scene unfolding with seismic intensity. The campaign to suppress the Three Feudatories reveals not only the precariousness of the political situation and the ruthless jostling for power, but also the brutal realities of warfare. Simultaneously, the imperial court becomes a crucible of white-hot intrigue, as princes scheme with lethal determination in their struggle for the throne. Similarly, *Emperor Yongzheng* depicts the escalating confrontation between Yongzheng and the Eighth Prince faction, as well as the bloody trajectory from relying on Nian Gengyao to his eventual elimination. The work masterfully lays bare the ruthlessness of political machinations, the fragility of human relationships, the subtleties of power plays, and the fratricidal strife among imperial brothers—each rendered with crystalline clarity and psychological verisimilitude. Particularly striking is Er Yuehe's sophisticated reconstruction of throne succession struggles within the imperial court, demonstrating his mature craftsmanship in handling grand historical themes. Consequently, these depictions of princely rivalry permeate with ever-present undercurrents of treachery, conspiracy, and deception—revealing the dark essence of power dynamics. In these court intrigues, Kangxi—determined to safeguard his throne—could depose and reinstate his own son, Crown Prince Yunreng, only to ultimately "re-demote him for offenses, confining him in Xian'an Palace." Yunti, aspiring to the crown prince position, resorted to witchcraft to eliminate his rival brother Yunreng. Meanwhile, upon seizing power, Yongzheng immediately imprisoned his political adversaries—brothers Yunti and Yunsi—among others. As Kangxi bluntly observed: “Imperial kinship holds no natural affection.”

Strictly speaking, these characters and events maintain authentic historical traces, and such life circumstances and details could indeed have existed. Yet they neither constitute the entirety nor necessarily the essence of historical life—not even the core of courtly existence. Thus, in a sense, they transcend the social reality of that era, representing the author’s typification—even simplification or dramatization—of history. This technique liberates characters and narratives from life’s tedium, rendering them in sharp relief with an almost transcendent quality. It allows readers immediate access to historical figures and events upon engaging with the work, revealing how history itself coalesces—how politics, power, and status are forged—thereby delivering profound narrative satisfaction. Er Yuehe addressed this narrative approach explicitly: “I indeed embrace a ‘transcendent’ perspective...This consciousness inevitably permeates my works. Whenever a character reaches the zenith of glory, I either eliminate them or orchestrate their downfall. Such sensibility stems from Daoist and Buddhist self-detachment—through this, I seek spiritual solace and a supra-conscious emotional state.”[①]

---

① Bai Wanxian & Zhang Shuheng, "*Records of the Er Yuehe Creative Symposium*". *Wolong Forum*, no. 4, 1993.

III. Dominant Discourse and Polyphonic Voices

The heroic complex and ambition for monumental achievements instilled in Er Yuehe since childhood often transmuted into a salvific vision for society. This ideological thread manifests throughout his various life phases—from his military service, where he harbored aspirations of generalship, to its inevitable dissolution upon civilian transition. Later, he aspired to become a scholar of *Dream of the Red Chamber* (Hongxuejia), but his incidental writings about Kangxi, Yongzheng, and Qianlong during this research unexpectedly launched his literary career. Consequently, this ideological thread naturally permeated his works. "Frankly, I originally sought an official career, dreaming of becoming 'an illustrious statesman of my generation'—or, more nobly put, a 'great public servant' to fulfill social responsibilities. But the bureaucratic path ultimately proved impassable, for I realized it required more than just moral character and scholarly acumen. When reality thwarted my ambitions, I turned to literary creation—transforming others' deeds into narratives for readers to ponder."① In crafting the *Emperor Series*, Er Yuehe consciously embodied the Confucian ideal of enlightened rulers and virtuous ministers. Through his narratives, he sought to portray sagacious monarchs and worthy chancellors who could rescue the nation from crises

① Er Yuehe, *"Correspondence with Professor Lu Shuyuan" in Selected Works of Er Yuehe*, Zhengzhou: Henan Literature and Art Publishing House, 1999, p.242.

and rectify societal ills—a sublimation of his own unrealized political aspirations. It was through his research on *Dream of the Red Chamber* that Er Yuehe gained entry into Qing history. Consequently, his ideals and aspirations found expression through the prism of Kangxi, Yongzheng, Qianlong, and their trusted ministers. In the *Emperor Series*, he portrays Kangxi as the "Emperor for the Ages," molding him from childhood as a heroic sovereign. Ascending the throne at age eight under the guidance of four regent-ministers, the prodigious yet politically vulnerable Kangxi faced immediate power struggles—particularly against Oboi's arrogance and insubordination. These very trials revealed Kangxi's extraordinary wisdom, courage, and statesmanship. *Great Emperor Kangxi* primarily showcases Kangxi's strategic brilliance and heroic stature through pivotal events like the intellectual duel with Oboi, the suppression of the Three Feudatories, and the recovery of Taiwan. Er Yuehe confessed: "Among the three emperors I portrayed, Kangxi holds my deepest admiration—the others are simply 'emperors,' but he alone merits the title 'Great Emperor.' I evaluate historical figures by three criteria: contributions to national unification and ethnic solidarity, advancements in productivity and livelihoods, and promotion of scientific, educational, and cultural development. By these measures, Kangxi achieved extraordinary feats."①

① Er Yuehe, "*Dialogue with Sun Haohui on 'Qin and Qing Dynasties*'". Publishing Reference, late April 2008.

Indeed, Er Yuehe's heroic narrative extends far beyond Kangxi. In terms of literary achievement, *Emperor Yongzheng* surpasses even *Great Emperor Kangxi*. Though Kangxi reigned for over six decades, making monumental contributions to national unification and ethnic cohesion, Er Yuehe's portrayal demonstrates that Yongzheng's dozen years of governance were no less crucial to shaping the Kangxi-Qianlong golden age—particularly in laying the groundwork for Qianlong's prosperity. Moreover, in some respects, Yongzheng's accomplishments required even greater fortitude than Kangxi's. Kangxi founded the dynasty, while Yongzheng preserved its legacy—and as the saying goes, founding is arduous, but stewardship is even more demanding, especially when preserving an empire burdened with accumulated malpractices from Kangxi's later years. More crucially, Yongzheng faced legitimacy challenges from the moment of his accession. Whether the throne was meant for "the Fourth Prince" or "the Fourteenth Prince," whether he rightfully inherited or forged the edict—these questions inherently undermined his rule. Through historical research, Er Yuehe refutes the popular narratives (both official and unofficial) that Yongzheng obtained the throne through Longkodo's alleged edict tampering (changing "fourteen" to "four"). Instead, he argues Yongzheng earned Kangxi's recognition through his diligent governance, exceptional competence, unwavering loyalty to the Qing empire, and benevolent care for the people, ultimately being chosen as the rightful successor. Thus, Er Yuehe dismisses as slander the accusations of Yongzheng "plotting against his father, oppressing his mother, killing his brothers, and slaughtering his siblings," as well as the characterization of him as "narrow-minded, cruel and ungrateful, shrewd and cunning, duplicitous." Upon ascending the throne, Yongzheng had to simultaneously rehabilitate his damaged public perception while implementing institutional reforms to eradicate systemic corruption and foster national prosperity. In *Emperor Yongzheng*, Er Yuehe boldly rehabilitates Yongzheng's historical legacy by portraying his rigorous governance: purging corrupt officials, banning factionalism, abolishing the "outcast" system, implementing bureaucratic reforms (gaitu guiliu), standardizing tax surcharges (huohao guigong), boosting production, strengthening border defenses, centralizing authority, and combating graft. This depiction transforms Yongzheng into a self-disciplined, reform-driven, and diligent ruler devoted to his people—a narrative that deliberately resonates with China's post-1980s societal currents. Conversely, Emperor Qianlong presents an ambitious monarch determined to surpass all predecessors and usher in an unparalleled golden age for the Qing dynasty. He steadfastly implemented a governance philosophy of "leniency as policy," abolishing the harsh measures of previous reigns. He valued upright and capable officials, promoted fresh talent, reorganized the bureaucracy, and severely punished corrupt functionaries. He reduced taxes to allow the people to recuperate, frequently traveled incognito to observe local conditions, dispatched competent officials to relieve disaster areas, and eliminated sources of unrest. He launched military campaigns to pacify rebellions in Jinchuan, the Western Regions, and Taiwan. He commissioned the compilation of the

Complete Library of the Four Treasuries to revitalize cultural heritage. Under Qianlong's rule, the dynasty gradually progressed toward a flourishing age of prosperity and productivity—a narrative that subtly harmonized with the contemporary themes of reform, opening-up, and national rejuvenation. "Writers inevitably develop an emotional inclination, hoping their literary creations might serve as exemplars for real life."① We may interpret Er Yuehe's historical narratives as articulating contemporary China's reform-and-opening and national rejuvenation through a dominant discourse framework. Yet this mainstream expression simultaneously resonates with popular social psychology, fulfilling collective needs—thus constituting polyphonic representation. As with all historiography being inherently contemporary, all literature is inevitably saturated with present-day consciousness. "As modern historical fiction, it roots itself in specific historical soil while remaining tethered to modern society's ideological psyche, forming a dynamic dialogue between past and present. In this sense, the past remains an integral part of the now."②

Indeed, the *Emperor Series*' polyphonic representation manifests equally in its focus on popular welfare. Yongzheng's policies—abolishing the "outcast caste" system, implementing the "tanding rumu" land tax reform,

① Wang Zengfan, "*Deficiencies in Er Yuehe's Emperor Series Novels*". *Zhongzhou Academic Journal*, no. 6, 2006.

② Zhu Shuiyong, "*Historical Echoes of Social Reformation and Cultural Transformation: Historical Novels of the 1990s Depicting the Ming-Qing Period*". Fujian Tribune (Humanities & Social Sciences Edition), no. 1, 1999.

and enforcing "mandatory civil service for all classes"—embodied historical emancipation for commoners. Similarly, Yongzheng and Qianlong's incognito inspections, where they directly engaged with grassroots life to understand popular grievances, articulated a proto-populist consciousness. Indeed, the Emperor Series' polyphonic representation manifests equally in its focus on popular welfare. Yongzheng's policies—abolishing the "outcast caste" system, implementing the "tanding rumu" land tax reform, and enforcing "mandatory civil service for all classes"—embodied historical emancipation for commoners. Similarly, Yongzheng and Qianlong's incognito inspections, where they directly engaged with grassroots life to understand popular grievances, articulated a profound concern for people's livelihood. The novels also construct moral exemplars like Henan Governor Tian Wenjing—an incorruptible and frugal official who devoted himself entirely to public service. Despite rising to the highest provincial rank, his eighty-year-old mother still supported herself by growing vegetables. Tian Wenjing would often roll up his trousers and labor on the Yellow River dikes, toiling through wind and rain until he ultimately collapsed dead at his post. Yet his rigid dogmatism and obstinate conservatism left him isolated in official circles—subordinates paid lip service while the populace suffered, culminating in his lonely demise. Li Fu, by contrast, combined outward rectitude with inner pliancy. His penchant for grandiose projects ultimately yielded no substantive achievements. Li Wei, Governor-General of Liangjiang (overseeing Jiangnan [later Jiangsu-Anhui] and Jiangxi provinces), rose to high office without formal imperial examination education. Unburdened by bureaucratic dogma, he implemented national policies with localized flexibility while maintaining compassionate governance. His personal integrity manifested in austere practices: only distinguished banquet guests merited chicken dishes, while imperial gifts were limited to homespun cloth shoes crafted by his wife. This maverick official—outwardly adaptable yet unyielding in principle—earned renown for blunt critiques grounded in pragmatic governance. The author portrays Li Wei as functionally illiterate yet surpassing many scholars in governance—a paradox resolved by his innate humanity and empathetic leadership. His grassroots origins fostered profound compassion for commoners; his intuitive understanding of human nature and practical wisdom in identifying shared interests far outshone the pedantic rigidity of Confucian classicists. This characterization embodies Er Yuehe's own affirmation of common people's lived experiences.

The Sociological Significance of Li Peifu's Plains Narrative

From his early works to the publication of the Plains Trilogy, Li Peifu developed a comprehensive narrative of the plains. In his writing, elements such as the Central Plains (flatlands), soil, sky, the Ying River, villages, wild grass, trees, dogs, donkeys, men, women, history, dialects, colloquial speech, tall tales, and folk stories serve not only as foundational components of rural society but also as essential literary constructs. More importantly, they function as critical semiotic codes for deciphering the plains narrative. These elements form an organic system within his works, and through the author's storytelling, they embody profound sociological implications.

Land, Wild Grass, and People

Li Peifu's narratives often emerge from the mundane minutiae of lives deemed as humble as weeds. "I am a seed. I have transplanted myself into the city." (*The Book of Life*) "The scent of tung blossoms lingers in my childhood memories. The flowers are faintly purple—a diluted hue that bleeds watery streaks toward the trumpet-shaped petals, tinged with lavender, while their stems glow milky white at the base, exuding a subtle sweetness from their tender cores." (*City Lights*) Such imagery stems from his unique perspective on society and human existence. Li Peifu's life has remained tethered to Henan—indeed, to the very soil and waters of the central plains region. Though born in a small town, he spent his formative years at his grandmother's rural home, later returning as an educated youth to serve as a production team leader during collective farming. Thus, his very existence and lived experiences are inextricably intertwined with that land and every grass and tree upon it. To some degree, he is a product of agricultural civilization—his life's foundation is that very earth. The land is life's primordial home, whether for plants and livestock or for upright-walking humans. In Li's consciousness, crops and vegetation constitute the true wellspring of life: the land nurtures plants, the plants sustain living beings, yet the soil itself cannot directly become nourishment for humans or animals.

Yet vegetation has never been accorded dignity—it is perpetually underestimated and scorned. Crops and wild grasses, especially the latter, are ubiquitous plants that wither and flourish with the seasons, deemed so ordinary that people trample them without thought. "On the plains, the most humble plants are the grasses." (*The Gate of Sheep*) Nevertheless, though deemed lowly, these plants possess astonishing resilience. However brutally people trample them, however barren the soil, they tenaciously sprout wherever a trace of moisture remains—even when crushed underfoot, cut down repeatedly, or burned to ashes, they never surrender their will to live. It is precisely these most commonplace plants that nourish countless living creatures, humans above all. For Li Peifu, humans and plants share an intrinsic, inseparable bond. "I've said that I write about people as if they were 'plants.' In this sense, The *Gate of Sheep*, *City Lights*, and the recently published *The Book of Life* form a 'plains ecological novel' series—or what might be called a 'botanical discourse' of the plains."[1] Why depict humans as plants? Because Li Peifu perceives in the humblest wild grasses a nobility of life, a nobility of spirit. On the Central Plains, the multitudes endure as plainly as common vegetation—flourishing and withering over decades or even a century. Human dignity is neither innate nor measured by lifespan, but rather by the spirit and values manifested through one's existence. In Li Peifu's literary world, trees and crops appear, but wild grasses dominate. In the opening chapter of *The Gate of Sheep*, Li Peifu meticulously catalogues over twenty varieties of wild grasses native to the plains, penetratingly revealing their essence: "The grasses of the plains survive through 'defeat' and persist through 'insignificance.'" These nameless plants—unremarkable yet innumerable—embody the diverse people of the plains. Though humble and often oppressed, they hold their heads high, collectively inscribing history through their tenacious existence, ultimately converging into the magnificent tapestry of Central Plains culture.

To extend the metaphor, the relationship between history and humanity mirrors that between humans and wild grasses. The Central Plains—the heartland of Chinese civilization—have witnessed millennia of pivotal historical events. Wars and catastrophes have rolled over this land like relentless wheels, crushing human lives as indiscriminately as wild grasses underfoot,

① Fan Huiqin, ed., *Li Peifu Studies*, Henan University Press, 2015, p.15.

mown down in successive generations. Yet the roots of life endure tenaciously. The people never abandon history; rather, like the humblest weeds, they silently and resiliently line the path of historical progression, sustaining its continuity. Fundamentally, all people are ordinary—no hierarchy of status can negate this universal condition. As Mao Zedong posited, "The people are the motive force in creating history."① History belongs not to deities or emperors, but to the daily lives of common individuals. The culture of a nation, particularly the enduring civilization of China's Central Plains, embodies this truth. It is the collective crystallization of millennia of ordinary lives—plain yet conventional, unpretentious yet refined, enduring yet ever-growing. Its nobility and profundity lie not in exalted origins, but in resilient vitality and ceaseless regeneration.

Whether through botanical allegory or wild grass narratives, Li Peifu's ultimate focus remains fixed on human stories. Using vegetation as metaphor, he probes the social substratum beneath history's wheels, chronicling ordinary lives inextricably bound to the Central Plains. These quintessential locals either devote their entire existence to this land or come of age within its embrace—all nurtured by its soil, all connected to it by unseverable blood ties. The plains and their history form the very backdrop of their lives. These

① Mao Zedong pointed out: "*The people, and the people alone, are the motive force in the making of world history.*" Selected Works of Mao Zedong, Vol. 3, p. 1031.

characters inhabit shared villages or fixed social orbits, living in daily intimacy where joys and sorrows intertwine. Together they work, live, struggle, and pioneer—sometimes sheltering and aiding one another, other times clashing in conflict or hatred. This tapestry of love and resentment weaves a life both richly layered and intensely pungent, like the complex flavors of the earth itself. Li Peifu intimately understands the dilemmas of rural China and the crux of interpersonal conflicts within its fabric. Writing from an insider's perspective, he narrates their visceral, authentic, and ecologically true stories, crafting characters steeped in the earthy essence of the Central Plains. "Depicting characters growing within specific cultural soil has always been a focal point of Li Peifu's creative endeavor."①

In *The Gate of Sheep*, Hu Tiancheng stands as Li Peifu's quintessential rural archetype. Though the author employs narrative restraint—deliberately withholding and mystifying through suggestive ambiguity—this rural figure's formidable energy permeates the text, revealing a colossus of the agrarian world. Assuming leadership of Hujia Village in his twenties, Hu spent decades transforming the impoverished community into a prosperous model through sheer audacity, tenacity, capability, and wisdom. He forged both a "rural kingdom" and an unshakable personal authority that attained mythical status in Hujia's collective consciousness. He studied the rural world metic-

① Fan Huiqin, ed., *Li Peifu Studies*, Henan University Press, 2015, p.152.

ulously—every blade of grass on the land, every individual under his governance. He scrutinized the gullies and expansive spirit of the plains, even delving into society and politics. From the plains, rural communities, and human relationships, he gleaned wisdom and experience that made his management of Hujia Village effortless. n Hujia Village, he was the pivotal center—everyone's life intersected with his, and his actions shaped the village's destiny and each resident's existence. Moreover, Hu Tiancheng was a figure who commanded celestial connections. Not only did he establish an impregnable network within Hujia Village, but he also cultivated an extensive web of influence beyond it. Thus, without even leaving his domain, he could sway county and municipal affairs. When Hu Guoqing's position teetered on the brink—even facing imprisonment—a single word or maneuver from Hu Tiancheng could reverse the crisis. Hu Tiancheng embodies both the product of Central Plains rural culture and the distinct imprints of contemporary China's sociopolitical landscape.

Gangdan (Feng Jiachang) and Diu (Wu Zhipeng) emerged from the very soil of the plains. Born and nurtured by this agrarian world, their veins pulsed with the essence of its earth. Feng Jiachang's father—a zhuixu (live-in son-in-law)—belonged to an insignificant clan with no standing in the village. After his mother's early death, his overwhelmed father thrust household leadership onto the boy's shoulders. Left no choice, he confronted every hardship. Barefoot since childhood (earning the moniker "Barefoot Immortal"), he stomped on thorny caltrops to toughen his soles into iron plates. The hardships forged his resolute and tenacious character. He endured, persevered, and nurtured a growing conviction within: to help his father raise his four younger brothers, to break free from this land of suffering, and to reach the longed-for city. The diligence, endurance, and resilience honed through adversity enabled him to fulfill his aspirations—establishing a family and career in the city, and eventually bringing his brothers there as well. Yet when they truly became urbanites, the rural complex etched in their bones inevitably resurfaced. Wu Zhipeng is "a willow wedge hammered into the city" (*The Book of Life*). Unlike others, he gained urban residency through higher education—university and postgraduate studies—qualifications that enabled his embeddedness. Yet becoming urban couldn't erase his rural roots or blood ties. He remained shackled by the cultural obligations of his rural heritage. Every villager was kin; every phone call carried familial imperatives he was bound to fulfill. Yet a rural seed scattered in urban soil neither claims the city nor gains power to solve every villager's plight. Thus, rural culture becomes an inescapable burden—he dreads phone calls, avoiding them like the plague. Ultimately, he chooses exile, fleeing to distant frontiers. Liu Hanxiang embodies a Qiaozhen-esque femininity—beautiful, kind, and loyal, yet assertively self-reliant. Feng Jiachang's grit and resilience captivate her; she willingly sacrifices and strives to help him overcome adversity. When Feng Jiachang secured urban status and took a new lover, Liu Hanxiang clung to her steadfast love yet resolutely severed ties, returning to her native soil. "She would sow this love upon the land!" Succeeding her father as village chief, she transmuted personal heartbreak into rural legend—a Zhongyuan "newly edited folktale" that reinterprets rural culture through matriarchal renewal.

Family, Village, and Society

The family is a relational unit bound by blood and kinship—one of humanity's fundamental forms of community. Families and villages often share an isomorphic relationship, with many villages essentially constituting extended familial networks. The village serves as the foundational spatial unit of rural society. "Villages are the basic cells of historical life and its primary vessels. Not only do they form the horizontal plane of history through interconnectedness, but they also penetrate its vertical depths. Like modern cities, villages intersect across historical coordinates, gathering within them the diverse elements of history—villages are, in essence, the history of agrarian society."[①] Villages thus function as both the stage for unfolding narratives and the primary spatial framework of the author's storytelling.

Li Peifu's human stories are invariably framed within village units—thus his rural narratives constitutes narratives of the village. He constructs fictional villages like Dali Village, Hujia Fort, Shangliang Village, and Wuliang Village, which collectively embody the rural society of the Central

---

① Wu Shenggang, "*On the Historical Texture in Contemporary Henan Writers' Works*". Journal of Xinyang Normal University (Philosophy and Social Sciences Edition), no. 3, 2013.

Plains. In agrarian societies, villages maintain inherent stability through their symbiotic relationship with traditional production modes. These settlements function both as cultural symbols and social entities. The adage "imperial authority stops at the county level," underscoring villages' pivotal role in pre-modern social organization. They serve simultaneously as rural homesteads for settled life and as hubs for social interaction and circulation. In Li Peifu's works, villages are neither mere points nor flat planes, but rather elongated corridors where time flows, lives intertwine, and people navigate countless twists and turns. One might say villages possess immense capacity, their lives brimming with boundless richness. They encompass the entirety of rural society—birth and death, labor and livelihood, economic and cultural activities, community governance, even matters of ethnicity, nation, and politics all become integral components of the village entity. Represented by the Plains Trilogy, Li dedicates expansive narratives to chronicling village transformations through characters' growth, struggles, and weathered experiences. Whether unfolding with sluggish inertia or tumultuous intensity, these journeys allow readers to glimpse the turbid weight of rural history and sense the vibrant diversity of Central Plains culture deeply rooted in this fertile land.

Hujia Fort is both an ordinary village on the Central Plains and a singularly unique one. Its distinction stems not from geographic advantage nor demographic peculiarity, but solely from producing an extraordinary individual—one who transformed the village and rewrote its history. In a sense, Hujia Fort functions as a familial entity. Though composed of multiple surnames, prolonged cohabitation has forged kinship-like bonds among its residents. Yet this relational entity is not always harmonious—it too has its problems. As the family's representative, Hu Tiancheng first organized the capture of "thieves," forcing them to display the "stolen goods" in public, thereby curbing the habitual petty theft and pilfering. Next, he had villagers collectively expose selfish motives, publicly air their shortcomings, lay bare their souls, cleanse ideological impurities, and shed undesirable behaviors. Hu Tiancheng proceeded to establish role models, formulate village covenants, promote new social norms, and cultivate a new villager ethos. During Hujia Fort's new village construction, he created an exhibition platform displaying the severed fingers of Mai Sheng and Xu Sanni to commemorate their sacrifice and inspire villagers to dedicate themselves to the village's development. He instituted a "Heroes' Roll" for Old Cao who died in the paper mill production, holding memorial services to honor him as a "hero" and "martyr," thereby reinforcing faith in Hujia Fort's cause. Hu publicly challenged superstitions by dismantling the "soul retrieval" ritual and decisively filled in the ten-acre pond that harbored these backward customs. He defied his mother's religious doctrines, insisting on burying her according to village regulations. Finally, he established the "Hujia Fort Code," ensuring the village operated entirely by its own rules. It was under Hu Tiancheng's leadership that Hujia Fort transformed from a poor, backward, and fragmented village into a new socialist village achieving common prosperity through collective economic development. The developmental trajectory and historical transformation of

Hujia Fort embody both the traditional Chinese ideal of wealth redistribution and the collectivist spirit of the new socialist era, all while preserving the enduring essence of national culture.

Compared to Hujia Fort, Wuliang Village is a more ordinary settlement on the Central Plains. Its village conditions, folk customs, production, daily life, and social interactions maintain broader consistency with typical Central Plains rural communities. Wu Zhipeng, though an orphan, received warm care and support from the villagers. He was nursed by women across the village and raised on communal meals, with the village Party secretary serving as his patriarchal guardian. The villagers collectively became his extended family, embodying the traditional Chinese virtue of aiding the disadvantaged while reflecting the blood-like bonds of rural communal life. It was precisely through this village nurture that Wu Zhipeng became a graduate student and university professor. Yet precisely because of this foundational upbringing, no matter how far he journeys, Wu Zhipeng remains tethered to this place by unbreakable ties—ties woven through present realities and historical legacy, flowing in his veins and etched into his psyche, mirroring the pervasive bonds among rural folk. Thus, Wu Zhipeng stands as their pride, while they also burden him with profound expectations and solemn trusts. Whether capable of bearing them or not, these represent an enduring cultural continuum—a legacy of earnest kinship and rural sentiment. Wu Zhipeng fled precisely because he recognized the problematic nature of these rural ties and burdens—a severe cultural and emotional overload. Yet he is no outright rebel against rural culture; in fact, he is himself a product of Central Plains rural society, remaining spiritually connected through multiple lingering threads. Of course, Wuliang is ordinary, and most Wuliang villagers persist tenaciously in their commonplace struggles and mundane lives. The old uncle—a military hero—married into Wuliang for love. While devoting himself to the village, he simultaneously wasted his life in marital strife, meeting a rather bleak end. Aunt Chong, despite life's relentless hardships, humiliations, and adversities, raised her children to successful adulthood through sheer feminine resilience, endurance, and fortitude—yet received none of the filial reciprocity culture and morality demand, embodying a painful civilizational paradox. Cai Weixiang represents the new generation of rural women—a rebel from childhood. She sought to break free from village and family, determined to forge her fortune in the city and rise above her station. Though her methods lacked propriety, her unrelenting, uncompromising pursuit undeniably reflects the tenacious striving of those at society's bottom rung. Cai Weixiang rose to become President Cai—her success redefined how others perceived her as she reshaped Wuliang through sheer force of will. These character evolutions parallel rural transformations; personal destinies intertwine with communal history. Rural life often unfolds with undisturbed calm, while history and culture accumulate beneath. Wuliang's apparent ordinariness precisely embodies the profound depth of Central Plains civilization.

Li Peifu excels at immersing himself in folk society. The land, people, and customs here feel intimately familiar, resonating deeply with his psyche.

When he enters this rural world, he steps into his narrative domain—a space where inspiration flows freely, creative breakthroughs emerge, vibrant characters come alive, compelling stories unfold, and local flavors flourish in rapid succession. *The Gate of Sheep* begins its narrative with "the scent of soil," then recounts the three-thousand-year tumultuous history of the Xu state: "Each yellowed page is stained with tears. With endless wars and frequent disasters, how did people survive?" Just as the story seems poised to focus on human lives, the author meticulously—almost relentlessly—introduces various wild grasses. This narrative design carries profound intentionality—to immerse readers completely in rural folk society, making them experience its people, elements, and stories through authentic folk perception. For this is the essence of the Central Plains: humanity's survival through millennia of disasters and warfare stems precisely from internalizing the wild grasses' tenacity—clinging stubbornly to the land, absorbing its nutrients and essence to perpetuate life, history, and culture. City Lights begins with the scent of tung blossoms. The tung tree, common across the Central Plains, carries memories of its "Imperial Concubine Fragrance"—a bittersweet nostalgia laced with hardship. When the father discovers the "walking" tung tree at dawn, he insists on "discussing this" with everyone: Village Head Guo Dou, other cadres, Old De, Grandma Sui'er, the entire village. Yet no one engages seriously; none can offer any explanation. The apparent indifference leaves him frustrated and helpless, casting an aura of desolation from the outset. This starkly portrays rural interpersonal dynamics—where gatepost strength (men tou) dictates unequal access to influence and resources. Meanwhile, the rural mentality of chasing benefits while avoiding troubles prevails—few wish to meddle in domestic squabbles or neighborly disputes lest they invite trouble. Thus, no one champions the father's cause. Wu Zhipeng's network of blood ties and *renqing* relationships in *The Book of Life* also typifies the social structure and interpersonal dynamics of rural folk society. China is a *renqing*-based society, and this is especially true in rural communities. As Fei Xiaotong noted, rural China is structured through a "differential mode of association".[①] In villages, where generations live together through intermarriage and proximity, most people are connected by kinship or familiarity. There are no formal boundaries—helping each other at home or abroad becomes an ingrained way of thinking for rural dwellers. Therefore, when Wu Zhipeng left Wuliang and gained "status" in the city, he inevitably became their spokesperson and reliance—all relational threads converged upon him.

The rural governance of Hujia Fort carries significant sociological implications. First, its "Ten Codes" represent all-encompassing village covenants—a creation of both Hujia Fort and its helmsman Hu Tiancheng. This innovation is not entirely original but rather a pragmatic adaptation, tinged

① Fei Xiaotong, *From the Soil: The Foundations of Chinese Society*. Beijing: Beijing Publishing House, 2005.

with elements of vulgar sociology. For instance, the village anthem comprises a morning song ("*The East Is Red*") and an evening song ("*Sailing the Seas Depends on the Helmsman*"), products of political secularization. "Village Rule (1): The bell toll is a command." "Village Rule (2): The 'broadcast boxes' installed above every household's door must not be turned off or privately removed. Hu Tiancheng said: 'We must heed the spirit.'" This reflects the operational methods of the collective era, bearing militaristic traces. "Review Method (3): 'Pants Removal'—Annotation: 'Pants removal' is a form of self-criticism." "Marriage Law, also called 'Traditional Law'—Annotation: Beyond state laws, Hujia Fort's marriages require 'team-led traditional education' for all weddings." This represents an extension of rural authority, a form of rural statecraft. Collectively, these rules embody folk wisdom as well as the peasants' cleverness, cunning, and obstinacy. Second is Feng Jiahe's Shangliang Dialect and its annotations. The author compiled nearly 30 commonly used terms from the rural "Shangliang" tradition, providing folkloric interpretations. These lexical items constitute a regional vernacular, yet their usage reveals the rich diversity of rural life and embodies pristine Central Plains cultures. City Lights presents this Shangliang Dialect compilation precisely because narrative alone cannot fully capture these folk customs. Through Feng Jiahe's persona and this linguistic artifact, the text achieves cultural preservation—fulfilling its mission as a symbolic vessel of cultural preservation.

History and Reality

Li Peifu is undoubtedly a realist writer. He engages not only with history but also maintains an intimate connection with contemporary reality. His works reflect decades of social life across the Central Plains—capturing both the richly textured rural existence and the rapidly evolving urban experience, while bridging the two to portray personal growth and destiny. Through these narratives, he maps the historical progression, development, and transformation of Central Plains society, unfolding a vast and monumental cultural panorama.

Henan in the Central Plains serves as a microcosm of China. Since the founding of the New China, particularly following the Reform and Opening, the land of Zhongzhou has undergone profound transformations. Li Peifu confronts reality, immersing himself in this historical shift. With fidelity, his pen traces the metamorphosis of this terrain in the new epoch—the evolving interplay between rural society and urban expansion, the sacrifices borne by the Central Plains' people, the contradictions and disquietudes encountered, alongside the hard-won felicities and exultations. The Ying River, Dali Village, Hujia Fort, Shangliang, and Wuliang serve as mirrors reflecting the rural society of the Central Plains. Works such as *The Golden House*, *The Li Family*, *The Gate of Sheep*, *The City's Light*, *The Book of Life*, *The Boundless Morning*, and *Tales of the Ying River* collectively chronicle the transformation of this region in the new era, embodying remarkable richness and depth. The Ying River, an unremarkable tributary of the Huai River system, flows through villages and communities that appear indistinguishable from elsewhere on the plains. Yet the lives of its people inevitably merge with societal progress, making them participants, contributors, and beneficiaries of epochal change. Thus, the tides of transformation will reshape their existence in full measure. Through generations of struggle, Hujia Fort emerged from poverty to become a moderately prosperous socialist collective farm. As the Party secretary of this model village, Hu Tiancheng cultivated extensive social networks while managing its affairs, operating within a carefully maintained "human arena." His connections extended directly to county, municipal, and provincial tiers—even reaching the capital. This network secured benefits for the village while simultaneously influencing power structures at local and regional levels, revealing the intricate rhizomatic growth of authority within Chinese society. Villages such as Dali, Shangliang, and Wuliang epitomize the rural reality of the Central Plains. Here, people strive and struggle for a better life. Some, like Feng Jiachang, Wu Zhipeng, and Cai Weixiang, have migrated to cities, but the majority remain—rooted in this land, multiplying, growing, and sowing seeds of hope. Whether Hujia Fort, Dali, Shangliang, or Wuliang, all have been swept into the rapid currents of transformation. Social change will alter everything—rural structures, family dynamics, individual ways of life—all profoundly reshaped. The agrarian heartland is now submerged under the tides of urbanization, marketization, and commodification. Even human bodies and minds endure the pressures and temptations of materialism, informatization, and technological rationality.

Works such as Waiting for the Soul and City White Paper reflect urban life, capturing the transformation of cities in the Central Plains. Whether the provincial capital of Pingyuan or the city of Xutian, these stand as symbolic representations of Central Plains urbanization.

Ren Qiufeng, the protagonist of Waiting for the Soul, is a man of vision, daring, and sharp business acumen. He has an instinct for seizing opportunities—bold enough to take over a failing state-owned department store, strategic in planning, and discerning in talent selection. With the support of the "Three Flowers of Business College," his bold creativity, exceptional public relations skills, and formidable commercial prowess allow him to navigate the cutthroat tides of commerce. Through relentless struggle, he engineers the store's miraculous rise, transforming it into a nationally unrivaled retail superpower. Yet the pinnacle of success bordered on a precipice—behind achievement lurked temptation, and victory often beclouded judgment, leading the soul astray. Driven by an insatiable hunger for power, Ren Qiufeng embarked on reckless expansion, overreaching in his pursuit of grandeur until the capital chain snapped, leaving him unable to manage the consequences. Thus, his painstakingly built "First Commercial Empire" collapsed in ruin. This narrative evokes a once-ubiquitous 1990s advertising slogan: "Where to go in the Central Plains? Zhengzhou Asia Mall." The rise and fall of Zhengzhou Asia Mall mirrors the fate of Ren's empire—an authentic fragment of urban reform in the Central Plains, a quintessential case study of market economy dynamics. *City White Paper* stands as an unflinching radiograph of urban existence. Amid rapid modernization and the advancement of Central Plains urban cluster strategies, cities have undergone voracious expansion. These concrete labyrinths offer not merely space, markets, and opportunity, but equally compression, risk, and traps—dazzling with modernity's glare yet festering with peripheral darkness, where tensions between contemporary and traditional forces simmer beneath the surface. Through the lens of an ailing girl's gaze, the work employs visceral sensory imagery—sound, light, color, odor—to dissect urban life's essence. With surgical irony, it exposes humanity's alienation under deteriorating ethics, irrational mechanisms, and incomplete legal frameworks within the market economy's ecosystem. Here, the ailing girl emerges as a potent metaphor—an embodiment of pathological urbanity. When experienced through the perspective of a beneficiary reveling in modernity's conveniences, the city may appear functional; yet through the eyes of the wounded, its fractures and maladies come sharply into focus. This shifting panorama of Central Plains urbanization is layered with the deep pigments of ancestral culture, overpainted with the garish hues of contemporary civilization.

Li Yuan Chun and the Ecology of Henan Opera

Henan Province stands as a bastion of traditional Chinese opera, home to a diverse array of regional genres dominated by bangzi theater. Historically, forms like Yu Opera served as both spiritual sustenance and cultural staple for the people of the Central Plains, permeating all levels of society. As one of China's principal operatic traditions, Henan opera constitutes a vital strand of the nation's folk arts. It has injected dynamic vitality and nourished the flourishing of Chinese theatrical heritage, contributing indispensable elements to its evolution.

However, with the advent of modernity, the emergence of new cultural genres and their accompanying modes of dissemination has fundamentally transformed how people consume and perceive culture. Like other traditional Chinese operatic forms, Henan opera has gradually faded from prominence, reaching a state where "the courtyard lies deserted, with few visitors arriving on horseback". The market for Henan's regional opera has drastically contracted, its developmental momentum severely weakened. Numerous local troupes have disbanded, their stages dismantled, as the art form's survival environment and ecological foundation rapidly deteriorate. Just as traditional opera's survival grew increasingly precarious, Henan Television—a modern media institution—launched Li Yuan Chun, marking a pivotal moment in the evolution of Henan's regional theater. At first glance, the marriage between television (a product of modern technology) and traditional culture appears incongruous. Yet historical logic underpins this fusion, as evidenced by its subsequent operational success. Li Yuan Chun essentially functions as a "television theater"—with its actual stage being the TV studio, while its spatial reach expands exponentially through broadcast signals. This creates a profoundly virtualized theatrical experience. Yet this virtuality neither obstructs nor diminishes television theater's role in propagating traditional opera. On the contrary, its very virtuality creates an expansive communicative field. The survival of any cultural form depends on a broad consumer base. Since its inception, traditional opera has thrived either on makeshift stages in crowded spaces or in established theaters—spaces where live audiences directly engage with performances, enabling cultural transmission. However, such physical stages impose inherent spatial constraints, limiting both audience reach and artistic dissemination. Meanwhile, television's ubiquity introduced a paradox: while its cultural richness and convenience have overshadowed and marginalized traditional theater, they have also filled the void left by opera's waning presence. The launch of Li Yuan Chun as a televised theater appears as an act of atonement—a medium assuming responsibility for the displacement it inadvertently caused. Li Yuan Chun transplants the theater into countless households, enabling audiences to consume opera as effortlessly as in physical venues—without stepping outdoors—thus reversing traditional theater's shrinking viewership. More significantly, the program's format disrupts the professional monopoly over stages. By elevating amateur enthusiasts (piaoyou) to protagonist status, it transforms passive spectators into active participants who now challenge each other in onstage competitions, subject to public appraisal. This paradigm shift has dramatically amplified popular initiative in both learning and disseminating traditional opera.

Today, Li Yuan Chun has become a flagship program of Henan Television, reigniting fervor for Henan opera not only across the Central Plains but also sparking a regional theater renaissance in multiple provinces. Once fading into obscurity amid modernity's cultural tides, these local operatic forms have now resurged into public consciousness through the program's popularity. More than mere revival, Li Yuan Chun has generated vital momentum for the art form's evolution, emerging as a driving force in contemporary regional theater production. It could be said that this modest television program orchestrates grand cultural currents—Li Yuan Chun is fundamentally reshaping the ecology of Henan's regional opera. Indeed, within modern cultural development, interactive relationships and reciprocal effects between diverse cultural forms persistently emerge. It is precisely this cultural interplay that maintains the broader ecosystem's equilibrium.

From this author's perspective, Li Yuan Chun's pivotal contribution to Henan opera lies in its market expansion—cultivating fertile ground for the art form's growth and creating developmental opportunities. Yet fundamentally, the program cannot generate opera itself. As we know, Chinese opera is a traditional composite art synthesizing literature, music, dance, visual arts, martial arts, acrobatics, and role-playing. Henan's bangzi-based regional theater traces its origins to Ming Dynasty *qinqiang* and *Puzhou bangzi*, which blended with local folk melodies to form this deeply rooted tradition①—one possessing profound cultural foundations and mass appeal. Traditional opera and television culture exist on vastly different historical timelines. Television can neither alter opera's past nor fundamentally dictate its future. The art form's evolution must follow its inherent logic and organic momentum—arbitrary external interventions often prove futile. Yet just as tradition and modernity are not irreconcilable opposites, television and traditional opera need not exist in isolation. Modern media can provide stages for opera, while opera enriches television's cultural repertoire. Li Yuan Chun exemplifies this symbiosis: by creating a contemporary platform for traditional theater (while simultaneously serving its own institutional needs), it bridges these temporal divides.

In truth, Li Yuan Chun merely harnesses television's expansive reach to aggregate and showcase traditional opera, reintroducing it to mass audiences. Consequently, its form and posture outweigh its artistic substance. The program compiles fragmentary excerpts—whether through competitive segments with audience participation or celebrity performances of renowned arias—stitched together by hosts. This format neither produces original op-

① Cihai: Arts Volume, Shanghai Lexicographical Publishing House, 1980.

eratic works nor presents complete dramas. Live viewers gain neither historical context nor the holistic artistic essence that unfolds through full productions. Yet crucially, Li Yuan Chun constructs a modern stage for opera, cultivating an ambiance that makes emotional engagement with traditional theater possible. Its significance lies in transcending temporal and spatial constraints—delivering opera's melodies and voices into households, permeating the auditory landscape. By facilitating exposure, understanding, and appreciation, it draws audiences back into opera's realm, generating ripple effects of renewed interest.

In summary, Li Yuan Chun has significantly reshaped Henan's operatic ecology. Primarily, its ripple effects have spurred renewed public engagement with traditional theater—rediscovering regional opera's history and reconnecting with its foundational roots. Modern visual media culture has increasingly monopolized cultural consumption, predominantly promoting popular and mass entertainment. Within this landscape, the absence of traditional culture (including opera) inevitably diminished its perceived significance, leading to widespread neglect. This systemic marginalization once relegated traditional opera to near-invisibility. Li Yuan Chun has guided the public toward recognizing traditional opera's vital place in national culture—revealing its profound heritage and vibrant artistic dimensions. This awakening fosters renewed interest and conscious efforts to preserve and revitalize regional operatic traditions. Secondly, the program has cultivated a dynamic ecosystem for Henan opera's dissemination. The "Henan opera sphere" encompasses not only the province itself but also neighboring regions and areas with significant Henanese diaspora communities. Through its lively format—particularly audience participation in competitive segments—coupled with satellite broadcasting, Li Yuan Chun intensifies interaction between performers, viewers, and society at large. A new operatic transmission paradigm is emerging. Finally—and most crucially—Li Yuan Chun has ignited a renaissance of operatic fervor across the Central Plains, driving the popularization of Henan opera. This constitutes the essential foundation for the art form's ecological revitalization and flourishing. The program's pervasive influence has sparked widespread public enthusiasm, giving rise to grassroots movements for opera study and performance. Today, whether in Henan's cities or villages, one encounters communal gatherings where young and old, men and women—especially younger generations—openly perform regional opera. This expanding participatory base demonstrates how traditional theater has reclaimed its role as a cornerstone of spiritual life. Simultaneously, Li Yuan Chun's touring performances extend the stage into broader society, further stimulating Henan opera's consumer market and nurturing public interest—acting as a cultural growth catalyst. Under its influence, previously shuttered regional troupes have resumed operations, gradually reclaiming their market niches. As primary vessels and transmitters of traditional theater, these professional troupes' revival proves pivotal: it facilitates both the excavation of classical repertoires and the creation of contemporary works attuned to modern demands. This dual capacity for preservation and innovation holds profound significance for Henan's operatic ecosystem.

The Spiritual Ecology of Contemporary Henan

I. Henan's Spiritual Ecology and Its Essence

Spiritual ecology refers to the dynamic value system, cultural configurations, and the nurturing milieu constituted by ideologies, consciousness, conceptual frameworks, and their representative symbols. It is composed of diverse, multifaceted spiritual elements. Every culture functions as a dynamic living entity with distinct characteristics. Countless cultural organisms—each with unique traits—interconnect to form an interdependent cultural ecosystem of mutual influence. The concept of ecology emphasizes four cardinal principles: First, it concerns not merely individual entities but more critically, populations; Second, it is dynamic—characterized by development and maturation; Third, it entails interconnectedness, mutual influence, and symbiotic coexistence; Fourth, its value derives not solely from individual units, but equally from their significance to others and the collective whole. Spiritual ecology thus constitutes a holistic cultural construct in the fullest sense.

The spiritual ecology of Henan refers to the dynamic value system and the historical/contemporary existential conditions of cultural communities within the Central Plains region, composed of multiple spiritual elements. This encompasses historical trajectories, contemporary developmental capacities, and cross-cultural influence. The historical stability of the "Central Plains" concept has fostered a degree of political, economic, and cultural homogeneity in the region. Such homogeneity fundamentally manifests as institutional, axiological, and spiritual consonance. The formation of such homogeneity was a protracted process extending to the present, inevitably giving rise to a distinct regional spiritual ecology. Chinese civilization, in reality, comprises numerous regional cultures—homogeneous in form yet heterogeneous in substance, or vice versa—such as Shangluo culture, Bashu culture, imperial capital culture, Shanghai-style culture, and Hong Kong-Taiwan culture. These regional ecosystems achieve relative stability and autonomy through their internal consonance of institutions, values, and spiritual orientations.

Henan, situated along the middle reaches of the Yellow River, bears the indelible imprint of Yellow River civilization within its spiritual ecology. The middle-lower Yellow River basin served as the earliest habitat of the Chinese nation. Current archaeological evidence indicates primitive human settlements in the middle reaches as early as the Paleolithic era. From an anthropological perspective, three primary factors governed habitat selection: 1. Access to sustenance; 2. Adequate water sources; 3. Natural ecological conditions providing disaster resilience and security. Historically, the middle Yellow River region's geomorphology and ecology perfectly satisfied these criteria. Henan's territory is shielded by the Taihang Mountains to the north, the Funiu Mountains to the west, and the Dabie Mountains to the south—a trilateral mountain barrier encircling the vast Huang-Huai Plain, providing natural defense against continental monsoons from three directions. The Yellow River, like a slender yet robust embracing arm, cradled its inhabitants.

Its waters not only sustained life but, through millennia of sedimentation and nature's geological alchemy, forged the Central Plains' fertile expanse—a testament to alluvial transformation. Simultaneously, the Central Plains historically sustained dense forests teeming with diverse fauna and flora—an ecosystem abundant in resources where both game and botanical yields provided sustenance. This ecological wealth rendered the region an ideal and poetic habitat for the Chinese nation. Legendary progenitors like the Yellow Emperor, followed by sage-kings Yao, Shun, and Yu, all lived and labored here, leaving enduring cultural imprints. Throughout recorded history, dynasties including Xia, Shang, Eastern Zhou, Eastern Han, Wei, Jin, Tang, and Song established their capitals in this heartland. For three millennia prior to the Southern Song, Henan remained the socioeconomic, political, and cultural nucleus—the crucible where Chinese civilization gestated and matured. "Henan, situated at the heart of the Central Plains, has since antiquity produced an unbroken succession of eminent figures, surpassing all other provinces in number."① Historically, this region birthed countless philosophers, literati, scientists, statesmen, strategists, and national heroes—including Mozi, Laozi, Zhuangzi, Shang Yang, Han Fei, Su Qin, Zhang Yi, Li Si, Fan Ju, Lü Buwei, Cai Yong, Jia Yi, Zhang Heng, Zhang Zhongjing, Xie Lingyun, Du Fu, Li He, Li Shangyin, Bai Juyi, Liu Yuxi, Cen Shen, Yuan Zhen, Han

① Hu Siyong. "Preface to Dictionary of Henan's Historical Figures." In *Dictionary of Henan's Historical Figures*, edited by Wang Tianxing, Wang Xingya, and Wang Zongyu. Zhengzhou: Zhongzhou Ancient Books Publishing House, 1991.

Yu, Cheng Yi, Cheng Hao, Wu Daozi, Bi Gan, Yue Fei, Fan Li, and Zhang Liang. Particularly, Mozi, Laozi, and Zhuangzi stand as peerless thinkers of the Spring and Autumn and Warring States periods, their philosophies attaining foundational significance for Chinese culture. Their works constitute the primordial canons of Chinese civilization. Thus, the Central Plains' profound cultural origins and luxuriant intellectual ecology have nurtured the richly layered spiritual ecology of Henan.

The spiritual ecology of Henan manifests both monolithic unity and pluralistic diversity through cultural permeation and synthesis. Historically, the Central Plains served as the most profoundly and comprehensively Confucianized region, where Confucian thought achieved an unshakable hegemony of supreme authority. It must be acknowledged that Confucianism constituted the core value system of the region's spiritual ecology for millennia, fundamentally shaping the cognitive paradigms of its people. However, waves of warfare, dynastic transitions, population migrations, and ethnic intermingling also facilitated the influx, transplantation, and hybridization of heterogenous cultural elements. During the Eastern Han to Wei-Jin periods, numerous ethnic groups from western and northern frontiers migrated inward, settling among Han communities in interlocking patterns. These "non-Han groups not only extensively assimilated Han feudal culture but also reciprocally influenced Han customs. By the Western Jin era, Luoyang's aristocracy had adopted nomadic practices—'using barbarian folding chairs and *mo*-style trays, preparing *Qiang*-style boiled and *mo*-style roasted meats, even wearing felt headwear, waistbands, and trouser piping.'"① This demographic fluidity catalyzed not only ethnic fusion but also political, economic, and cultural exchanges—particularly the intermingling and coexistence of divergent worldviews, behavioral patterns, and lifestyles. These cross-currents continuously infused the Central Plains culture with novel elements, sustaining its pluralistic equilibrium.

From a cultural-ecological perspective, no culture can be monistic—monistic cultures is hard to endure. As spiritual constructs, cultures exhibit even more profound interdependence than natural species. For any culture to sustain its vitality and competitive edge, it must ceaselessly incorporate new elements. Such renewal necessitates openness to external cultural currents, achieving revitalization solely through cross-cultural exchange, friction, and eventual grafting, hybridization, and synthesis. The spiritual ecology of the Central Plains exemplifies this process—its historical vibrancy emerged precisely through such dialectical engagement with other cultures, forging an ecological panorama of remarkable dynamism.

① Jian Bozan, ed. *An Outline of Chinese History*, vol. 2. Beijing: People's Publishing House, 1982, 30-34.

II. The Spiritual Ecology of Contemporary Henan

The spiritual ecology of contemporary Henan refers to the current state of existence, growth, and development of spiritual and cultural elements—their essence, extensions, and interrelationships—within the region.

"Contemporary" is a dynamic temporal concept. In this context, it primarily denotes the period from the Reform and Opening-up to the present ongoing era. Since the Reform and Opening-up, China has undergone transformative changes that have captivated global attention. Henan, as a microcosm within China's macro-framework, has undergone changes inextricably synchronized with the nation's broader transformation. This metamorphosis first emerged through shifts in ideology, institutions, and systems, subsequently permeating all facets of society—every sector, stratum, and even the daily lives of ordinary people. In turn, these societal changes have further stimulated new ideological and institutional reforms. Material and spiritual dynamics are fundamentally intertwined: the emergence, evolution, and transformation of spiritual ecology remain inextricably linked to shifts across the entire social landscape.

Henan, situated inland within contemporary China—neither coastal nor bordering—has long relinquished its historical socioeconomic primacy, lacking most advantageous conditions for modern development. Moreover, it bears a weighty historical legacy: whether glory or suffering, triumph or setback, all weigh heavily upon its people. Yet Henan progresses nonetheless, advancing with accelerating momentum toward the ultimate goal of Central Plains revitalization. This socioeconomic development constitutes the material foundation for the formation of Henan's contemporary spiritual ecology.

The formation of contemporary Henan's spiritual ecology has unfolded through three primary pathways. First, historical inertia. Cultural and spiritual resources, as historical accumulations, possess greater resilience and vitality. Compared to material resources, they are intangible, stable, transmissible, shareable, and enduring. Consequently, cultural resources are less susceptible to destruction or eradication than material ones. Once ideas and spirits take form, they crystallize into psychological imprints—persistent convictions that exert lasting influence on individuals and society. In this sense, culture itself constitutes an enduring human tradition, inherently possessing developmental inertia. While external forces significantly influence cultural trajectories, benign cultural ecosystems foster greater flourishing—yet even cultural marginalization cannot abruptly terminate its existence or evolution. As the primary cradle of Chinese civilization, the Central Plains have cultivated deeply rooted cultural ecosystems over millennia. Despite recent relative stagnation in economic and cultural development, the historical inertia generated by this ancient, continuous civilization remains the fundamental impetus for Henan's cultural advancement. First, the historical memory of Central Plains culture has been engraved into the very marrow of Henan's people, becoming foundational to their cultural imagination and interpretive frameworks. Second, the enduring excellence of this tradition constitutes both a vital component and the core substance of contemporary Henan's spiritual ecology. Third, the cultural virtues forged through millennia—profundity, breadth, resilience, and enterprising spirit—serve as boundless energy for material and spiritual creation. Finally, the rich cultural atmosphere cultivated over centuries provides fertile ground for the growth of Henan's modern spiritual ecology.

Second, endogenous development. This refers to the spiritual resources generated by Henan people themselves—as the primary agents of regional progress—through creative activities in both material and spiritual production. Generally speaking, whether for a nation, an ethnic group, or a defined region, spiritual ecology constitutes a localized spiritual resource. This very localization defines its essential nature. Moreover, the formation of any spiritual ecology must principally arise from the autonomous creative acts of its native people—the fundamental DNA that distinguishes one spiritual ecosystem from another. Undoubtedly, the spiritual ecology of contemporary Henan has been principally forged by its people. Fundamentally, it crystallizes their creative labor—both material and spiritual. Since the Reform and Opening-up, Henan's populace has striven tirelessly to transform its historically disadvantaged conditions. The government has charted developmental blueprints for regional revitalization, while the people demonstrate unwavering conviction and industriousness. Through pragmatic, persistent efforts, Henan has achieved substantial socioeconomic progress. Concurrently with socioeconomic advancement, Henan has vigorously strengthened cultural development—implementing strategies to revitalize through education and empower through culture. This underscores the catalytic role of spiritual and cultural forces in driving progress. Building upon the historical momentum of Central Plains culture, the province has: 有 expanded new frontiers in cultural development; actively cultivated contemporary spiritual ecology; continuously infused it with fresh vitality and substance. This constitutes the very core of Henan's modern spiritual ecosystem.

Third, external derivation. This refers to the influence of factors outside Henan's region on the formation of contemporary Henan's spiritual ecology. While the spiritual ecology of contemporary Henan is primarily created by Henan's people and is endogenously developed, it is simultaneously influenced and permeated by cultural factors beyond Henan's region—these constitute the external elements in its formation. There is no doubt that any culture possesses its own essential attributes; yet it is equally undeniable that no culture is monistic, as a monistic culture would lack the advantages of hybridization and robust vitality. Therefore, the essential attributes of any culture inherently possess multidimensional extensions and rich connotations. Since the Reform and Opening-up, development across China's regions has been uneven. Coastal areas, border regions, southern provinces, early open cities, and political-economic-cultural centers—whether in terms of productive forces or spiritual elements like ideas and concepts—have all progressed ahead of inland regions like Henan. The experiences and values from these pioneering reform zones undoubtedly hold vanguard and paradigmatic significance for inland areas. In reality, throughout China's 30-year reform journey, regional development has existed in a state of competition. To gain advantage in this competition, the decisive factors are: whose thinking is more emancipated, whose concepts are more open, whose soft/hard environments are more favorable, and whose measures are more effective. In essence, it boils down to whether the spiritual dimension can provide sufficient support for people's practical activities. Located in China's central inland region, Henan has long remained relatively enclosed, with ideological emancipation lagging behind. The development of coastal areas and neighboring regions has exerted tremendous impact on Henan. Consequently, under external pressures and through internal reflection, Henan's ideologies, concepts, and spiritual conditions have undergone continuous transformation. A determined will for development and revitalization has gradually taken shape, propelling Henan forward with great strides in China's modernization process. It can be said that through collisions and assimilation with external ideas, concepts, and value orientations, contemporary Henan's spiritual ecology has forged a solid core and root system, while simultaneously developing an outward form imbued with modern consciousness.

The spiritual ecology of contemporary Henan can be broadly categorized into three content systems:

The Ideological Framework. Ideological concepts represent relatively unstable yet dynamic elements within humanity's spiritual constitution. Typically latent in human consciousness yet emergent at the forefront of mental activity, these concepts often manifest as both established realities with certain universality, while simultaneously reflecting specific thoughts and behaviors as unformed spiritual products. Their markedly individualized characteristics consequently render them inherently fluid. However, precisely because of their individualized and distinctive nature, ideological concepts possess exceptionally rich connotations. They permeate the consciousness of every member of society, with each person's ideological framework capable of forming a complete system unto itself. While each individual's ideological concepts inevitably differ and can never be entirely identical, their constant influence on human behavior remains undeniable. That said, when examining the ideological framework within contemporary Henan's spiritual ecology, our conceptual focus is on the collective ideological paradigm of Henan as a whole, rather than individual constructs. The ideological framework of Henan exhibits distinct characteristics within China's overall system of thought. Situated in the nation's heartland, Henan bears profound influences from traditional Chinese culture, with Confucian ideals and agricultural civilization deeply rooted in the mentality of its people. From modern times through the Reform and Opening-up period, Henan has not been at the forefront of modern civilization's surge or modernization's advance. Consequently, the transformation and renewal of ideological concepts in Henan have naturally lagged behind other regions of the country. Henan's ideological framework retains relatively more orthodox elements, such as traditional Confucian thought, agricultural civilization's cognitive patterns, and value judgments stemming from the planned economy era. Nevertheless, it must be acknowledged that traditional culture still contains rational and excellent elements. Through integration, transformation, and alignment with modern civilization, these elements can enrich the ideological framework of contemporary Henan's spiritual ecology. Simultaneously, as a transitional zone between eastern and western China, Henan plays a pivotal bridging role. This geographical position significantly contributes to enriching and refining Henan's ideological system. In fact, during the nearly 30 years of reform and opening-up, Henan has placed great emphasis on renewing its ideological framework. Government and various social strata have organized discussions and campaigns to promote ideological renewal, disseminate modern civilization concepts and scientific knowledge, and reshape Henan's image. These efforts have permeated all levels of Henan society, particularly through concrete transformations in ideological perspectives during the province's construction and development initiatives, all of which have vigorously advanced the development of Henan's ideological framework. Today, Henan's ideological framework has undergone fundamental transformations. Within China's modernization process and against the backdrop of global economic integration, Henan's ideological system is achieving full alignment with modern civilization. The province's rapid and comprehensive development in recent years best exemplifies the profound changes in its ideological framework.

The Spiritual Coordinate System. As the core pillar of contemporary Henan's spiritual ecosystem, this system represents both the culmination and sublimation of the people's ideological concepts—a fully formed spiritual construct. Spiritual coordinates never emerge spontaneously; they are consciously and deliberately forged through cultivation. Within human spiritual activities, ideological concepts exist abundantly and diversely, typically manifesting as rich, distinctive individual expressions. In contrast, spiritual coordinates synthesize, consolidate, and elevate these individual thought patterns into composite formations with specific conceptual depth. Undoubtedly, spiritual coordinates find their solid foundation in the widespread individual ideological concepts existing within society. As composite formations with specific conceptual depth, the cultivation of spiritual coordinates values not quantity but essential connotation. People nurture spiritual coordinates to establish faith, set goals, and provide orientation for both spiritual and practical activities—ultimately enabling human life to propel practice through consciousness and achieve aesthetic fulfillment through practice. During its socioeconomic development and modernization drive, Henan has coalesced the progressive ideologies of its people, cultivating a rich spiritual coordinate system through transformative practices. This system includes: Revolutionary ethos from historical milestones (the 1923 Railroad Strike, revolutionary struggles in the Hubei-Henan-Anhui base, the LIU-Deng Army's Thousand-

Mile Advance into the Dabie Mountains, Taihang Mountains anti-Japanese resistance, and Huaihai Campaign) that continue to inspire patriotism and heroism; Constructivist spirits like the Jiao Yulu Spirit and Red Flag Canal Spirit forged during peacetime; Exemplary Communist Party members and heroic model figures like Shi Laihe, Wu Jinyin, Chang Xiangyu, Ren Changxia, Li Liancheng, Zhao Ming'en, Wang Hongbin, Zhang Rongsuo, Liu Wengong, etc., embodying public service and selfless dedication—each constituting a towering spiritual coordinate that enriches Henan's modern spiritual ecology. If the ideological framework represents the soil nurturing this ecology, the spiritual coordinate system forms its robust trunk and branches.

(III) The Artistic-Humanistic System. As the foliage and blossoms of contemporary Henan's spiritual ecosystem, this system represents the artistic and aesthetic expression of the people's ideological concepts and spiritual coordinates.nComprising a series of formalized works across diverse genres, categories, and forms, art simultaneously reflects both human societal practices and the conceptual/emotional dimensions of thought—crystallizing spiritual activities. Thus, the growth of this artistic-humanistic system remains inextricably intertwined with both the ideological framework and spiritual coordinate systems. The artistic-humanistic system encompasses literature, arts, journalism, publishing, theoretical research, and related fields. As these are all formalized works, this ecosystem constitutes not only a tangible spiritual ecology but also one with enduring impact—a perpetual spiritual presence. Overall, contemporary Henan's artistic-humanistic system demonstrates robust developmental momentum, holding nationally pivotal influence that showcases the substantive strength of Henan's spiritual ecology. In literature, the "Henan School" has demonstrated remarkable achievements over the years, producing nationally renowned writers such as Li Zhun, Yao Xueyin, Bai Hua, Wei Wei, Zhang Yigong, Zhang Yu, Qiao Dianyun, Tian Zhonghe, Liu Zhenyun, Zhou Daxin, Eryue He, Su Jinsan, and Wang Huairang. Notably, Eryue He's "Qing Emperor Series" novels have caused a sensation at home and abroad in recent years, becoming a vibrant growth point in Henan's cultural landscape.

In opera arts, Henan's distinctive opera traditions have flourished magnificently. Yu Opera, Qu Opera, Yue Diao, and other genres compete in splendor, with widely acclaimed productions like *Hua Mulan*, *Mu Guiying Takes Command*, *Sunny Gulch*, *The Snowstorm Match*, and *Capturing Jiang Wei* enjoying nationwide popularity. A constellation of master artists—including Chang Xiangyu, Ma Jinfeng, Yan Lipin, Tang Xicheng, Niu Decao, Zhang Xinfang, Hai Lianchi, Shen Fengmei, and Mao Ailian—have attained profound artistic mastery, captivating audiences with peerless performances. In music and dance, Henan has implemented the "Zheng-Bian-Luo Artistic Excellence Project" with distinction. Monumental productions like the symphonic poem *Mulan's Ode*, grand dance dramas *Shaolin in the Wind* and *River-Luo Rhythms*, and the opera *Along the River During Qingming Festival* showcase profound cultural depth. As a powerhouse of calligraphy and painting, Henan boasts vigorous brushwork and solemnly substantial artistry, with the "Central Plains Calligraphic Style" influencing nationwide. The province also treasures abundant folk narratives—myths, ballads, nursery rhymes, folktales, and ditties—constituting invaluable artistic-humanistic ecosystems. Henan's broadcasting, television, and news publishing sectors rank among China's foremost. In 2002, the province placed fifth nationally in book publishing output and first in distribution outlets. *Henan Daily* has maintained leading national circulation for years, while *Dahe Bao* entered the "World's Top 100 Newspapers by Circulation," becoming a globally recognized cultural brand. *Cartoon Monthly* is acclaimed as "China's Premier Comic Publication." Henan's humanities and social sciences research exerts significant national influence. For years, the province has consistently ranked among China's top performers in securing National Philosophy and Social Sciences Foundation projects, with numerous research achievements exerting considerable impact within their respective academic fields nationwide. In summary, these artistic and humanistic achievements have played a vital role in nurturing the growth of contemporary Henan's spiritual ecology.

The Heroic Essence in *The Grand Mansion Gate* and *The Dyehouse*

The tides of change bring forth new opportunities. As the new century dawned, China's television production and cultural landscape became a spectacle of buzzwords and gimmicks—flashy yet ultimately superficial. Few works, in this observer's view, managed to penetrate audiences' minds with truly seismic impact. Yet two productions stand apart: The Grand Mansion Gate (CCTV, 2001) and The Dyehouse (CCTV, 2003), which demand our critical attention.

The quiet yet profound impact of The Grand Mansion Gate and *The Dyehouse*—achieved without hype—stems not merely from artistic craftsmanship, but fundamentally from their heroic essence and its mode of expression. While hero-worship reflects a universal social psyche, the crucial factors lie in how heroic archetypes are crafted, the narrative opportunities seized, and the expressive methods chosen to ensure heroes resonate within collective consciousness. These two dramas represent exemplary paradigms of such storytelling.

I. Historical Context

History forges heroes, and heroes in turn shape history. Thus, history constitutes not only the spatial-temporal realm for heroic existence and action, but also the very substance of their lives—and ultimately, the vessel for cultural production and continuity. Whether examining heroes or ordinary figures, our acceptance of specific individuals inherently demands acknowledgment of their historical milieu. Yet our historical inquiry seeks not simplistic deconstruction, but rather to illuminate the fertile soil from which figures emerge and reveal the foundations of cultural existence.

Both *The Grand Mansion Gate* and *The Dyehouse* extract pivotal segments from China's modern history. *The Grand Mansion Gate* spans nearly a century, from the late Qing Dynasty to the founding of New China, while *The Dyehouse* unfolds between the early Republic era and the Japanese occupation of Jinan during the Anti-Japanese War. This historical period—universally recognized as one of profound national tribulation and resilient resistance—provided fertile ground for heroism. As turmoil breeds heroes, these decades witnessed an extraordinary emergence of talent and heroic figures. By selecting this historical backdrop, both dramas inherently secured optimal conditions for heroic portrayal. What merits attention is that both dramas present this historical background primarily through major historical events rather than specific dates—similar to Mo Yan's Red Sorghum, where beyond the red sorghum fields of Qilu region and the overarching context of Japanese invasion as grand stage setting, we encounter no concrete temporal or spatial markers, nor precise eras for characters and events. However, this approach of obscuring historical specifics fundamentally departs from traditional hero narratives that strictly adhere to documented timelines, locations, or even real-life figures. While superficially sacrificing certain factual authenticity, it effectively dismantles creative constraints, providing expansive freedom for character and story development. This technique liberates audiences from binary authentication thinking, endowing narratives with measured fictionality and enhanced legendary qualities. Consequently, stories gain vividness and characters acquire deeper spiritual dimensions.

It must be emphasized that history is essentially stories; history is culture. The vividness of history inherently manifests through the vividness of its narratives and characters. We cannot deny the cultural significance of any historical period, nor can we negate the inherent dynamism of history—even its most uneventful chapters. However, different historical contexts give rise to narratives of varying intensity, and nurture characters of distinct types, temperaments, and capacities. Conversely, the depth of historical substance and cultural resonance embedded within artistic stories and characters serves as the crucial criterion determining a work's success. *The Grand Mansion Gate* and *The Dyehouse* employ modern Chinese history as their fundamental stage and props, thereby constructing narrative depth at a profound level and endowing the works with significant historical and cultural resonance. We recognize that modern China faced monumental socio-historical dilemmas: the dual imperatives of national survival and modernization, the tension between preserving cultural heritage and assimilating Western knowledge to develop new culture. This historical multiplicity and profundity inherently shape narrative complexity—where intricate social contradictions inevitably manifest through historical figures. The thoughts and actions of individuals in such contexts cannot but exhibit historical multidimensionality. Their struggles against calamities, breakthroughs beyond historical constraints, and liberation from societal/personal predicaments all bear historical profundity while radiating heroic brilliance. Thus, while history forges heroes, we must equally acknowledge that extraordinary historical periods possess intrinsic epic qualities. This explains why *The Grand Mansion Gate* and *The Dyehouse* consciously selected an epoch that constitutes nothing less than a heroic epic.

II. Story (Signification)

The stories of The Grand Mansion Gate and The Dyehouse serve as fundamental vehicles for signification. Admittedly, the narratives selected by these works represent but one historical possibility among many within their modern Chinese setting. Objectively speaking, given the nature of China's modern history—where monumental sociopolitical issues like national survival, independence, and liberation could have spawned more politically charged narratives—these dramas consciously eschewed overtly prominent historical themes. Instead, they focused on a relatively latent historical thread: the stories of industrial and commercial enterprises. While we cannot accuse the creators of evading weighty historical themes, we may discern their deliberate inclination toward contemporary narrative sensibilities.

It must be acknowledged that economic activity constitutes the lifeblood of national development, with commerce and enterprise forming its foundation. Yet during existential crises for the nation, business affairs inevitably recede from urgent prominence. Consequently, heroes and their narratives are invariably forged in the crucible of history's most turbulent junctures. Conventional wisdom suggests that during periods of radical social transformation, heroic figures rarely emerge from the business world—and when they do, only those who transcend commercial spheres to confront epochal challenges, whether through glorious success or noble sacrifice. Why, then, did the creators of *The Grand Mansion Gate* and *The Dyehouse* select business narratives? What signification do they convey, and what cognitive frameworks do they offer? These questions compel us to ponder within the vast interstice between history and contemporaneity. The reality is this: while we cannot deny past heroes their heroic status today, we must recognize that the urgent concerns of turbulent eras may lose contemporary relevance. Conversely, historically latent themes—like commercial enterprise—can assume new prominence, just as figures once excluded from heroic pantheons may now be thus honored. Naturally, any claimant to heroism must possess its essential attributes.

In contemporary society, the nation is vigorously establishing a market economy system, where economic development and the enhancement of comprehensive national strength through economic prowess constitute the central mission. Undoubtedly, economic advancement and entrepreneurial endeavors have become defining themes of our era—those who strive valiantly within these economic currents may rightly be recognized as models and heroes of our time. *The Grand Mansion Gate* chronicles the vicissitudes of traditional Chinese medicine—specifically the herbal enterprise "Hundred

Herbs Hall," a century-old establishment beneath the imperial capital's walls—depicting its processing, production, and commercial triumphs and tribulations. *The Dyehouse* traces the rise and fall of Shandong's textile industry, from humble workshops to its ultimate destruction under Japanese artillery. Though both narratives intertwine with pivotal modern historical events, they consciously retreat from battlefield carnage and political upheavals, choosing instead to illuminate history through commercial lenses. Yet the creators' intentionality is unequivocal: these narratives demonstrate that heroism manifests not only on battlefields during national crises, but equally within commerce during peacetime. Social progress and historical development result from the synthesis of multifarious forces—a dynamic aligning with history's plural potentialities. Indeed, Marxist orthodoxy positions economic foundations as society's determining factor, though this recedes secondary during acute social contradictions—never negating its fundamental role. Indeed, whether in extraordinary historical periods or peacetime, the business sector and broader economic domain have consistently made foundational contributions to social progress—contributions deserving unwavering societal recognition. This thematic essence in the works constitutes a restoration of historical veracity. Such signification perfectly aligns with modern societal currents. Today's value orientation has decisively shifted from profit-aversion: individual entrepreneurship and wealth-building, alongside national economic development for prosperity, now command universal esteem. The paradigm of "wealth-bringing heroes versus poverty-keeping losers" has firmly taken root. However, we must never prioritize wealth accumulation alone—the moral dimensions of its process demand equal emphasis. Pursuing profit must not eclipse righteousness; prosperity should benefit others, not just oneself, and crucially, must never compromise national integrity. Consider The Grand Mansion Gate's Seventh Master: when Japanese forces pressured him to co-manage Hundred Herbs Hall, he chose potential death over compliance; he risked his life smuggling medicinal supplies to support the Eighth Route Army's resistance. By intertwining business narratives with epochal historical choices, these works underscore commerce's moral imperatives and historical figures' value orientations. *The Grand Mansion Gate* and *The Dyehouse* narrate such stories with dual intentionality: First, they reveal how the business community made indelible contributions to national liberation during existential crises. Second, they demonstrate that even under dire historical circumstances, merchant forebears never abandoned ethical principles. Though profit-seeking dominates contemporary values, these works affirm that gain must never supersede righteousness—a moral stance resonating profoundly with Chinese cultural ethos, thus earning widespread audience endorsement.

It is noteworthy that both *The Grand Mansion Gate* (大宅门) and *The Dyehouse* (大染坊) incorporate the character "大" (grand) in their titles. Regardless of the creators' shared intent, this lexical choice fundamentally accentuates the heroic essence of their narratives and characters. In Chinese culture, "大" carries profound connotations: As an honorific (e.g., 大爷 "elder uncle", 大娘 "aunt"); Denoting leadership (e.g., 老大 "chief" in traditional guilds); Signifying extraordinary heroism (e.g., 大侠 "gallant knight", 大儒 "eminent scholar", 大圣 "sage"). Thus, we must never interpret this "大" superficially—its deliberate usage unmistakably conveys the creators' heroic vision.

III. Characters (As Symbols)

The Grand Mansion Gate and *The Dyehouse* feature numerous characters, but their protagonists—Bai Jingqi and Chen Shouting respectively—stand paramount. If any secondary figure demands equal attention, it is the Second Madam of the Bai family in *The Grand Mansion Gate*. These three exemplars possess extraordinary intellect, courage, and moral fortitude that transcend ordinary measure. While the Second Madam lacks backstory, Bai and Chen's childhood experiences immediately reveal their exceptional natures. Bai Jingqi emerges as a man who laughs but never weeps—unyielding, indomitable, and obstinate to the core. Traditional tutoring couldn't tame him; he tormented tutors into resignation. His childhood mischief knew no bounds: distributing his own urine as "elixir" to playmates, brandishing a knife against his uncle, enduring brutal floggings from the Second Madam without uttering a sound. Such episodes—marking his juvenile obstinacy and fortitude—ultimately left even his disciplinarian mother at a loss. Similarly, *The Dyehouse*'s Chen Shouting endured an extraordinary childhood. Orphaned and destitute, he survived by begging until collapsing from starvation—only to be rescued by a benefactor, foreshadowing his "great survival presages great fortune" destiny. A steamed bun and bowl of soup pulled him back from death's brink, catalyzing his metamorphosis: adoptive parents, apprenticeship in dyeing. This seismic fortune reversal manifests his exceptional vitality and indomitable character.

As adults, Bai Jingqi and Chen Shouting proved truly remarkable. Like legendary heroes across art and history, they embodied competence, wisdom, and courage—yet infused with distinctly personal traits. Bai, despite aristocratic origins, defied the idle-rich stereotype. His family's cultural nurture, the Second Madam's influence, and his innate tenacity forged an extraordinary life of dramatic reversals. When his self-chosen marriage provoked maternal disownment, exile to Jinan left him destitute—until a stroke of genius (trading feces for silver dollars) launched his renowned ejiao business. He salvaged Hundred Herbs Hall from crisis after the Second Madam's demise, confronted Eight-Nation Alliance troops with drawn blades, and chose potential execution over collaborating as a puppet pharmaceutical association head during Japanese occupation. Bai Jingqi embodied audacious love and hatred, moral ambiguity incarnate. Though wedded, he brazenly pursued Yang Jiuhong—a courtesan beloved by his sister's father-in-law, the Jinan governor. With two concubines already, he threatened kin with blades to marry maid Li Xiangxiu. His tyrannical patriarchy broke his son's leg, yet he indulged his sister utterly. This paradox of iron-willed dominance and chivalrous softness—ever defending the vulnerable—defined his complex heroism. Chen Shouting stands in stark contrast to Bai Jingqi as a complete embodiment of truth, kindness, and moral excellence. Having endured childhood hardships, he gained profound understanding of suffering and joy, evil and goodness. Despite achieving remarkable success and wealth as a prominent business tycoon in Qingdao and Jinan, he never forgot the benefactors who saved his life, treating them as his own parents. Though witnessing others keeping concubines, he steadfastly adhered to his principles of taking no concubines or secondary wives. When rescuing the beautiful Shen Yuanyi from distress, he maintained complete propriety without any improper thoughts. In business, while employing shrewd strategies, he always upheld integrity as his foundation, being ever ready to help others and repay kindness. Yet towards Fujii, the Japanese who militarily ravaged and economically invaded China, he sought nothing less than utter annihilation. Chen Shouting demonstrated remarkable acumen, maneuvering through the business world with masterful prowess. His enterprises expanded seamlessly from secluded villages to coastal Qingdao and then to Jinan, Shandong's provincial capital, as he successively outmaneuvered competitors—even the Japanese Fujii would have faced utter defeat without the artillery backing of imperialist aggression. The life trajectories of Bai Jingqi and Chen Shouting are undeniably epic, marking them as legendary business heroes. To heighten this mythic quality, the creators deliberately engineered dramatic vicissitudes in their narratives, creating profound psychological resonance that aligns with audiences' latent aspirations.

Yet both Bai Jingqi and Chen Shouting ultimately function as narrative symbols. We recognize that all literary works and their woven tales fundamentally comprise essential elements—temporal settings, locales, characters, events, and outcomes—which constitute storytelling's basic codes. Among these, characters reign as the most pivotal semiotic units. For no story exists without personae, nor can any narrative achieve vitality without vividly rendered characters. As previously established, historical vitality determines narrative vitality—yet all history fundamentally comprises human lives and deeds. Without exceptional human expressions, history would lack richness and profundity. For *The Grand Mansion Gate* and *The Dyehouse*, Bai Jingqi could have been "Black Jingqi" or "Blue Jingqi"; Chen Shouting might have been "Zhang Shouting" or "Sun Shouting." Their heroic essence remains immutable, for these narratives derive their heroic nature precisely through their protagonists' deeds. Strip away this heroism, and the stories forfeit their defining attribute. Bai Jingqi and Chen Shouting impeccably fulfill their symbolic functions as heroic narrative vessels. To accentuate this semiotic role, the creators endowed them with quintessential heroic attributes—competence, sagacity, daring, and profound historical consciousness—precisely to orchestrate their exemplary enactment of heroism.

IV. Narrative (Methodology)

Heroes, by definition, emerge during extraordinary historical junctures as exceptional figures—whether commanding storms to save nations or igniting transformative sparks with their lives to alter history's trajectory. Consider iconic exemplars: modern-era heroes like Li Dazhao, Mao Zedong, Huang Jiguang, Dong Cunrui, Lei Feng, and Wang Jinxi; historical paragons including Yu the Great, Su Wu, Yue Fei, Wen Tianxiang, Li Zicheng, Lin Zexu, Hong Xiuquan, Deng Shichang, and Sun Yat-sen. Their heroic legacies were self-fashioned, their narratives self-authored through historic deeds. Yet *The Grand Mansion Gate* and *The Dyehouse* subvert conventional heroic paradigms. Though set during China's tumultuous modern era—typically fertile ground for heroism—their protagonists lack extraordinary traits. These narratives, rooted in pharmaceutical and dyeing commerce, feature protagonists thoroughly immersed in mercantile pursuits: ordinary individuals navigating business complexities, their identities saturated with commercial pragmatism. Moreover, these narratives and characters are fictional constructs. Unlike historically authenticated heroes, such artificially crafted stories demand performative enactment—ultimately realized through characterization. Truthfully, transmuting ordinary merchants into heroic vessels is by no means an easy task.

We profoundly sense how *The Grand Mansion Gate* and *The Dyehouse* first intensify their narratives' legendary qualities. In *The Grand Mansion*

Gate, the eldest son's medical mishap at court leads to his decapitation; the patriarch collapses under familial ruin; as the ancestral business teeters toward collapse, the sister-in-law Second Madam emerges to salvage the crisis—a radical exception to traditions prohibiting female inheritance, especially by daughters-in-law. More crucially, the Second Madam's intervention steered Hundred Herbs Hall from brink to prosperity. Through exhaustive strategizing—combining meticulous planning with uncompromising resolve—she not only reclaimed the Bai family's flagship pharmacy but propelled the household to renewed glory. This narrative turn delivers dual astonishment: unanticipated plausibility and artistic brilliance. Equally startling is Bai Jingqi's fecal entrepreneurship during destitution in Jinan—another masterstroke of improbable yet convincing storytelling. It must be noted that these success processes—even the secret formulas and techniques involved—are never fully disclosed in the narratives. We, as audience, can only acquiesce to their artistic arrangements. Secondly, the works amplify characters' chivalric ethos. Chen Shouting—kidnapped for his expertise yet unyielding to torture and death threats—embodies the legendary gallant battling through Jianghu. Illiterate but undaunted, he conquers Qingdao and Jinan amidst turmoil, while his loyalty and righteousness epitomize quintessential martial virtues. Bai Jingqi, though fundamentally a pharmacist, was deliberately crafted by the creators with a mentor equally versed in letters and martial arts, resulting in him carrying a sword throughout his life—ever ready to brandish blades or firearms, even fearlessly confronting Japanese soldiers from the Eight-Nation Alliance. His lone-wolf demeanor and heroic audacity command universal admiration: demonstrating his mettle as the young master during his inaugural medicinal procurement in Anguo; creating miracles after being cast out from his family; enduring two imprisonments with vows to "rather wear out the prison floor" than submit, leaving opponents both frustrated and impotent. Third, the works employ fictional storytelling to expand interpretive possibilities and aesthetic dimensions. Conventional heroes typically derive from historical figures—their authenticity beyond doubt—yet this very fact constrains artistic license. By opting for non-traditional protagonists, *The Grand Mansion Gate* and *The Dyehouse* achieve unprecedented creative freedom, allowing unfettered character development that yields the dramatic potency of legendary tales and historical romances, maximizing both literary and visual appeal. Fourth, the works deconstruct heroic mystique, democratizing their appeal. By centering on business figures—whose activities intimately connect with commoners' daily existence—The Grand Mansion Gate and The Dyehouse eliminate the traditional distance between heroes and audiences. While heroism inherently elevates, conventional heroes often operate in enigmatic realms. These protagonists, however, radiate populist accessibility: Chen Shouting's boardroom cunning coexists with familial tenderness; Bai Jingqi's righteous fury blends with roguish charm. Such complexity enhances relatability without fully replicating legendary tropes—marking the creators' masterful narrative innovation.

Form and Meaning
— A Critique of CCTV's Spring Festival Gala

Since its inception in 1983, the CCTV Spring Festival Gala has become an indispensable cultural feast and consumable in the lives of the Chinese people, particularly during the Lunar New Year celebrations. With advancements in electronic technology and the proliferation of broadcast television and computers, the Gala's influence and impact have grown exponentially. oday, no fewer than several hundred municipal and regional television stations across the nation produce Spring Festival Galas of varying scales and quality, among which CCTV's flagship broadcast remains the most representative. Moreover, propelled and catalyzed by the Gala's influence, variety-show specials have proliferated like bamboo shoots after rain across broadcasters of all tiers. These entertainment spectacles—particularly the Spring Festival Gala—now constitute a singular phenomenon within China's media landscape. This essay examines the formal paradigms and cultural significations embedded in such media artifacts through the lens of the Gala.

I. Event and Paradigm

In 1983, responding to the climate of Reform and Opening-Up, the burgeoning vitality of cultural spheres, and the liberated, exuberant psyche of the populace, CCTV produced what would later be recognized as a seminal cultural event—the Spring Festival Gala. Its debut instantly captivated the nation, garnering widespread acclaim. The Gala's immediate acceptance across social strata stemmed from the convergence of objective and subjective conditions for such an event. By then, China's Reform and Opening-Up, initiated in 1978, had achieved measurable momentum, with rapid revitalization permeating politics, economics, culture, and the broader social fabric. The populace, emancipated from prolonged ideological constraints, found themselves invigorated in both spirit and morale. In 1983, Comrade Deng Xiaoping's call to "eliminate spiritual pollution" in cultural domains prompted swift introspection and rectification within arts circles regarding liberalization tendencies—a move that served, to some degree, as both warning and corrective against certain deviations from the central trajectory of cultural development and even Reform and Opening-Up. Thus, this cultural event at the year's outset acquired extraordinary significance: it simultaneously manifested cultural liberation while serving as a paradigmatic model for purifying artistic expression. Crucially, its timing—the Spring Festival, that quintessential node of traditional Chinese temporality—ensured public reception akin to the unquestioned acceptance of New Year's Eve reunion dinners, rendering institutional and mainstream societal endorsement self-evident.

If the birth of the Spring Festival Gala in 1983 was a product of its historical circumstances, environment, and zeitgeist, then its transformation into an annual cultural institution—maintaining undiminished relevance across two decades and beyond—testifies to the program's inherent vitality. CCTV's inaugural Gala in 1983 might have been a contingent occurrence, with no predetermined guarantee of annual repetition from 1984 through 2002 and thereafter. Yet twenty years of historical development ultimately rendered it an inevitability. From the perspective of cultural evolution, the broadcaster had discovered both its distinctive role and a dynamic new vessel for carrying forward China's cultural development. Following the Industrial Revolution in 18th-century Britain, Western nations embarked on their historical march toward modernization. The 20th century witnessed an acceleration of this process with advancements in modern science and technology. By the 1960s-70s, most developed nations had largely completed their modernization. After the founding of New China, the country gradually initiated its transition from an agrarian to an industrial society. During the 1970s, China formally articulated its objectives for achieving the Four Modernizations. However, due to the disruptions caused by the Cultural Revolution (1966-1976), the Four Modernizations initiative (encompassing agriculture, industry, national defense, and science/technology) failed to gain proper traction and were derailed from their intended developmental trajectory. The Reform and Opening-Up initiated at the Third Plenary Session of the 11th CPC Central Committee in 1978 marked an acceleration of the Chinese nation's modernization drive and its gradual integration into global modernization processes. China's rapid industrialization and modernization (or what might be termed its transition toward post-modernity) profoundly transformed daily life while triggering mutations across all societal strata. This social metamorphosis created complex variables in the interplay between different societal levels, with historical progress yielding both achievements and unintended fissures that many found disquieting. The complexities of modernization demand more than unbridled optimism and euphoria—they require the fortitude to withstand historical pressures while grasping the essence of developmental trajectories. Profound societal transformations inevitably alter regulatory mechanisms, presenting the crucial contemporary challenge of navigating ever-shifting social paradigms. The experience of early-modernized nations reveals modern media's dual role: both as catalyst for societal modernization and as its defining hallmark. The launch of CCTV's Spring Festival Gala signaled Chinese modern media's conscious intervention into contemporary life. Prior to this, the network's most influential program had been *Xinwen Lianbo* (News Simulcast). While *Xinwen Lianbo* equally represented a forceful media incursion into modern society, its fundamental purpose stemmed from state-political objectives—an extension of state power and authoritative discourse into media spheres. Precisely these national imperatives created optimal institutional conditions for *Xinwen Lianbo*'s dominance.

However, as the most influential mass medium in modern society, television can never achieve the requisite depth and breadth of social engagement through news programming alone. It must transform its discursive modes—not merely conveying messages directly, but mastering multidimensional, polyphonic expression to meet the evolving communicative demands across social strata. In essence, a television network must transcend its role as news broadcaster to become a cultural medium—an aspiration shared by all contemporary mass media. The creation of the Spring Festival Gala represents CCTV's pioneering attempt to transition from a news broadcaster to a cultural medium. This symbiosis—where media articulates culture and culture enriches media—epitomizes the modernist trajectory of television's evolution. Traditionally, Chinese cultural expression had relied on conventional forms; the intervention of mass media, particularly television, birthed radically new modes of cultural manifestation. Significantly, this experiment proved remarkably successful. Amid widespread acclaim, the public discovered television's alternative visage—a revelation of the medium's contemporary significance. Thus, as society modernized, people abruptly realized that contemporary life had become inseparable from television—and particularly from the Spring Festival Gala format—to the point where they eagerly anticipated its annual return: that specific moment, distinctive form, unique atmosphere, and singular emotional experience. By 2003, twenty full years had passed. Though much had changed, and though audiences held diverse opinions about the Gala, no one fundamentally questioned its existence. One could state with certainty: the Spring Festival Gala would endure for another twenty years.

CCTV's Spring Festival Gala pioneered the variety-show format in Chinese television, triggering transformative shifts in both media content and expressive modalities. Its success not only cemented its own cultural dominance but also spawned numerous derivative programs on the national broadcaster—including *Comprehensive Arts*, *Zhengda Variety*, and *Quyuan Zatan*, along with specialized New Year galas (opera, dance, comedy sketches) and holiday specials for National Day, Labor Day, Mid-Autumn Festival, and New Year's celebrations. Regional stations nationwide soon emulated and innovated upon this model. Today, televised variety programming has evolved into a robust media cultural formation, with the Spring Festival Gala remaining the foundational archetype for China's entertainment television ecology.

II. Artistry and Narrative

As a curated gala of performing arts, the Spring Festival Gala has always prioritized artistic excellence—both as its founding principle and enduring objective. Undeniably, CCTV's Gala maintains the highest artistic standards among similar nationwide programs. This preeminence stems firstly from the network's unparalleled advantages: formidable technical capabilities, nationwide coverage, and institutional prestige that enable maximal mobilization of cultural resources across China. Secondly, the continuous elevation of artistic quality reflects both the fervent expectations of hundreds of millions of viewers and the program's very raison d'être. For a televised arts spectacle, artistic merit remains the paramount concern.

The Gala's artistic excellence manifests foremost in its meticulous conceptualization. Since CCTV's inaugural Spring Festival Gala, each edition has undergone an arduous creative gestation—particularly in design planning. Every aesthetic decision demands exhaustive deliberation: the program's visual identity, narrative throughlines, thematic focus, atmospheric tonality, artistic caliber, performance genres, and even anticipated audience reception become neuralgic points that torment producers. The greater challenge—conjuring innovative approaches annually while elevating artistic standards—requires nothing short of visionary ingenuity. Secondly, the Gala's artistry manifests in its rigorous creative production and meticulous programming. Historical evidence demonstrates that content creation remains the most crucial yet challenging aspect—where difficulties emerge in achieving innovation, elevating quality standards, producing refined works, and generating sensational impact. Consequently, beyond mobilizing renowned industry figures through institutional channels, the production team actively solicits public submissions nationwide, ensuring the gala's repertoire benefits from premium source material. Moreover, the Gala's program refinement process demonstrates extraordinary exactitude. Our investigation into its production history reveals each selected performance undergoes rigorous evaluation and meticulous curation—followed by comprehensive staging design, casting, rehearsals, and aesthetic packaging. Even approved programs face potential replacement due to deficiencies in content, form, linguistic appropriateness, technical execution, or performer proficiency. While employing uniquely stringent selection criteria, the Gala's curation paradigm exemplifies perfectionism in cultural production. Thirdly, the Gala assembles an unparalleled constellation of renowned performers and artists. Ultimately, exceptional artistic forms demand masterful interpreters—and the Spring Festival Gala has become the preeminent national (indeed international) stage for artistic demonstration. To achieve its exacting standards, amplify artistic impact, and maximize audience appeal, the production recruits celebrated artists from across China—including Hong Kong, Macau, Taiwan—and overseas diasporic communities. This stellar convergence transforms the Gala into a veritable galaxy of cultural luminaries, with many performers considering participation the ultimate barometer of their artistic prowess and societal influence. Fourthly, the Gala aggregates the highest achievements across China's artistic spectrum. From traditional opera, dance, xiangsheng comedy, skits, and acrobatics to pingtan narrative singing, contemporary fashion, and folk customs—the event constitutes nothing less than a grand exhibition of Chinese performative arts. Whether featuring new creations or canonical repertoire, each presentation arguably represents the apex of its respective form. Indeed, over these two decades, numerous iconic works either achieved fame through the Gala or leveraged its platform to amplify their reach—particularly songs that became nationwide (and pan-regional) sensations after their performances. Representative examples include Zhang Mingmin's *My Chinese Heart* and Fei Xiang's *A Fire in Winter*. This phenomenon simultaneously validates the works' artistic merit and testifies to the Gala's unparalleled cultural authority.

If artistic excellence constitutes the Gala's eternal pursuit, then narrative potency represents its ultimate objective. Art has always served to reflect and amplify social realities while articulating the human condition. As a cultural spectacle staged on Lunar New Year's Eve, the Gala transcends mere artistic aggregation—its historical and contemporary discourses demand rigorous engagement. Why does the Chinese nation celebrate Spring Festival? While retaining primordial significance, the tradition's semantic core and peripheral practices have undergone profound hermeneutic evolution across time. From a contemporary perspective, the Spring Festival's paramount significance lies in commemorating the past while envisioning the future—or more succinctly, in bidding farewell to the old and welcoming the new. Consequently, regardless of how one celebrates, what truly matters are the symbolic meanings and thematic essences embedded in the observance. The Spring Festival Gala essentially constitutes a communal platform—constructed through televisual artistry with mainstream societal endorsement and popular consensus—where all social members collectively perform this ritual. Thus, its fundamental value resides not in the platform's structural completeness or aesthetic refinement, but rather in the scope, depth, and qualitative substance of the narratives it facilitates. Indeed, the Spring Festival Gala has effectively constructed a collective discursive space for national Spring Festival narratives. It transforms private celebratory rituals into public cultural articulation, enabling the thematic essence of communal celebration to achieve heightened clarity and penetrative resonance.

The Gala's narrative themes are unequivocally clear: they deliver the aspirational symbolism and emotional catharsis people crave during the New Year. This significance isn't artificially imposed by the program itself, but fundamentally springs from the public's inherent need for festive emotional expression—which the Gala's producers have astutely channeled and synthesized. Consequently, the event's narratives achieve both maximum legitimacy and universal resonance, to the extent that the Gala has nearly monopolized contemporary Spring Festival storytelling. A thorough examination of the Gala's evolution reveals how it has maximized its narrative potency by wielding the cultural mandate granted by society and audiences. As a traditional national festival, the Lunar New Year naturally dominates the Gala's thematic framework—yet mere celebratory motifs have long proved insufficient to contain its expanding significance. In reality, beneath the festive veneer, each edition articulates deeper thematic concerns. While perennial elements like jubilation, unity, auspiciousness, and motifs of progress and vigor form the consistent foundation, each year introduces its own grand theme. For instance, 2001 proclaimed "New Century, New Aspirations," while 2002 declared "Uniquely Splendid Vista Here." Within these grand themes, orchestrating epic narratives serves both as the Gala's critical breakthrough point and the ultimate test of directorial prowess. Consequently, macro-level thematic architecture becomes imperative, while simultaneously demanding meticulous coordination between grand narratives and intimate storytelling—constructing sweeping arcs without neglecting finely-woven vignettes.

Objectively speaking, through years of refinement, this narrative approach has achieved remarkable expressive power. When each year's Gala unfolds before us, we engage not merely with a variety show, but with a dual historical-contemporary discourse. The Spring Festival Gala employs its celebratory platform to articulate narratives meticulously cultivated over a full year—harvesting material from international affairs to domestic milestones, from grand spectacles to neighborhood vignettes, from state discourse to grassroots chatter. For instance, 1998's unprecedented floods and the Asian financial crisis inevitably became central to 1999's Gala narrative. Hosts emphasized the year's exceptional challenges while screens projected recurring footage of national leaders at floodfronts and military-civilian alliances forming impregnable defenses to safeguard lives and property. Furthermore, flood relief directly inspired several program segments. The 2002 Spring Festival Gala foregrounded China's Olympic bid success, World Cup qualification, and WTO accession as its core narrative pillars. Hosts repeatedly channeled irrepressible euphoria to amplify audience excitement, while archival footage of these milestones looped relentlessly—maximizing the event's discursive agenda. Beyond these macro-themes, individual programs wove micro-narratives that enriched the Gala's expressive tapestry through heightened emotional resonance. *On the Field of Hope* captured rural reform's vitality; *The Story of Spring* and *Entering the New Era* extolled the CPC's socialist construction leadership; *Love My China* and *Greater China* embodied ethnic solidarity; while *Chinese Kids*, *Chinese Kung Fu*, and *The Foolish Old Man* showcased civilizational spirit. Skits like *The Family Planning Guerrillas*, *Repackaging*, *Migrant Worker's Adventure*, and *The Race* distilled profound allegories—with *Yesterday·Today·Tomorrow* even satirizing Clinton's impeachment alongside societal commentary. Educational, scientific, and familial themes further demonstrated how intimate narratives articulate grand historical discourses. While deploying artistic performances for celebratory entertainment, the Gala strategically incorporates distinguished figures emblematic of annual achievements—scientific pioneers, Olympic medalists, flood-relief heroes, model workers, overseas scholars, diplomats, and even foreign dignitaries—whose New Year greetings collectively exhibit, proclaim, and transmit the nation's annual reckoning. This synthesis transforms communal aspirations and international goodwill into a curated spectacle. ... Through artistic embellishment of seasonal rituals, the event aesthetically articulates collective sentiments while manifesting societal ideals.[①] Here, artistry functions as narrative apparatus, transmuting popular discourse into state idiom—rendering the Spring Festival Gala dually characterized by aesthetic production and political semiosis.

① Wu Wenke: *Interpreting the Spring Festival Gala's Cultural Significance*, China News Service: https://www.chinanews.com.cn/2002-02-20/26/163110.html, accessed February 20, 2002.

III. Significance and Impact

It must be acknowledged that as a cultural institution refined over two decades, the Spring Festival Gala has achieved profound significance and far-reaching influence. Its paramount importance lies in having accomplished a televisual miracle—transforming a variety show into cultural mythology. From its foundational conception, the Spring Festival Gala was originally designed as nothing more than a festive artistic gathering during the Lunar New Year—akin to traditional celebratory customs. While it inherently carried narrative elements, these narratives were predominantly rooted in vernacular discourse. The contemporary Gala, however, has been burdened with excessive mainstream ideological content, amplifying its narrative functions to monumental proportions—a developmental trajectory entirely unforeseen by its creators. The question of whether the Gala would become an annual institution initially lacked definitive resolution. Yet today, not only has it become a permanent fixture, but it has fundamentally transcended its original identity as mere artistic entertainment. Consequently, the Gala's cultural impact and significance have become multidimensional phenomena.

First, the Spring Festival Gala has fundamentally transformed how Chinese people celebrate the Lunar New Year. Historically, Lunar New Year celebrations were characterized by vibrant yet localized customs—community operas, dragon dances, land-boat processions, couplet postings, and fireworks—all spontaneously organized and modest in scale. These traditions predominantly emphasized material consumption and tactile ritualism. The national broadcaster's institutionalization of New Year rituals through the Gala has precipitated a paradigm shift: contemporary celebrations now prioritize cultural consumption and metaphysical fulfillment over material indulgence. This transition represents nothing less than the modernization of a millennia-old folk tradition through televisual mediation. This transformation undoubtedly stems from historical imperatives, yet television media's agency has served as the most immediate catalyst. In our television-dominant modernity, the medium's allure proves irresistible—its technological sophistication having exponentially amplified coverage breadth, cultural radiation, and societal permeation. Through fluid programming, vivid imagery, and dynamic presentation, television creates profoundly immersive experiences. The Spring Festival Gala leveraged these very attributes to revolutionary effect: it awakened public consciousness to the existence of cultural dimensions beyond material feasting—dimensions far more captivating and affectively resonant. Indeed, the millennia-evolved Spring Festival customs embody profound cultural sedimentation that transcends mere gastronomic indulgence. At this pivotal juncture of temporal renewal, individuals and collectives—from familial units to the nation-state—harbor complex affective constellations: nostalgia, aspiration, and unarticulated discursive urgencies that historically remained confined to private spheres, never fully expressed. On Lunar New Year's Eve, the Spring Festival Gala utilizes television's unique capacity to construct, through artistic means, a communal discursive space—

simultaneously warm, joyous, harmonious, and aspirational—for over a billion Chinese descendants worldwide. It synchronizes the consumption of reunion dinners with artistic appreciation and modern televisual revelry, while articulating year-long accumulated (and often still-gestating) collective sentiments through hosts, performers, and programming—achieving that rare synthesis of intergenerational appeal and pan-social accessibility. Moreover, the Gala meticulously articulates both societal and state-level imperatives, serving as a conduit for national policy dissemination while amplifying the collective aspirations of all social strata. This dual articulation has elevated the event into a cultural necessity—demanded not merely by domestic audiences across classes, but by the global Chinese diaspora. The Spring Festival Gala has now achieved the status of indispensable New Year ritual, standing alongside dumpling-making and firecrackers as constitutive elements of contemporary Spring Festival praxis. We must acknowledge that the "Gala complex" has become a widespread phenomenon. It's truly difficult to imagine how people would celebrate the Spring Festival without it twenty years from now.

Secondly, as a grand-scale variety show, the Spring Festival Gala has become a powerful engine driving the development of contemporary Chinese culture. In modern society, cultural evolution increasingly trends toward popularization and accessibility, aligning with the rhythms and lifestyles of contemporary living. Cultural consumption has emerged as a defining characteristic of modern cultural development. Consequently, the relationship between culture and market forces has grown increasingly symbiotic—where there are consumers, a market follows; where a market exists, it generates production incentives; and these incentives in turn make cultural production and reproduction sustainable. The leveraging effect of market forces on cultural development has become profoundly pronounced. Within the cultural sphere, different art forms and cultural products cater to distinct consumer demographics—the size of these consumer bases directly determines market scales. When a particular cultural form secures an expansive market, it gains essential material foundations and favorable conditions for development. However, cultural products fundamentally differ from material commodities in their intrinsic attributes. An overreliance on market mechanisms to steer cultural development would inevitably precipitate structural imbalances in cultural ecosystems. While markets can open vital channels for cultural production and advancement, they equally possess the capacity to constrict these very channels. Take pop music and mass-market literature as examples—their expansive consumer markets suggest tremendous growth potential. However, we must never allow unfettered market forces to drive unchecked expansion that could potentially submerge the development of refined cultural products. Conversely, premium cultural works face inherently limited markets; were their development dictated solely by market logic, their very survival would be jeopardized. The Spring Festival Gala's significance for cultural development lies in its strategic leverage of its massive societal influence to provide an unparalleled platform for showcasing diverse ethnic arts, creating vital growth opportunities. Over its twenty-year history, the Gala has brought virtually all traditional Chinese art forms—even endangered and nearly extinct varieties—into the spotlight before billions of viewers. This monumental exposure has both highlighted traditional arts' intrinsic value and exponentially amplified their cultural reach. Throughout its annual editions, the Spring Festival Gala has showcased not just contemporary song-and-dance performances, but a veritable encyclopedia of Chinese cultural heritage: traditional opera, cross-talk comedy, skits, acrobatics, calligraphy, ink wash painting, paper-cutting, embroidery, batik, ethnic instruments, vocal mimicry, folk dances, martial arts—even culinary arts and rare craftsmanship. This amounts to nothing less than a grand exhibition of Chinese artistic traditions. It is no exaggeration to state that the Gala's monumental influence has single-handedly revived declining art forms and safeguarded endangered traditions on the brink of extinction.

Third, the Spring Festival Gala holds paradigmatic significance for the evolution of China's media culture. As previously established, mass media—especially technology-driven television and digital platforms—play pivotal roles in modern society. However, modern media's societal impact stems not from the technological apparatus itself, but rather from two fundamental factors: its capacity to bear socio-historical content, and its ability to cultivate media cultures with substantive depth and intellectual richness. While television has achieved near-global saturation, with its tendrils penetrating households worldwide, this ubiquity guarantees neither audience acceptance nor content quality. Paradoxically, television's omnipresence often breeds formulaic programming and mediocre content—outcomes far more likely to trigger viewer aversion than engagement. Thus, media's meaningful societal intervention demands more than technological reach; it hinges fundamentally on content substance, requiring both intellectual depth and cultural resonance. The Spring Festival Gala stands as a paradigmatic success story in media culture. While television's audiovisual richness and instantaneous reach provide crucial technical advantages, the Gala's true triumph lies in its curated content—a cultural feast meticulously timed for the Chinese people's most symbolically charged moment. This offering masterfully blends folk traditions with contemporary trends, artistic excellence with narrative depth, creating an irresistibly diverse banquet that satisfies both nostalgic cravings and modern sensibilities. After two decades of evolution, though rising aesthetic standards have made it increasingly difficult to satisfy all tastes, the Chinese people's unwavering demand for and ever-growing consumption of the Spring Festival Gala remain undeniable. This explains why CCTV's annual gala continues to break its own viewership records year after year—indeed, the Spring Festival Gala now commands what is arguably the world's largest single-audience event. It is highly probable that no television network worldwide has ever produced a program comparable to CCTV's Spring Festival

Gala in terms of sheer scale, consistently expanding viewership over two decades, and truly mass appeal. In this sense, the Spring Festival Gala stands as an unparalleled milestone in global television history.

IV. Challenges and Strategies

Having evolved over two decades amidst public acclaim and soaring expectations, the Spring Festival Gala's cultural significance remains indisputable. Yet in recent years, it has also become a contentious subject of widespread debate. While some applaud its achievements, others level pointed criticisms. Regardless of perspective, as a media-cultural phenomenon, it commands sustained attention unmatched by most social events. The intense public scrutiny stems precisely from its revered status in the audience's psyche. This very prestige breeds ever-escalating expectations, inevitably creating a gap between anticipations and the Gala's actual delivery—a disparity that fuels viewer dissatisfaction. Realistically, as an event bound by temporal constraints (the Spring Festival context) and thematic continuity, certain repetitive elements in content and format become virtually unavoidable. Year after year, it must: showcase culturally sanctioned art forms, extend established narrative traditions, and deliver celebratory entertainment. This cyclical nature, while structurally necessary, risks being perceived as creative stagnation. What's more crucial is that given its variety-show nature—being an amalgamation of brief artistic segments—the Gala inherently cannot achieve the same level of specialization, depth, and artistic coherence as dedicated single-genre performances. Admittedly, when judged by pure artistic standards, certain program segments may indeed fall short of representing their respective art forms at the highest professional level. From the audience perspective, different social strata naturally hold divergent expectations for such a large-scale variety show. As a cultural product specifically tailored for the Spring Festival season, the Gala must prioritize the holiday's unique atmosphere and collective emotional needs—inevitably leaving some viewers' specific demands unfulfilled, which breeds dissatisfaction and critique. Moreover, the Spring Festival Gala has long transcended its identity as a mere artistic event, evolving into a narrative vehicle that employs artistic means. As the Gala has grown and developed, the narrative burdens imposed upon it by the state, society, and audiences have escalated to near-unmanageable proportions. These cumulative factors inevitably contribute to declining satisfaction rates among viewers.

How then should this two-decade-old, culturally entrenched media institution evolve? The fundamental solution lies in continuous innovation and quality improvement—innovation encompassing both artistic and narrative dimensions, and quality enhancement involving both artistic excellence and narrative depth. Historical precedents demonstrate that quality elevation springs fundamentally from innovation. This creative renewal must germinate at the conceptual stage—only genuinely original blueprints can yield transformative programming capable of reinvigorating the Gala's cultural relevance. Of course, innovation should not be confined to the conceptual stage alone—it must permeate the entire production process. Each year's Gala should strive for novel approaches, creative breakthroughs, innovative methods, and revitalized energy. In contemporary terms, it must keep pace with the times to maintain vitality while elevating quality through this renewal. Regarding artistic quality, the Gala's inherent format constraints naturally limit radical transformations in its artistic components. Achieving artistic innovation and quality enhancement without overhauling its fundamental structure is undoubtedly challenging. The key lies in enriching the artistic substance within existing frameworks—preserving the distinctive charm and ethnic character of traditional arts while infusing them with contemporary relevance. As for the Gala's narrative quality, this dimension offers substantial untapped potential. Not only can the linking scripts and hosts' dialogues be further refined, but program content also warrants meticulous polishing to achieve greater concision, incisiveness, and intellectual depth—elevating its cultural resonance and impactful delivery. The effectiveness of hosts' language particularly depends not on verbosity, but on precision, aptness, and penetrating insight—qualities that determine its emotional potency and discursive force. In summary, as a flagship brand within China's televisual culture, the Spring Festival Gala has established remarkable developmental momentum. The crucial challenge now lies in fortifying its vitality while amplifying its cultural impact and efficacy—an imperative demanding rigorous scholarly examination.

On the Evolution of Literary Consciousness in the New Era

Any substantive discussion of this issue must be situated within China's—indeed, the world's—broader historical context. The Reform and Opening movement emerging in the late 1970s irrevocably integrated China into the trajectories of modernization and, ultimately, globalization. Over the past three decades, historic transformations have permeated every stratum—from state apparatuses to societal microcosms, from dominant institutions to grassroots communities—reshaping both collective ideologies and material realities.

In the realm of literature and art, while the Party and state's guiding principles have undergone no fundamental alteration—and while the literary traditions, historical legacies, and theoretical foundations sustaining contemporary Chinese literature remain essentially unchanged—the developmental landscape has nevertheless shifted profoundly. From the era of the "Three Prominences" and model revolutionary operas to today's flourishing diversity of artistic expressions, China's literary policies have implemented significant recalibrations, precipitating a tectonic reconfiguration of literary consciousness.

Naturally, the transformation of literary consciousness can never manifest as a unilateral or simplistic endeavor—it invariably intertwines with multifaceted and intricate literary praxis. Though we measure literature against exacting standards and expectations, the rules and market forces imposed upon it remain, whether for scholars or readers, merely extrinsic factors in this evolution. The true catalyst for metamorphosis resides invariably within writers and their creative praxis.[①] Hence, to trace the trajectory of contemporary Chinese literature's conceptual shifts, one must invariably begin with the writer's creative labor and the textual forms it generates.

Yet contemporary literary praxis manifests in overwhelming volume and variety—evident in the annual publication of over 1,000 novels, countless short stories in periodicals, and the deluge of essays, poetry, and flash fiction across print and digital platforms. When our gaze fragments across these disparate, kaleidoscopic textual specimens, we risk losing sight of the fundamental trajectories underlying literary consciousness's evolution. Thus we have elected to examine the shifting conceptual lexicon of Chinese literature across these three decades as our methodological entry point.

Concepts refer to the distillation and summation of established phenomena. Within literary creation, certain conspicuous creative tendencies, aesthetic philosophies, narrative techniques, and value systems—having achieved critical mass and cultural resonance—coalesce into collectively recognized formulations. When such phenomena attain precise definition through widespread acknowledgment, they crystallize into what we term "literary concepts."[②]

---

① Wu Shenggang. *Ecological Expression and Literary Value.* Journal of Xinyang Normal University (Philosophy and Social Sciences Edition), no. 3, 2005.

② Jiang Xiaohu. *"Literary Consciousness" Over Three Decades: From Intellectual Currents to Commercial Labels*. People's Daily Online. http://culture.people.com.cn

The three decades spanning from the conclusion of the "Cultural Revolution" in 1976 to the present (2006) have witnessed Chinese literary development achieve—if not globally remarkable accomplishments—at the very least a state of undeniable vitality. Most notably, contemporary Chinese literature has shed its rigid, monolithic frameworks to embrace a polycentric developmental paradigm characterized by pluralistic expression. It must be acknowledged that contemporary Chinese literature has yet to enter an era yielding world-class authors, monumental works, or comprehensive flourishing. Even among currently active writers, none can definitively claim vanguard status, nor can any works be decisively identified as seminal. The literary scene resembles rotating sovereignty—where each figure dominates the spotlight briefly, some through absurdist posturing, provocative sensationalism, or manufactured commercial appeal—collectively inflating artificial literary valuations and constructing illusory literary spectacles. Yet this phenomenon itself constitutes an organic accumulation within contemporary Chinese literature—precisely demonstrating the current literary market's unconstrained openness and the profound transformation of literary consciousness. Within this liberated creative ecosystem, writers' ideological banners proliferate and reconfigure through constant aggregation and dispersion, crystallizing into distinct literary concepts. These formations collectively trace the developmental trajectory of our national literature, fundamentally embodying the metamorphosis of literary consciousness in the new era.

From a macroscopic perspective, the evolution of literary consciousness in the new era has progressed through the following key phases:

I. Reflection on History and Reality: The Rise of Rational Discourse in Literary Creation

The year 1976 marked the conclusion of the "Cultural Revolution" and a pivotal historical turning point for contemporary China. As the barometer of the nation's intellectual climate, literature inevitably underwent profound transformation during this period. The literary transformation first manifested in the critical reappraisal of the recently concluded "Cultural Revolution"—a systematic interrogation of its guiding artistic principles, creative dogmas, and representational paradigms. What merits particular attention is how this shift emerged from methodical rationalism, constituting both a historical paradox and an historical inevitability. The "Cultural Revolution" period represented an era of collective frenzy and irrationality. Its abrupt termination left an ideological and psychological vacuum—one that, upon awakening from this collective delirium, necessitated sober reckoning with the traumatic experience. In 1977, Liu Xinwu's *The Class Teacher* and in 1978, Lu Xinhua's *The Scar* exposed the lingering shadows cast by the "Gang of Four" on Chinese society. These seminal works triggered seismic reverberations across the literary landscape, ultimately crystallizing as defining texts of the Scar Literature movement. Other influential works included: Ru Zhijuan's *The Misassembled Story*, Chen Guokai's *What Should I Do?* Jin He's

Reencounter,Ye Weilin's *On the Unmarked River*, Feng Jicai's *Ah!* Gu Hua's *The Ivy-Clad Cottage*, Lu Yanzhou's *Legend of Tianyun Mountain*, and Lu Yao's *Life*.① "Scar Literature" emerged as the first truly consequential literary movement in post-1949 China. The very nomenclature—diverging radically from previous literary categorizations—embodied an intrinsic rebellion against the panegyric tradition epitomized by the "Three Prominences" during the "Cultural Revolution".

The literary stage then welcomed Educated Youth Fiction. As the monumental, world-shaking "Up to the Mountains, Down to the Villages" movement concluded, the intellectuals once rooted in vast rural landscapes returned en masse to urban centers. Writers—particularly those with firsthand zhiqing experience—initiated profound retrospection. Works like: Liang Xiaosheng's *The Snowstorm Tonight*, *Growth Rings*, *Snow City*, Zhang Chengzhi's *The Golden Pasture*, Cong Weixi's *Grasslands of the North*, Ye Xin's *Debt of Love*...interrogated the movement's seismic societal impacts, preserving irreplicable narratives of joy and suffering unique to that historical moment. Educated Youth (Zhiqing) Literature achieved its conceptual breakthrough by transcending binary judgments. In revisiting this collective historical experience, writers simultaneously captured the movement's romantic

① Meng Fanhua and Cheng Guangwei. A History of Contemporary Chinese Literature Development. People's Literature Publishing House, 2004, pp. 204-206.

grandeur and heroic pathos alongside the inescapable hardships of extraordinary circumstances, ultimately reflecting the post-fever rationality that emerged. This dual perspective marked an intrinsic evolution in contemporary Chinese literature's consciousness. By the early 1990s, as newer Educated Youth fiction waned in influence, the genre solidified as a historical-literary signifier—a unique marker of ideological transformation in China's literary development.

Reform Literature emerged in lockstep with the nation's transformative pulse, its very soul intertwined with the zeitgeist of change. The watershed Third Plenary Session of the 11th CPC Central Committee in 1978 unleashed reform currents that surged from rural household contract systems into urban centers, eventually permeating every corner of the land. As China's seismic societal shifts reverberated through individual consciousness, writers gradually shifted their gaze from historical retrospection (like the Educated Youth Movement) toward the living realities of reform and development. The seminal work inaugurating this genre was undoubtedly Jiang Zilong's The New Factory Director. Other paradigmatic texts included: Gao Xiaosheng's *Li Shunda Builds a House* and *Chen Huansheng Goes to Town*, Zhang Jie's *Heavy Wings*, Li Guowen's *No. 5 Garden Street*, and Lu Wenfu's *The Wall*. Reform Literature holds particular significance as the first post-transition literary movement to directly engage with contemporary social realities. By unflinchingly portraying both the arduous struggles and inherent contradictions of the reform process, it resonated profoundly across mainstream society and all social strata. The movement's cultural impact ultimately transcended conventional literary boundaries, generating societal reverberations far exceeding typical artistic influence. It must be acknowledged that Reform Literature's seismic impact stemmed directly from its symbiotic relationship with societal transformation. Though the term itself has faded from discourse, its legacy persists in contemporary anti-corruption narratives—sharing the same intellectual lineage. The movement's conceptual significance remains inextricably bound to the reformist ethos it embodied, cementing its role as a catalytic force in the evolution of New Era literary consciousness.

Root-Seeking Literature most profoundly embodies the New Era's rational literary consciousness. By the mid-1980s, as China's reform and opening deepened across all dimensions, societal transformations permeated every sphere. Confronting this historical watershed, a cohort of culturally concerned writers and humanistic scholars began intense interrogation of Chinese literature's developmental trajectory—fundamentally questioning both its ontological foundations and future directions. The year 1985 witnessed Han Shaogong's seminal manifesto *The "Roots" of Literature*—effectively the intellectual charter for what became known as the Root-Seeking Movement. Writers embarked on rigorous excavations of national traditions, cultural memory, and collective consciousness, operating under the conviction that "only the authentically national can become truly global." This philosophical orientation positioned cultural rootedness as the essential pathway to world literary recognition. Notable works from this period include: Liu Xinwu's *The Bell and Drum Towers*, Feng Jicai's *The Three-Inch Golden Lotus*, Deng Youmei's *That Fifth*, Han Shaogong's *Pa Pa Pa*, A Cheng's *The Chess Master* and *The King of Children*. Many achieved cross-media success through acclaimed television adaptations, further amplifying their cultural impact. This phenomenon undeniably stems from the writers' profound engagement with traditional, ethnic, and regional cultural particularities. When viewed through the longitudinal development of contemporary Chinese literature, Root-Seeking Literature may ultimately prove to possess unique significance—for it represents the first systematic attempt to interrogate literature's essence (cultural and aesthetic) within both Chinese and global contexts. Such deliberate, clear-eyed cultural introspection suggests an inevitable magnification of literature's societal role and, more crucially, a return to its fundamental nature.

II. Avant-Garde Experimentation: Literature's Non-Rational Frontiers

As a manifestation of collective consciousness, literature inevitably evolves alongside societal transformation. By the mid-1980s, China's deepening reforms had catalyzed comprehensive structural fluidity, precipitating subtle yet seismic shifts in value systems: market forces began asserting tangible influence while their role as constitutive mechanisms within China's opening society remained conceptually unformalized. Yet the rupture of established equilibriums and recalibration of interests birthed a transitional epoch—where nascent orders gestated amidst socioeconomic duality, mirroring the price double-track system's inherent tensions. As mainstream discourse recognized, reforms had entered their decisive phase, confronting society with existential choices. This historical juncture accelerated literary consciousness' self-renegotiation: while some writers gravitated toward popular fiction's mass appeal, others intensified their focus on literature's autonomous realm, galvanizing experimental impulses.[①]

The manifest trajectory of literary transformation reveals a distinct non-rationalization of both literary consciousness and expression—a phenomenon mirroring the era's sociopolitical landscape. Society's semi-ordered state engendered overwhelming existential complexity, where reform's convulsions provoked collective anxiety amid powerlessness. The cacophony of daily life and psychosocial disarray rendered rational cognition nearly impossible, while the new societal architecture being drafted by political architects remained indeterminable. Literature, fundamentally a medium of sensorial perception rather than systematic exposition, could only function as

① Hong Zicheng. A History of Contemporary Chinese Literature. Peking University Press, 2009, p. 335.

society's nervous system—registering tremors rather than interpreting blueprints. This epistemological position necessitated the non-rational paradigm evidenced across emerging literary concepts.

Neorealism first signaled this shift. Where writers had previously fixated on societal macroclimates and grand transformations, authors like Chi Li began elevating the minutiae of urban mundanity to central thematic status. This movement's macro-to-micro pivot particularly resonated with women writers—whose acute sensitivity, nuanced perception, and concrete thinking often surpassed abstract reasoning—effectively creating a creative breakthrough. Chi Li—universally recognized as a Neorealist pioneer—authored *Life Full of Troubles* and *Coming and Going*, while Fang Fang's *The Landscape*, Liu Zhenyun's *A Land of Chicken Feathers*, and Liu Heng's *Damn Grain* and *Fuxi Fuxi* transformed quotidian trivialities into literary art. By adopting an omniscient free-agent narrative perspective, these writers uncovered profound existential resonances within mundane realities. Neorealism ultimately functioned as a tactical detour in literature's evolutionary trajectory—allowing writers to circumvent the representational quandaries posed by society's radical transformations, while preventing literary muteness amidst chaotic realities. By channeling creative energy into depicting sanctified banality, the movement preserved literature's discursive dignity during this interstitial epoch.

Next emerged the Avant-Garde—marking literature's first conceptual paradigm divorced from sociopolitical imperatives, instead pursuing aesthetic autonomy as its ultimate objective. These writers, profoundly influenced by Western cultural currents, privileged experimental forms like stream-of-consciousness and magic realism, forging China's inaugural purely aesthetic literary movement. Chen Rong's *At Middle Age*, Xu Xing's *Variations Without a Theme*, Ma Yuan's *The Temptation of Gangdisé*, and Liu Suola's *You Have No Choice*—alongside emerging voices like Mo Yan, Ge Fei, Yu Hua, Su Tong, and Ye Zhaoyan—collectively redefined literary horizons. Having spent their formative years during the "Cultural Revolution" without absorbing its traumas, these Avant-Garde writers pursued formal innovation as their primary breakthrough, eventually transcending the movement itself to forge individualized creative paths. The Avant-Garde, while ostensibly pursuing aesthetic ideals, rooted its creative praxis fundamentally in subjective perceptual frameworks—as evidenced by its radical formal choices. This ontological positioning ultimately precluded the movement from achieving genuine rationalized pursuit, despite its intellectual pretensions.

Then came New Historical Fiction. Traditionally, history had been confined to monolithic narratives. Following the Avant-Garde's experimental interlude, writers rediscovered the investigative rigor and critical consciousness that had characterized classical literati—transcending the traditional *literature-as-moral-vehicle* paradigm to reinterrogate historical constructs.

This epistemological shift birthed the New Historical Fiction movement. Su Tong's *Wives and Concubines*, Chen Zhongshi's *White Deer Plain*, Mo Yan's *Red Sorghum* and *Big Breasts and Wide Hips*, along with Ye Zhaoyan's *Moon-Chasing Pavilion*, collectively demonstrate authors' courageous reframing of historical narratives. These works not only displaced traditional historical fiction but gradually established the aesthetic norms that continue to govern the genre's contemporary practice. New Historical Fiction constitutes less a representation of history than its radical deconstruction—eschewing all pretense of rational historiography. Like Red Sorghum's narrative strategy, it fragments historical continuity into visceral vignettes: magnified character studies sutured together by cinematic violence.

The fourth trend is Satirical Literature (Beijing-Style/Punk Literature). As China's New Era literature underwent upheavals and reconstruction amid societal collisions, it shed its solemn rationality. Readers now demanded new literary voices—forcing literature to reinvent its "persona" for relevance. Thus emerged satirical literature, epitomized by Wang Shuo's works, blending Beijing dialect with anti-establishment wit. The "Punk Literature" phenomenon (a defining 1990s movement exemplified by Wang Shuo's *Looks Pretty* and *I'm Your Daddy*) reached its zenith with the author's iconic declaration: "As a ruffian, who do I need to fear?" Its irreplicable linguistic verve—combining unfiltered prose with deadpan satire—dethroned literature from its institutional pedestal. Wang Shuo and Wang Xiaobo became the twin pillars of this trend, embedding satirical writing into China's literary consciousness. To this day, devoted adherents continue its subversive legacy, cementing punk literature's role in accelerating literary non-rationalization.

III. Corporal Sensuality: Literature's Sensualist Era

The 1990s witnessed China's formal establishment of a socialist market economy, with market mechanisms permeating all societal spheres. As the nation deepened global integration, unprecedented material abundance transformed consumption into modernity's defining feature—an era where material desires inflated perceptual horizons, fundamentally altering literary sensibilities. Amid slogans proclaiming "living is sensation, happiness is sensation, even health is sensation", we plunged wholesale into the Age of Sensualism. This paradigm birthed an eminently perceptible world—where modern technology's visual turn birthed an image-centric era, transforming audiovisual constructs into dominant cultural landmarks.[1] Modernity itself seemed reduced to a collage of proliferating images. The aestheticization of everyday life legitimized audiovisual constructs as modernity's imperative, while marketization subsumed all human experience under transactional logic—where even cultural production bears appreciation potential. Literature, inevitably, became enmeshed in this market calculus.

---

① Wu Shenggang. *Audiovisual Constructs: Cultural Significance and Spiritual Deconstruction*. Journal of Xinyang Normal University (Philosophy and Social Sciences Edition), no. 3, 2004.

More crucially, literature's horizons of possibility underwent radical reconfiguration. Market forces now dictated not just how to write, but what to write—transforming all marketable human experiences into legitimate literary material. No longer merely intelligible intellectual output, literature became sensorial commodity. Thus inevitably, literature too succumbed to the sensualist paradigm.

Corporeal Writing. This movement marked a radical descent from metaphysical spirituality to uncompromising materiality—where sensory physiology replaced intellectual abstraction. Celebrating perfumed sensuality and corporeal aesthetics, it privileged erotic games and sexual phenomenology as literature's new cardinal motifs. Emerging like thunder in the 1990s, Corporeal Writing sought spiritual emancipation through physical transgression—shattering literary conventions. Mian Mian's *Candy* and Wei Hui's *Shanghai Baby* epitomized this movement, though subsequent imitators increasingly catered to voyeuristic appetites, culminating in the so-called "Erotic Literature" phenomenon. While criticized for graphic depictions, the movement's seismic impact undeniably signaled literature's newfound aesthetic libertinism and market-driven permissiveness.

Beauty-Writer Phenomenon. While overlapping with Corporeal Writing, this concept diverged fundamentally. Where the latter focused on textual transgression, Beauty-Writers (later including Male Beauty-Writers like Shanghai University's Ge Hongbing) subverted literary norms by prioritizing physical allure over textual merit—establishing authorial image as the primary cultural commodity. Paraphrasing Qian Zhongshu's famous analogy: "Never mind the nutritional value of eggs—what matters is the hen's photogenic qualities." (These writers—not all conventionally beautiful—shared defining traits: youth, boldness, unwavering self-regard as beauties, prolific self-expression, thematic repetitiveness, and official disfavor. The cohort—Wei Hui, Mian Mian, Annie Baby, Chun Shu, Zhang Yueran, Yan Ge, Gu Xiang, Jiang Lizi, Su De, Zhou Jianing, Jiang Fangzhou—were predominantly post-80s millennials.) Today, these labels have become such cultural anachronisms that being called a "Beauty-Writer" would provoke vehement denial.

Post-80s Generation. The Post-80s label surged in 2003, designating writers born in the 1980s—mostly emerging from online platforms or the New Concept Literature Contest. Their works, often constrained by limited life experience, exhibited hyper-sensitivity to interiority. While Han Han, Guo Jingming, and Zhang Yueran gained fame independently, they became the movement's unofficial triumvirate. By late 2004, many began disavowing the label. After launching figures like Li Shasha, Sun Rui, and Chun Shu, the term had exhausted its historical valence. The Post-80s Generation's legacy might best be described as ephemeral cultural froth—their youth and uncharted creative horizons, unshackled by labels, promise limitless potential. The movement's canonical figures include: Jiang Feng (*Lest We Forever Grieve*), Zhang Yueran (*Distant Cherries*), Sun Rui (*Grasslike Years*), Guo

Jingming (*City of Fantasy*), Han Han (*Triple Gate*), Li Shasha (*Red X*), Chun Shu (*Beijing Doll*), and Jiang Fangzhou (*In Development*).

Pathography. Following Bi Shumin's controversial *Saving Breasts* (on breast cancer), Zhejiang Literature Press published Zhao Yuhong's *China's Number One Disease* (on hepatitis B), while Shanghai Century Publishing released Taiwanese writer Xu Yousheng's *Goodnight, Melancholy* (on depression)—heralding a wave of illness-themed narratives. These works shared pathological frameworks, with patients as protagonists, leveraging disease's sociocultural resonance for profound reader engagement. Pathography will endure as a vital conceptual framework—where literary works serve merely as the medium, ultimately striving to cultivate societal conscientiousness toward patients and foster discrimination-free environments.

IV. Metamorphosis and Literary Value Reconstruction

The New Era literature has undergone profound conceptual transformations—yet this evolution remains unfinished. Contemporary Chinese literature continues to develop, with its paradigms still in flux. The following concepts represent emerging trajectories in this ongoing value reconfiguration.

Neo-Romantic Literature. Emerging as a deliberate counterpoint to Corporeal Writing, this genre eschews all carnal descriptions between genders, resembling the chaste sensibility of Korean family dramas. It champions love's redemptive power, celebrating lifelong commitment while awakening readers' yearning for idealized affection. Though rich in emotional portrayal, it prioritizes spiritual catharsis over sensory titillation, transforming romantic narratives into vehicles for moral elevation. Current reader favorites like *Heart-to-Heart, Love-to-Love* and China Women Publishing House's *Who's Hotter Wins My Heart* exemplify Neo-Romantic Literature. The works of Xi Juan, the "Floral Dress" writing collective, and the "Flower Rain" series collectively embody this movement—its refreshing ethos radiating enduring cultural warmth.

Youth Wuxia. This emerging trend distinguishes itself from the Jin Yong/Gu Long tradition and the "Wen Rui'an/Li Liang/Huang Yi New Wuxia" wave. Unlike prior movements with manifestos, Youth Wuxia coalesced organically when a new generation—Han Han, He Yuanwai, Dai Lili—simultaneously produced wuxia epics, creating an unspoken literary alignment. Youth Wuxia retains only superficial vestiges of traditional sectarianism—mentioning Emei, Wudang, and Shaolin yet eschewing martial techniques, violent conflict, and clichéd tropes like cliffside discoveries. This paradigm embodies unconstrained creativity, as post-80s writers forge their own paths beyond canonical constraints.

The conceptual evolution of literature has grown increasingly fast-foodized and arbitrary. Nearly every new publication now manufactures its own marketing label—from ephemeral trends like "Youth Scar Literature" or "Chest-Writing" to even established figures like Yu Qiuyu's "Memory Literature" and Zhou Guoping's "Spiritual Autobiography" during their memoir promotions. These coinings, as transient as rain dampening mere surface dust, briefly stir discourse before vanishing into oblivion.

Why this conceptual churn so frequently? Four tectonic shifts explain it: the state's relaxed cultural governance that increasingly respects literature's autonomous development; society's growing pluralistic tolerance; literature's democratization from sacred to popular; and the market mechanism's colonization of literary production, where conceptual volatility mirrors acute market sensitivity. Beneath these surface mutations lie deeper paradigmatic transformations in literary consciousness—the true engine driving creative evolution.

Thus, while we view the haphazard conceptual labeling with measured concern, our focus remains fixed on literature's value reconfiguration and the tectonic shifts in China's literary consciousness. Riding the express train of modernization and globalization, New Era literature has undergone radical metamorphosis—today's conceptual diversity dwarfs both the first 30 years of contemporary Chinese literature and even the modern literary period. The emerging aesthetic ethos, increasingly characterized by openness, freedom, and equality (albeit with diminishing autonomy), resists premature judgment.

What we ultimately anticipate is the spiritual renaissance of Chinese literature through this dual evolution of concepts and paradigms, laying the foundation for its global ascendance.

The Theory of Cultural Fashion

I

Two prevailing trends in contemporary reality have catalyzed the rise of cultural fashion as a societal phenomenon, simultaneously charting the fundamental trajectory for our investigation into this subject. First, since the 1980s, humanity has grown acutely conscious of the clash between epochs—the turn of both century and millennium propelling us toward a pivotal historical juncture. While we cannot fully reconstruct the psychological contours of past transitional eras, one certainty remains: modern individuals, with their deepened understanding of temporal cycles and societal rhythms, exhibit heightened sensitivity to this duality of decay and emergence. At this chronotopic crossroads, nostalgia contends with futuristic yearning as the dominant collective sentiment. The twentieth century witnessed unprecedented upheavals, yet the post-1980s era delivered truly unfathomable transformations that ultimately reshaped the global order. Take China: where the 1949 revolution brought earth-shaking changes, the post-80s period accelerated into hyper-evolution—changes not by geological epochs but by breathless days and moons. Reform and Opening-up propelled China onto the global stage, where economic and political restructuring unleashed productive forces, catalyzing unprecedented developmental achievements and modernization. Rising living standards and enhanced comprehensive national power all stem from these transformative dynamics. “Novelty” has undeniably become the hallmark of this epoch—while nostalgic undercurrents persist, the prevailing zeitgeist overwhelmingly celebrates innovation and anticipates change. Second, the latter half of the 20th century witnessed the knowledge explosion, the new technological revolution, the "Third Wave," and the digital transformation—particularly through computers and networking—fundamentally reshaping human existence. These forces precipitated radical shifts in lifestyles, social paradigms, and value systems, prompting declarations of humanity's entry into the information society and knowledge economy, with the world marching toward globalization and integration. The planet has effectively condensed into a global village inhabited by billions, its changes unfolding at dizzying speed. Yet even this relentless conceptual churn struggles to encapsulate the transformations underway. Yet this remains our reality: the knowledge explosion, technological revolutions, and lightning-fast digital information flows render yesterday's wisdom obsolete, turn morning headlines into afternoon archives, and devalue freshly acquired data before utilization. This relentless cycle manifests a singular mantra—"novelty"—with all its allure, efficacy, and market value. In our so-called information society, this cult of the new wields undeniable hegemonic influence.

The world's lightning-paced transformations and life's burgeoning diversity have created fertile ground for fashion's proliferation. By definition, "fashion" constitutes emergent forms and ideas that rupture established material and conceptual paradigms, characterized by three cardinal traits: novelty (fresh, avant-garde), divergence (departing from norms), and singularity (unconventional, extraordinary). The lexicon of fashion—"trendy," "vogue," "new," and "wave"—typically denotes pioneering concepts that break conventions. Yet semantically, trendy/vogue occupy a more avant-garde stratum: though innovative, they lack broad consensus. New aligns closer with true fashion, requiring dual manifestation—as novel phenomena and socially validated movements with measurable (albeit non-decisive) cultural traction. The concept of "wave" carries deeper historical resonance. When we speak of "epochal waves" or "historical tides," these currents invariably mirror the essence of their eras, embodying the fundamental trajectories of societal evolution.

As the most dynamic element within social phenomena, culture reflects a society's political and economic foundations while constituting its superstructure. This superstructure exerts active, transformative influence upon the economic base—though ultimately determined by it. Consequently, all human social praxis and historical movements inevitably imprint themselves upon collective consciousness. Given the inexhaustible diversity of social practice and the perpetual motion of societal change, consciousness remains in constant renewal, generating conceptual innovation with boundless potential. As a spiritual manifestation of societal politics and economics, culture perpetually guides collective existence—with cultural fashion operating at its vanguard. To define it precisely: cultural fashion constitutes a cultural modality that mirrors prevailing political-economic formations and embodies developmental trajectories, characterized by novelty, avant-gardism, and dynamic vitality—the lifeblood coursing through society's veins. While capable of crystallizing epochal cultural traits—and potentially evolving into cultural trajectories when cultivated—cultural fashion doesn't inherently embody developmental directions. Fundamentally, it's merely novel cultural vessels carrying ideological content, deriving value primarily through novelty's allure. Yet this "newness" remains ancillary to culture's essence. To genuinely enter the cultural mainstream, such fashion must deepen its substantive content, authentically manifesting culture's core attributes—only thus can it become epochally vital and developmentally aligned.

II

Cultural fashion operates at the vanguard of cultural evolution. Yet however dynamic culture may be, it cannot self-generate fashion—for culture is ultimately the crystallized yield of human creative praxis. Divorced from social practice, from humanity's material and spiritual production, no cultural phenomena can emerge. Thus cultural fashion remains fundamentally anthropogenic, born of societal dynamism and historical development.

Cultural fashion has existed as an objective reality since humanity's dawn. In early societal stages, constrained by primitive culture, technology, and—critically—limited means of transmission, its production remained rudimentary, cycles protracted, and dissemination sluggish, preventing rapid mass adoption as spiritual commodities. Modernity's socioeconomic progress, technological leaps, and digital ubiquity have since furnished optimal conditions for its accelerated production and viral spread, with mass media emerging as the primary epicenter of cultural fashion's generation and propagation. First, mass media inherently function as ideological apparatuses, tasked with news production, information dissemination, and cultural commodity manufacturing. As modernity's primary psychic factories, they leverage journalistic imperatives—novelty, authenticity, veracity, and speed—to maximize audience penetration. These institutions perpetually process raw data into formatted consciousness, meticulously calibrated to both hegemonic ideological demands and the cross-class material and spiritual needs of society. Moreover, owing to their privileged societal position, mass media inherently focus on emerging social currents and nascent trends—their production processes and outputs thus acquiring an inherent futurity and novelty-seeking impulse. This predisposition readily transforms their cultural commodities into venerated fashion, rendering mass media the principal "factories" for cultural fashion's design, manufacture, and replication.

Second, mass media's comprehensive informational reach and voluminous data acquisition engender substantial public trust, rendering their manufactured and replicated products readily assimilated by audiences. With its cellular-level societal penetration and transnational media symbiosis, contemporary media aggregates staggeringly diverse intelligence—from presidential campaigns to civilian routines, from insurgent operations to sporting events, even tracking rare species' appearances, fashion shows, or regional culinary trends. This panoptic capture, enhanced by immersive video, real-time broadcasting, and fax technologies, achieves unprecedented verisimilitude, forging visceral connections with daily life that command instinctive public credence.

Third, equipped with cutting-edge technologies, sophisticated infrastructure, and globally interlinked intelligence networks—augmented by computerization and digital networks as the "Fourth Media"—modern mass media have consolidated their position as society's epistemic nuclei: the dominant hubs of public discourse, information aggregation, and cultural dissemination. Through its ceaseless manufacture, relentless replication, and ubiquitous dissemination of social information—from vitally relevant events to cultural products—modern media's perpetual operations (24/7 broadcasts, special newspaper editions, etc.) create an inescapable informational vortex. This high-frequency ideological bombardment has crystallized a dominant "media discourse system", or more succinctly, "media culture"—an omnipresent force demanding cognitive surrender. Indeed, barring willful denial of reality, modern mass media have effectively become society's secondary power center, subordinate only to formal political institutions. This hegemony breeds escalating dependence—studies indicate over 88% of contemporary informational intake derives from newspapers, magazines, broadcasting, and digital platforms. Such cognitive colonization demonstrates media's unparalleled penetrative influence across human consciousness.

Fourth, mass media predicate their existence on audience need-fulfillment—actively calibrating content to popular psychology, consumption preferences, and aesthetic trends. This manifests as strategic news fabrication, selective information engineering, and deliberate fashion construction, all designed to harvest goodwill, secure ideological buy-in, and maximize consumption metrics. Take these operational paradigms: media mass-produce social vignettes to exploit ideological escapism; voraciously curate global exotica to feed audiences' novelty cravings; and churn out escapist entertainment—game-show hybrids, soap operas—tailored to prevailing aesthetic and consumption trends. Given media's psychic monopoly, such engineered cultural products, once consumed, readily metastasize into mandated fashions.

III

While numerous factors drive cultural fashion's emergence and permeation, the fundamental catalyst remains latent consumer desire.

Post-1980s China—with its political democratization, economic vibrancy, and social openness—fostered ideological pluralism, diverse identity pursuits, and heterogeneous lifestyles. Concurrently, economic growth and material abundance elevated living standards, transforming multifarious aspirations into tangible possibilities. The knowledge revolution and technological advances—particularly in information technology and dissemination methods—have further facilitated this consumption pluralism. Since China's distinctive entry into market economy processes, the market's fundamental resource-allocation role has grown increasingly pronounced. Its mechanisms have not only optimized factor mobilization to spur economic growth and satiate consumer demand, but also achieved totalizing penetration into social life's every stratum. This manifests most acutely in its hyper-stimulation of material desires and consumption fantasies, simultaneously distorting social relations and devaluing spiritual pursuits. This transformative process "harbors a latent ideological stance: the outright rejection of 'political-moral monism' in favor of celebrating mass society's hedonistic entitlements—prioritizing direct, quotidian fulfillment of individual material desires over abstract cultural ideals"①. In essence, all human aspirations now manifest through consumption rituals. Setting material consumption aside, cultural consumption operates under three paradigms: First, the erasure of cultural essence—where developmental trajectories matter less than need-gratification. Second, the flattening of historicity—replacing depth and sublimity with hedonistic immediacy. Third, the sensualization of mass culture—where affective pleasure dominates both production and consumption circuits.

Cultural fashion arises and exists precisely from these conditions. In any case, what exists is reasonable—the greatest justification for the existence of cultural fashion lies in public demand. We may say that human desires constitute demand, which can be either material or spiritual in nature. Spiritual

① Wang Desheng. *The Aesthetic Landscape of Secular Life: Understanding China's 1990s Aesthetic Transformations*. Thought Front, no. 10, 1998.

needs, in turn, can be classified as higher-level or lower-level. While we cannot definitively categorize the demand for cultural fashion as high or low, it undeniably represents a genuine need in people's lives. In modern society, rampant material desires saturate every facet of human existence, eroding spiritual foundations. People find themselves overwhelmed—externally besieged by market forces and internally drained by life's demands—leaving their psyches hollowed out by consumerist erosion. Society's breakneck development and accelerated rhythms have multiplied uncontrollable variables—particularly with the deluge of new technologies, knowledge, and phenomena—breeding widespread self-doubt about one's ability to remain epochally relevant. This existential uncertainty traps individuals in perpetual agitation, trepidation, and disorientation. Amidst such fierce competition, people need to recharge, uplift their spirits, and strengthen their will—seeking strength from culture. Yet while they wish to understand history, they lack the time and energy to read complete historical works, turning instead to dramatized versions in newspapers, films, and TV shows. Life's uncertainties and spiritual thirst call for theoretical guidance, but without the luxury of deep study, they rely on media summaries, translations, and commentaries. Meanwhile, the practical burdens of material consumption create a longing for spiritual fulfillment, aesthetic balance, and psychological entertainment. Yet expecting the masses to immerse themselves in serious art's sanctum, bathed in the grandeur of humanity's masterpieces, remains an unrealistic proposition. Instead, consuming pop music charts, indulging in martial arts films and romances, or tracking celebrity gossip and beauty pageants offers more tangible gratification—delivering immediate sensory stimulation and visceral thrills. Mass media has astutely capitalized on these societal needs—mass-producing and replicating fast-food-style cultural products. Through meticulous planning, packaging, promotion, and marketing, it aggressively pushes these goods to bestseller status, cementing their dominance in cultural consumption. Indeed, the formation of today's cultural trends is inextricably linked to media amplification. Otherwise, we cannot explain why mass media is saturated with consumptive, entertainment-driven, and instant-gratification content—from sports events to pop music and TV dramas. Once a product demonstrates marketable hooks ("readability," "selling points," or "visual appeal"), media outlets at all levels swarm to replicate it, fueling a cycle of oversaturation until the trend exhausts itself. For instance, when a TV drama becomes popular, channels of all sizes rush to rebroadcast it—even conducting fawning interviews to manufacture media dominance. Similarly, if an event shows viral potential, outlets aggressively mine it for "news within news."

This media-imposed discourse often forcibly reaches audiences, yet due to their deep trust and psychological reliance on mass media, few actively resist it. Thus, people willingly or unwillingly internalize these narratives—a testament to media's unchecked persuasive power. "Under the combined influence of power and ideology, media completely monopolizes the entire process of information handling. In this scenario, the social radar function of mass communication becomes altered—the signals (information) it transmits often do not reflect real-time conditions and rarely provide fully truthful accounts of reality."[①] Yet fundamentally, no cultural trend can exist without first being accepted and recognized by its audience. In this sense, it is the collaboration between mass media and the public that jointly creates cultural fashion.

IV

Cultural fashion's broad audience demonstrates its significant social impact. As a cultural phenomenon primarily targeting consumption, its widespread consumer base inherently reveals the cultural significance it embodies. Culture encompasses both elite culture (high-end culture) and mass culture (popular culture). Given its distinctly mass appeal, cultural fashion inherently embodies the attributes of popular culture. Yet whether elite or mass-oriented, all cultural forms share the same fundamental significance. In the writer's view, culture serves three essential purposes: first, an educative role—teaching morality, kindness, and aesthetic appreciation; second, a formative role—subtly shaping national character and spirit through its pervasive influence; and third, an entertainment role—refining temperament and providing mental and physical enjoyment. Cultural fashion rides the crest of cultural development, charging at its forefront—its defining traits being relentless novelty

① Li Yan. *The Alienation of Mass Communication Processes*. China Radio & TV Academic Journal, no. 10 (1997).

and audience captivation. While public engagement with cultural trends is not entirely indiscriminate, modern audiences (excluding children lacking basic discernment) generally exercise value-driven selection and informed judgment in their consumption. Whether as individuals or collectives—the driving forces of social progress—people's cultural value orientations operate within a core normative space, largely insulated from ideological extremes when detached from mainstream ideology. While novelty remains cultural fashion's most compelling allure, this represents merely one facet of its complex appeal. The other vital factor behind cultural fashion's persuasive power lies precisely in its cultural substance and inherent significance. Thus, the longevity and impact of cultural trends fundamentally depend on the depth of their cultural content and the meaningful values they embody.

What role does cultural fashion play in society? In the writer's view, it manifestseducational, formative, and recreational functions—though to varying degrees. In reality, modern cultural fashion profoundly shapes both cultural consumption patterns and, to some extent, the very trajectory of sociocultural development. For instance, the Misty Poetry movement of the late 1970s to mid-1980s significantly influenced the evolution of New Era poetry. The rise of reportage literature since the reform period imbued narrative genres with documentary traits. The global dominance of pop music—especially through electronic instruments—revolutionized musical artistry. Meanwhile, the popularization of sports culture, the mainstreaming of fashion, and even evolving hairstyles have collectively reshaped cultural consumption patterns, lifestyles, and behavioral norms—sparking profound shifts in aesthetic sensibilities. Ultimately, the depth and breadth of cultural fashion's impact—whether on cultural evolution or broader societal progress—hinges on its intrinsic cultural substance and spiritual essence. Fundamentally, a cultural trend's ability to endure and integrate into mainstream culture signifies its possession of essential cultural attributes, carrying meaningful cultural depth and philosophical resonance. Conversely, trends lacking such substance and spirit inevitably fail to take root or achieve mainstream assimilation.

On the other hand, we must soberly recognize that cultural fashion also carries negative consequences. Its defining trait—relentless novelty—demands constant trend-chasing, which inherently limits cultural sedimentation. This lack of sedimentation results in superficiality, where form eclipses substance, ultimately reducing cultural trends to hollow shells devoid of deeper meaning. The implications of such hollow cultural trends are predictable: they fuel obsession with surface aesthetics while obscuring true cultural meaning. Moreover, cultural fashion often becomes inextricably fused with consumerism—frequently manifesting as materialistic desire. This fusion risks eroding cultural substance, reducing engagement to mere sensory stimulationand consumption-driven gratification, devoid of profound spiritual resonance. Moreover, once cultural fashion becomes entrenched in consumerism, it inevitably succumbs to market mechanisms, enabling mass production and endless replication. In this process, cultural trends degenerate into commercial slogans and sensory triggers—tools for stimulating consumption rather than conveying meaning—while diluting cultural substance to its most tenuous form. Furthermore, the aggressive promotion of cultural trends can spawn "bubble culture"—creating an illusion of cultural flourishing that obscures true progress. Like "viewing flowers through fog or the moon reflected in water," this phenomenon distorts perceptions and muddies the trajectory of authentic cultural development. The commercial success and buzz surrounding cultural fashion may create an illusion of cultural prosperity, yet behind this hype often lies cultural depletion and hollow trends. Without rational guidance, such phenomena can distort genuine cultural development, leading to substantive losses. Worse still, the distortion within cultural fashion risks influencing broader aesthetic trends, misdirecting spiritual pursuits and imposing hidden costs on those chasing trends—a reality society must confront.

In analyzing the drawbacks of cultural trends, we do not deny their positive social impact but rather highlight this duality: while injecting novelty and vitality into modern life, they also impose certain burdens. Thus, we must cultivate the wisdom to remain discerning amidst chaos—guiding cultural fashion rationally to harness its potential as a genuine catalyst for cultural progress.

The Audio-Visual Construct: Cultural Signification and Spiritual Dissolution

This proposition spans a temporal framework extending from the late 20th century into the 21st—and continues to unfold within the present moment. We delineate the conceptual framework of this proposition through the following trajectory: Over two decades of China's reform and opening-up have yielded monumental economic growth; the gradual consolidation of a socialist market economy has amplified the role of market mechanisms across all facets of social life; globalization trends, compounded by China's accession to the WTO, have further integrated the nation into the globalized order; the accelerated pace of modernization has abruptly rendered Chinese society symptomatic of both industrial and post-industrial conditions; alongside economic prosperity, social existence has grown increasingly fragmented and kaleidoscopic, with all phenomena manifesting as materialized, reified entities. Nor is this phenomenon confined to material goods—mental productions are equally ensnared. The tide of reification has inundated every domain of modern existence. Against this backdrop, does contemporary life manifest as profusion or affliction? This inquiry seeks, through an examination of the quintessential symptom of modern reified society—the sonic-visual construct—to elucidate its cultural signification and spiritual valence.

I. Audiovisual Construction: Modern Cultural Landscape

Following the established framework, we delve into the core of our inquiry. As officially articulated in mainstream discourse, China's developmental trajectory follows this logical sequence: reform and opening-upestablished market mechanisms to drive economic growth, which in turn serves as the foundation for achieving societal modernization. Modernization is fundamentally a multidimensional concept, encompassing economic, political, cultural, and social imperatives. Yet humanity's actual modernization trajectory has deviated from idealized, balanced development. The current reality reveals a paradox: while modernization accelerates globally, counter-modern forcessimultaneously proliferate. Increasingly, modernization manifests as material obsession—where rampant consumerism dominates industrial and post-industrial societies, eclipsing its broader aspirations.

Consumption inevitably breeds its own display, stimulation, and promotion—and the most effective channels for these inevitably colonize our visual and auditory spaces. As Hegel observed, among human senses, only sight and hearing qualify as cognitive senses, while others remain secondary. This forms the philosophical foundation for today's audiovisual-dominated reality, where modern life unfolds within an inescapable sensory matrix of images and sounds. A walk through the city reveals towering skyscrapers—symbols of modernity's grand ambition yet equally stark monuments to its material excess. Vivid advertisements, splashed with seductive slogans and celebrity imagery, dominate every surface: buildings, transit hubs, alleyways. This sensory onslaught simultaneously proclaims urban prosperity and amplifies consumerist desire, saturating public space with competing narratives of aspiration and commodification. From metropolises to small towns, streets are lined with shops overflowing with goods—a kaleidoscope of packaging that mirrors both the excess of modern materialism and the chaotic charm of a child's Rubik's cube. The relentless flow of pedestrians and vehicles in public spaces forms a powerful material current, symbolizing the collusion between people and objects in modern society. More crucially, beyond the massive industrial structures and their accompanying noise, we are perpetually immersed in an unending stream of electronic sights and sounds. Electronic billboards in stations, docks, stores, parks, and squares ceaselessly scroll, flooding public sightlines with repetitive visual noise. Neon lights flicker erratically, while laser beams slice through the urban core—rendering cities incapable of nocturnal respite, their rhythms synced to the relentless pulse of commercial spectacle. Simultaneously, cities roar ceaselessly—a cacophony of industrial clatter, shrieking sirens, vendor cries, and the deafening blare of celebrity vocals from storefront speakers. High-decibel noise and murmuring chatter, frenetic beats and languid melodies, all merge into an oppressive soundscape that drowns out both the city's inner voice and any semblance of tranquility. People drift through this chaos—disoriented and mentally frayed —buffeted by relentless soundwaves. Yet the dominant sensory assault now emanates from screens: televisions, computers, even smartphones ensnare usersin a perpetual audiovisual siege, whether in offices or private homes. With advancing technology, television production has evolved to deliver high-frequency, ultra-HD, and immersive audiovisual experiences—programs so captivating they command undivided attention. Meanwhile, computers lure users with vast data storage and networked information platforms, creating an equally irresistible digital pull. Moreover, the trajectory of electronic devices manifests as televisions becoming computer-like and computers television-like—a mutual assimilation that perfects their audiovisual capabilities. This technological symbiosis only deepens human immersion within the constructed audio-visual worlds they generate. Mobile phones—as the quintessential electronic communication tools—have rendered audiovisual stimuli perpetually trailing behind individuals, clinging to their very bodies. People now move as if tugged by invisible strings, or more precisely, experience the constant sensation of being shadowed. Thus, they can never truly sever connection with this world. Nor is this phenomenon confined to urban spaces; modern audiovisual saturation has now permeated rural territories in totality. Industrial manufacturing long ago identified rural areas as prime markets for expansion. Household appliances now permeate village homes, ceaselessly dumping the grandiose audiovisual world upon relatively unadulterated countrysides. Beyond this, colossal billboards advance into rural territories—a colonization accelerated by small-town development strategies. What were once tranquil villages now march toward urbanization and cacophony. Rural decibel levels escalate; rural spaces distend unnaturally.

It must be emphasized that the audiovisual world we inhabit today bears no resemblance to the ecologically balanced, naturally emergent audiovisual environment of humanity's early epochs. Ours is an artificial sonic-visual construct of human making. In the era of natural economy—where one might "pluck chrysanthemums beneath the eastern hedge, then gaze contentedly at southern mountains"—the visual field consisted exclusively of elements in their primordial state: heaven and earth, celestial bodies, mountain ranges, rivers, forests, plains, humans and creatures alike. This organic tableau included only the most essential human structures—basic living facilities, cultural installations born of productive activities, and accumulated cultural relics. These phenomena existed as manifestations of ecological equilibrium in its natural state. Though encompassing babbling streams and roaring floods, lightning flashes and howling gales, the cries of tigers and lamentations of apes, the clucking of fowl and barking of hounds—even the clamor of human activity—they remained fundamentally emergent from nature itself: authentic sounds of the earth, cadences of primal creation. The modern audiovisual world, by stark contrast, is entirely of human manufacture. Consider photoelectric technology: the paramount force and foundation underpinning modern society's creation, the most significant achievement of human ingenuity since the industrial revolution, and above all, the essential building block of our constructed audiovisual world. Advertisements are meticulously engineered to colonize consciousness with commodities. Product packaging is honed to trigger consumptive desires. The towering, grid-like proliferation of skyscrapers serves to intensify worship of urban civilization. High-decibel loudspeakers in every public space hijack attention and ensnare potential customers. Deliberately crafted computer interfaces and television programming construct inescapable audiovisual environments—digital quicksand where mental escape becomes impossible. Thus, the modern audiovisual world emerges as humanity's self-engineered cage—forged to satiate its own desires and impulses. In philosophical terms, this constitutes "conscious" volitional action. Herein lies modern society's distinctive cultural paradox.

II. The Ontology of Audio-Visual Being: A Universe of Meaning

We identify the audio-visual construct as modern society's distinctive cultural phenomenon precisely because it has actively molded modernity itself. Should one seek the fundamental demarcation between contemporary society and earlier historical epochs, it lies in the relentless ascendance of metropolitan centers—where modern technology has facilitated the creation of an ever-expanding audio-visual universe.

The advancement of audio-visual technology has fundamentally transformed modern society. The expansion of this audio-visual realm has enriched contemporary existence, rendering it more vibrant, more kaleidoscopic, and more dynamically complex. This proliferation of sensory diversity and cultural abundance undeniably marks societal progress. Humanity can never—and should never—retreat to monochromatic desolation. Thus, we affirm: the audio-visual dimension constitutes our modern reality, the very atmosphere of contemporary life, embodying in profound ways the essential character of modern existence.

The audio-visual dimension comprehensively defines modern existence. What, then, constitutes the essence of contemporary life? While multiple interpretations exist, those immersed in modern society would likely identify sensory abundance and radical diversification as its paramount characteristics—precisely the qualities manufactured by audio-visual technology. Moreover, propelled by globalization, this phenomenon accelerates toward configurations beyond our predictive capacities with unprecedented momentum. As we have demonstrated, modern societal development exhibits a defining characteristic: the perpetual escalation and satisfaction of insatiable consumer desires. This reality manifests as total materialization—a wholesale reification where every individual is inevitably swept into the relentless logistics of commodification. Advanced technology and intensive operations now generate mountainous accumulations of material goods at every moment—yet these ever-growing peaks of commodities remain perpetually unconsumed. Material obsession and compulsive consumption have become the unquestioned axioms of modern existence. Contemporary humanity moves with neither the unburdened ease nor the vigorous resilience of our recent forebears. Such is the inexorable reality we now inhabit.

Inescapable material cravings and perpetual consumption inevitably cultivate a materialist sensibility, fueling modern humanity's worship of commodities. This material veneration fundamentally constitutes a form of thirst—yet such thirst neither demands environments choked by material excess nor burial beneath possessions. For modern individuals, these extreme conditions would annihilate both the sensuous and rational dimensions of existence. Precisely as perpetual exposure to delicacies—be they rare mountain treasures or oceanic delicacies—fails to sustain appetite or inspire culinary delight, so too do modern individuals require material stimulation. Yet this stimulation increasingly manifests not necessarily through physical objects, but through endlessly proliferating, kaleidoscopic symbols of materiality. Consider currency—that supreme embodiment of material value—which typically exerts far greater stimulative power over consumption than concrete goods. Money, after all, manifests as the pure abstraction of generalized value, a privileged signifier. In truth, modern existence unfolds entirely within a universe of signs, and the audio-visual realm we inhabit constitutes nothing less than modernity's semiotic sphere. Every commodity and phenomenon in modern society undergoes meticulous semiotic packaging, emerging as pure signification. As we traverse urban spaces—streets, train stations, docks, stores, hotels, plazas—the dazzling oversized imagery, vibrantly crafted visuals, deafening acoustics, and frenetic rhythms all mask the brutal material infrastructure: the relentless logistics and mountainous material accumulations they merely signify. Moreover, societal evolution has precipitated the radical sophistication of semiotic systems. The colonization of daily life by signs now enjoys universal cultural sanction. Street signage, traffic lights, and road symbols efficiently condense linguistic information—while an ever-expanding array of commercial semiotics actively stimulates desire and engineers demand. Modern individuals instinctively recognize signifiers of commerce—specific symbols denote banks, stores, or product categories. Yet this semiotic system operates at a deeper level: life itself becomes categorized, homogenized, and proceduralized, even extending to uniform aspirations and value systems. Consider how happiness has been algorithmically defined as material abundance, life's purpose reduced to wealth accumulation, and living itself equated with consumption. The trajectories of modernization, urbanization's relentless march, the synchronization of daily rhythms, and mass media's ceaseless propaganda have collectively rendered existence startlingly formulaic: endless work cycles fueling endless consumption, all culminating in solitary diversion within identical "matchbox" dwellings.The forces of global integration now accelerate what amounts to cultural synchronization—with Western lifestyles and developmental paradigms aggressively promoted as universal templates. This campaign for homogeneity finds eager adherents even within our immediate communities. Should this trajectory persist unaltered, our world will be threatened to polarize civilizations into binary opposition. Clearly, the trend of symbolization in modern society continues to spread deeper and wider, to the extent that even humans themselves have become symbols. People deliberately package themselves—choosing specific clothes, hairstyles, speech, eyebrow shapes, lipstick colors—to highlight individuality and express personal identity. While individuality seems amplified, people are gradually turning into symbols.

We must acknowledge that the symbolic world before us carries both material and cultural significance. This world, constructed primarily through audio-visual elements, constitutes a vital aspect of modern culture and embodies its defining characteristics. We recognize that in primitive cultures, where language remained underdeveloped, visual symbols held paramount importance in humanity's understanding of self and nature. Following this primal epoch until recent history, linguistic culture dominated human civilization. Although artistic expressions like painting, sculpture, dance, and vocal music emerged early, culture remained fundamentally language-centric. Fundamentally, language itself constitutes a form of visual symbolism—particularly evident in Chinese characters. Yet linguistic signs have achieved complete abstraction, becoming inextricably intertwined with human cognition as instruments of thought. As Aristotle observed, man is the animal possessing logos—ultimately, the linguistic animal. The crux lies in this: as education becomes universally accessible, language ceases to be an elitist privilege. "In recent history, both Western and Chinese cultures manifest an increasingly evident trajectory: visual signs are surpassing—or have already superseded—linguistic signs as the dominant cultural paradigm."[①] In the 1980s, Daniel Bell presciently identified this cultural shift in The Cultural Contradictions of Capitalism: "The dominant modality in contemporary culture is now visual. Sounds and images, particularly the latter, now organize aesthetics and command audience attention. This appears all but inevitable in mass society.[②]" He asserts: "Two salient dimensions of contemporary life demand emphasis on visual elements. First, the modern world constitutes an urban reality. Metropolitan existence—with its structured stimuli and social configurations—affords unparalleled opportunities for seeing and being seen (rather than reading or hearing). Second, the very character of contemporary inclinations manifests through: the lust for action (versus contemplation), the pursuit of novelty, and the craving for sensationalism. Nothing satisfies these urgent desires more effectively than visual components in art."[③] Bell analyzes the inevitability of visual culture superseding linguistic culture through dual frameworks—objective and subjective. Objectively, urban civilization undeniably provides expansive domains for images and graphics to flourish. Subjectively, metropolitan masses no longer revere the traditional aesthetic ideals of "con-

① Tao Dongfeng, Jin Yuanpu & Gao Bingzhong (eds.). *Cultural Studies*. Tianjin: Tianjin Academy of Social Sciences Press, 2000, p.124.

② Daniel Bell. *The Cultural Contradictions of Capitalism*. Translated by Zhao Yifan, Pu Long & Ren Xiaojin. Beijing: SDX Joint Publishing Company, 1989, p.154.

③ Daniel Bell. *The Cultural Contradictions of Capitalism*. Translated by Zhao Yifan, Pu Long & Ren Xiaojin. Beijing: SDX Joint Publishing Company, 1989, p.154.

templative stillness" or "passive observation," instead craving dynamic participation and immersion. Hence Bell's definitive conclusion: "I maintain that contemporary culture is becoming predominantly visual rather than print-based—an indisputable reality."①

Bell's theoretical framework expands our perspective, revealing contemporary culture's dual transformation into not merely a visual but equally an auditory culture. The audio-visual realm constitutes both the lifeworld and cultural-artistic sphere of modern existence. We now viscerally witness the flourishing of this audiovisual culture and its artistic manifestations. Advanced technologies have exponentially enhanced humanity's capacity for figurative representation. Where traditional methods required meticulous manual creation using brushes and ink, modern photographic and videographic techniques now achieve greater expressive power with unprecedented simplicity. These technologies paradoxically enable both hyper-realistic reproduction and deliberate artifice—employing close-ups, cuts, and other cinematic techniques to heighten emotional resonance, allure, and seduction. Facial close-ups amplify subtle emotional fluctuations; strategic framing accentuates bodily aesthetics; advertisements deliberately hypersexualize through sensory overload—combining provocative imagery with pulsating lights and saturated colors to push technological manipulation to its limits. The advent of cinema and television transformed static images

① Ibid., p.156.

into dynamic visual narratives, seamlessly integrating imagery with sound. In auditory arts, electronic instruments—coupled with advanced amplification, broadcasting, and particularly high-fidelity technologies—have exponentially intensified music's penetrative power. Any individual with unimpaired hearing now receives continuous musical stimulation during waking hours. Modern auditory art's psychological impact rivals, if not surpasses, that of visual art in its influence upon contemporary consciousness. Most crucially, the synergistic integration of modern visual and auditory arts has achieved unprecedented potency in its captivating, stimulating effects on human perception. Within Chinese cultural traditions, early operatic forms—combining vocal performance, dialogue, and physical acting—undeniably constituted primitive audiovisual synthesis. However, contemporary fusion represents an exponentially more sophisticated integration, achieving sensory orchestration of unparalleled complexity. These art forms achieve complete audiovisual synthesis—combining photorealistic motion imagery, precise voice-overs, and engineered soundscapes into seamless perceptual realities. Cinema, television dramas, and music videos exemplify this total integration. Such technological perfection explains their irresistible allure, inducing voluntary prolonged immersion where temporal awareness dissolves.

The proliferation of modern audiovisual arts stems directly from contemporary psychological demands. In our hyper-consumptive society—marked by material obsession, inflated consumption, accelerated rhythms, and existential pressures—material and consumptive desires form two inexorably expanding dimensions. These forever-elusive pursuits leave individuals psychologically emaciated ("wasting away") and neurally exhausted. Yet this self-inflicted captivity persists. When material corrosion erodes the psyche, the paradoxical remedy remains material: only renewed consumptive stimulation can generate the illusion of motivational energy. Thus, audio-visual art (audio-visual signs) that mirrors our hyper-material reality ceaselessly floods modern perceptual spaces. The immediacy, intuitiveness, and intense seductiveness of audio-visual media grant inherent superiority over textual communication, establishing cultural hegemony where the audio-visual dominates the literary. Culture fundamentally reflects human modes of production and ways of living. Contemporary audiovisual consumption patterns epitomize modern lifestyles, particularly in how cultural consumption itself has been transformed. Research indicates that urban Chinese residents now spend most leisure hours engaged with televisual content, newspapers, music, and digital devices. Parallel surveys reveal over 50% of urban consumers prioritize purchasing information appliances—a behavioral shift precipitating fundamental transformations in aesthetic preferences. The audio-visual domain has undeniably emerged as the paramount sphere of contemporary aesthetic engagement. Indeed, as reification intensifies, audio-visual culture's dominance over linguistic culture has become institutionalized. Contemporary art devoid of audio-visual elements would cease to qualify as modern; likewise, modern individuals deprived of audio-visual artistic consumption would find themselves alienated from contemporary existence. Thus, we say that the audio-visual realm constitutes both our material and artistic reality.

III. Audio-Visual Inflation: The Dissolution of Spirit

The audio-visual realm constitutes an artistic domain. Audio-visual culture embodies the defining characteristics of our era. As both artistic and cultural phenomena, these developments demand rigorous examination through dual critical lenses—aesthetic and cultural.

As previously noted, audio-visual constructs now permeate every sphere of modern social existence. The dominance of audio-visual culture over linguistic culture has solidified into cultural hegemony, emerging as the paramount paradigm of contemporary society. This audio-visual veneration continues to intensify—or more precisely, modern humanity's dependence on and obsession with this sensory culture grows ever more inexorable. This very dynamic fuels audio-visual culture's accelerated proliferation. From the perspective of modern economics, within consumer societies, any growth in demand instantly stimulates corresponding production and manufacturing expansion. Crucially, audio-visual proliferation coincides with cutting-edge technological advancement. Thus, audio-visual culture emerges as the quintessential high-tech artifact—saturated with both material density and technological sophistication. The ever-growing demands of modern society serve as the precondition for audio-visual expansion, while technological advancements enable mass reproduction at scale—making this proliferation an inevitability. Yet the crucial question remains: beyond adapting to contemporary rhythms and satisfying sensory cravings, what deeper consequences does this audio-visual inflation impose upon us?

We must indeed acknowledge the profound significance of audio-visual constructs in modern society. These technological formations have enriched contemporary existence while becoming fundamental prerequisites for artistic production—propelling cultural development into unprecedented realms. Consider how photographic art now threatens to eclipse painting; how cinema and television dramas proliferate, transforming literary classics and new textual art into audio-visual formats, as audiences increasingly prefer screens over pages, leaving masterpieces forgotten. Similarly, electronically synthesized music overshadows traditional instruments—particularly ancient ones—rendering them obsolete. More crucially, audio-visual technology's advancement and proliferation have stripped artistic production of its mystical veil. As technical accessibility enables mass participation, life becomes aestheticized while art becomes democratized—or perhaps more accurately, de-artified through total assimilation into the everyday. Consider how ownership of a camera or camcorder enables those devoid of painting knowledge or technique to produce images rivaling professional artworks. Similarly, individuals lacking literary mastery can employ "audio-visual language" to craft cinematic narratives, while even vocally untrained persons generate artistic enjoyment through karaoke technology, etc.

Audio-visual constructs transform impossibility into reality, banish solitude and silence from daily life, saturate existence with stimulation and passion, and render the world perpetually clamorous and restless. Yet this very excitation erodes tranquility and rationality—irrevocable losses, though we can no more return to the era of "plucking chrysanthemums beneath the eastern hedge" than reverse time itself. Nevertheless, we must persistently seek to recreate that poetic unity where "painting dwells within poetry and poetry within painting," and steadfastly pursue art's essential nature and culture's spiritual core. We cannot claim audio-visual art lacks capacity to stir human souls, provoke rational contemplation about human existence and worldly essence, or elicit aesthetic resonance. Yet audio-visual proliferation has undoubtedly rendered our world more cacophonous and agitated—this sensory deluge fundamentally impedes tranquility and rational engagement. As replication technologies mass-produce sensory stimuli, audio-visual products inevitably succumb to mediocrity, superficiality, and ephemerality. To satisfy increasingly ubiquitous demand and achieve maximal accessibility, audio-visual products must suppress artistic specificity, dilute cultural substance, and erode rational qualities while amplifying sensory appeal. Consider the prevailing genres: historical farces, romantic dramas, entertainment shows, and commercial advertisements—all remarkably effective at fulfilling heightened sensory cravings and alleviating fatigue from accelerated lifestyles. Yet consumers become entrapped in this vortex of mediocre, ephemeral content, squandering precious time. While achieving superficial "delight" and addictive escapism, they grow oblivious to cultural purpose, indifferent to artistic essence, until their spiritual core dissolves in mindless amusement. Even comparatively serious audio-visual works construct constrained artistic atmospheres, offer limited aesthetic dimensions, and provoke only circumscribed rational reflection. Consider film and television adaptations like *Dream of the Red Chamber*: while undeniably conveying certain thematic elements of the original text through creative interpretation, the inherent divergence between audio-visual and literary languages inevitably creates gaps—whether in thematic depth or the cultivation of aesthetic space and sensibility. Following the release of *Dream of the Red Chamber* film and television adaptations—with their vivid immediacy, two-dimensional flow, and heightened visual impact (sensory stimulation)—countless viewers, particularly youth, abandoned the original text. Satisfied merely with moving images, they forfeited both comprehensive engagement with the novel's artistic universe and access to its complete aesthetic dimensions.

More alarmingly, audio-visual proliferation increasingly erodes human agency. While industrialization's material "alienation" has long been critically examined, we now confront a parallel phenomenon: the dissolution of selfhood within expanding audio-visual constructs. Confronted by overwhelming audio-visual saturation, modern individuals face diminishing autonomy. Television and radio barrage viewers with endless content—dramas, variety shows, commercials—regardless of preference. Urban spaces assault vision with relentless signage. Most critically, digital technologies transform homes into mediated platforms where audio-visual stimuli dictate existence. This virtual existence inverts the subject-object relationship: do we control these signs and images, or have they come to control us? he erosion of selfhood inherently restricts cognitive liberty. In truth, modern individuals often exist as mere receptors—enslaved by the very audio-visual signs they consume. This represents an advanced stage of alienation, where reclaiming agency and achieving genuine emancipation within the symbolic order has emerged as the paramount spiritual challenge of our era.

The Transformation of Literary Theory in the Age of Images (the Information Era)

The premise of our inquiry is this: as we enter the 21st century, the existential condition of humanity has undergone profound transformation. The observable panorama reveals that economic globalization and integration have largely materialized and continue to proliferate, while modernization and post-modernization advance at an accelerated pace. The concept of a "global village" is no longer an abstraction—time and space have contracted, human interaction has reached unprecedented frequency, and the economic, political, cultural, and even quotidian ties between nations and ethnic groups have grown closer than ever before. Within this near-universal unified market, commodities saturate existence, material desires run rampant, and consumption stimulates every fiber of human sensibility. The alteration of human lifestyles thus follows as an inevitable consequence. This manifested reality owes its entirety to the advancement of modern science and technology. Since the 20th century, progress in these fields has surged forward with unprecedented momentum. In the macroscopic realm, trains, automobiles, aircraft, and spacecraft have contracted time and space; in the microscopic domain, radio, film, television, computers, and the internet have expanded human horizons boundlessly. We must acknowledge that, during specific historical phases, science and technology exert a determinative influence upon humanity's modes of existence. Science functions simultaneously as both means and end—human production, daily existence, and all correlated activities must now conform to scientific principles. It has become the paramount capital of our epoch, with scientific rationality emerging as the fundamental methodology and logic of human survival. Under the hegemony of instrumental rationality, profound transformations in humanity's material production modes, intellectual production modes, and corresponding lifestyles have become inevitable. Nowhere is this more evident than in the realm of consciousness, where changes over the past century have been particularly tectonic. First, books have ceased to be the exclusive medium and commodity for intellectual transmission and consumption. Broadcast, cinema, television, computers, and the internet now constitute far more potent media, capable of satisfying increasingly diversified intellectual demands. Second, paper and pen no longer serve as primary instruments for mental creation and production; contemporary technological means can generate thought-products combining superior audiovisual elements with textual sophistication. Empirical reality demonstrates that humanity has irrevocably entered the Age of Images. This constitutes the fundamental environment of modern existence—and by inevitable extension, the essential ecosystem for literature itself.

I. The Domain and Boundaries of Literature

"The development of practical reality and the transformation of cultural paradigms, coupled with the emergence of novel phenomena and objects, have overflowed traditional disciplinary confines, rupturing the epistemological frameworks of established fields. This has necessitated the expansion or displacement of academic frontiers—'boundary migration' has become a shared recognition among scholars across disciplines."[①] In the Age of Images, the conceptual domain and territorial boundaries of literature inevitably undergo metamorphosis.

Traditionally, the domain of literature has been primarily defined by paper-based and textual criteria, broadly divided into two categories: first, printed textual literature, mainly referring to literary works formalized in writing and produced in printed form, including both classical literature and popular mass-market literature; second, orally transmitted protoliterary forms with distinct literary qualities, encompassing stories, legends, myths, folk songs, moral precepts, and xiehouyu (folk witty sayings)—essentially what is conventionally termed folk literature. The fundamental types of literature fall into three major genres: narrative literature, lyrical literature, and discursive literature, with principal forms including novels, poetry, prose, reportage, and essays.

Contemporary literature can no longer be strictly delineated by paper-based or textual criteria. On one hand, traditional printed literature remains a vital component of the literary domain; on the other, just as modern science and technology have caused seismic shifts in our world and human existence, literature itself is undergoing a massive transformation toward visual expression, with its boundaries expanding at an unprecedented pace.

---

① Jin Yuanpu (ed.), *Cultural Studies: Theory and Practice*, Henan University Press, 2004, p. 3.

As both phenomenon and historical fact, the advent of photographic technology indisputably marked a pivotal event in ushering in the Age of Images, enabling the true-to-life reproduction of objective reality. The vanguard of literature's visual transformation, however, emerged in cinema. Through the sequencing of lens-captured imagery, films construct plotlines, weaving multiple narrative threads into complete stories that achieve holistic narration. Early silent films relied entirely on image montage, requiring audiences to comprehend narratives purely through visual juxtaposition. The subsequent synchronization of sound with moving images brought unprecedented clarity to cinematic storytelling, rendering plot trajectories distinctly perceptible. Yet at its core, cinema's primary narrative medium remains the image—it constructs plots through the intrinsic relationships between visual frames. Sound and on-screen text serve merely as auxiliary devices, enhancing rather than replacing imagery's storytelling dominance. For the first time in human expression, continuous flowing pictorial language supplanted written words as the vehicle for historical and contemporary narratives. The advent of television technology significantly enhanced the capacity of visual storytelling. Unlike film projectors requiring physical screening, TV converted images, sound, and text into broadcast signals transmitted to receivers, exponentially expanding narrative reach. Subsequently, the ubiquity of computers and digital networks created a unified medium combining aural, verbal, textual, and visual elements—simultaneously becoming both a vehicle for literature's dissemination and an instrument for its creation.

To be precise, modern society constitutes an audiovisual universe—the digital era① has merely rendered imagery more conspicuously dominant within contemporary existence. The emergence of a comprehensive visual semiotic system now exerts seismic impacts across both material and cognitive spheres of human life, exerting determinative influence over behavioral patterns at every phase: initiation, progression, and culmination. This imagistic paradigm's aggressive incursion into human perception inevitably fractures traditional cultural territories, instigating relentless competition for discursive dominance. What truly matters is how visual semiotic systems and digital technologies rapidly seek entry points into people's lived reality and perceptual horizons, establishing themselves as indispensable agents in modern life through multiple dimensions: serving instrumental functions in daily existence, interpreting new configurations of both the physical and symbolic worlds, and reconstructing narratives of history and contemporary experience. The emergence of this new system has precipitated a cultural reterritorialization—where the concession and gifting of cul-

① Wu Shenggang, "*Audiovisual Constructs: Cultural Significance and Cognitive Dissolution*," Journal of Xinyang Normal University (Philosophy and Social Sciences Edition), no. 3, 2004.

tural territories and spaces coincides with the relative contraction of traditional domains, forming what appears to be an inevitable logical progression. "Literature's once-hereditary territories," as observed, "have now been massively eroded and voraciously consumed by the overwhelming onslaught of visual media."①

Amid widespread lamentations over literature's marginalization and territorial losses, we must recognize this phenomenon as both reality and illusion. Objectively speaking, while the status and influence of print-based textual literature have indeed transformed—primarily due to visual semiotic systems' incursion into the literary domain—these changes cannot solely substantiate claims of literature's decline. Paradoxically, the very infiltration of imagistic systems has expanded literature's conceptual boundaries, effecting a substantive territorial enlargement rather than contraction. It must be emphasized that current reservations about the literary legitimacy of visual semiotic systems remain transitional rather than fundamental—a provisional stance that evolving cultural practices will inevitably rectify. Without engaging in comparative evaluations of textual versus visual literature's expressive capacities, we need only examine the substantive literary roles imagistic systems now fulfill within contemporary society to recognize their indisputable claim to half of literature's reconfigured territory.

① Peng Yafei, *The Pictorial Society and the Future of Literature*, Literary Review, no. 5, 2003.

Over its centennial evolution, cinema has transcended its primitive stage of stitching images into rudimentary narratives, ascending to the realm of high artistic expression capable of profound lyricism, emotional catharsis, and aesthetic refinement. Television, within mere decades, has staged a full-scale invasion into literature's domain, mastering diverse literary techniques—from narrative-driven series to lyrical video-poems, from discursive documentaries to intimate interviews. Digital technologies have achieved even swifter hegemony: the computer and internet, through their unique fusion of text and image, simultaneity and diachrony, stasis and motion, now command literature's very essence with unparalleled informational capacity, compelling literature's rapid assimilation into their ecosystems—witness the rise of internet literature as a formidable new paradigm. Even photography cultivates its literary derivatives: photo-novels, photographic essays, and deliberately crafted art photography. Nor should we overlook radio's century-long literary engagement, whose radio dramas and poetry broadcasts once wielded unprecedented cultural influence. It is undeniable that within today's literary marketplace, audiovisual literary consumption now commands substantial market share, while print-based textual literature experiences corresponding contraction—a natural evolution of cultural metabolism. Crucially, aggregate demand for literary experience remains undiminished; what has emerged is merely a strategic diversification across consumer demographics, aesthetic hierarchies, and generic categories.

Consequently, any contemporary examination of literature must take as its fundamental objects of study the emergent literary phenomena, practices, and materialized realities of our time—transcending the prescribed boundaries of print-based textual tradition to redefine literature's potential frontiers. This conceptual expansion forms the essential foundation for advancing literary theory and sustaining meaningful scholarly inquiry.

II. Literary Writing (Creation) and Production

The transformation of literary creation and production methods constitutes the fundamental impetus behind literature's internal evolution. The current literary reality manifests as a coexistence of print-based textual literature and audiovisual literary forms. The traditional production model of print literature follows an established procedure: authors compose with pen and paper—the so-called "boxed-character crawling"—before submitting to journals or publishing houses for review and eventual publication. With the widespread adoption of computers, the writing tools for print literature have largely shifted from paper and pen to mouse movements and keyboard strokes, as texts now materialize on computer screens and storage devices. Authors can interact with editors via email, enabling effortless collaborative editing through cutting, modifying, or deleting content. More significantly, the internet's global connectivity has dramatically lowered the threshold for literary circulation by linking computers worldwide. Works composed through keystrokes can now bypass the gatekeeping of traditional literary "power institutions" like journals and publishers, flowing directly into online distribution channels. This simplification and truncation of literary production processes has subverted existing literary systems and power structures, while drastically shortening the production cycle.

The evolution of literary writing tools transcends mere alterations in textual production methods and procedures—it fundamentally transforms the cognitive paradigms, structural configurations, intrinsic qualities, and modes of existence characteristic of written literature. For centuries, the act of wielding brushes and splashing ink on paper became literature's entrenched orthodoxy, generating meticulously theorized processes: from conceptual germination and compositional execution to revisionary refinement and final crystallization. Computer-aided writing eliminates the traditional process where strokes and lines gradually transform into characters and phrases through manual execution. By merely striking keys, writers now generate words, phrases, even complete clauses through direct digital output—a radical convenience that has fundamentally altered the deliberate, measured rhythm of literary composition. This technological acceleration has precipitated a corresponding intensification of creative cognition, modifying the neural throughput of literary components within the writer's consciousness. Such cognitive recalibration may ultimately transform the author's phenomenological engagement with every facet of the creative process. In chemistry and physics, any alteration in conditions or processes invariably transforms outcomes. By the same principle, modifications in literary methodologies inevitably reshape literature's formative patterns. Primarily, the newfound conveniences—of composition, revision, and textual recombination—have significantly lowered the technical barriers to writing. The once-arduous tasks of text manipulation and manuscript processing no longer constrain creators, potentially enabling more flexible textual architectures and facilitating extended narrative expanses. Secondly, the elimination of handwriting's deliberate tempo—where words materialize through meditative contemplation and thoughts unfold gradually—may enhance cognitive fluidity and emotional intensity in creators, yet potentially at the expense of conceptual vortices, reflective detours, and hermeneutic depth. Furthermore, while digital tools facilitates unfiltered spontaneity, it risks attenuating the distilled rationality and cultivated wisdom traditionally requiring sustained intellectual sedimentation. Thirdly, as computer networks redefine literary connectivity, paper ceases to be textuality's exclusive medium—a dual transformation simultaneously restructuring literature's internal architecture and external manifestations.

The creation of visual literature constitutes a fundamentally distinct process from textual literary creation—one that traditional literary theory has largely failed to address. Yet having acknowledged the indispensable position of visual semiotic systems within literature, we must now investigate the governing principles of imagistic literary forms. The most salient characteristic of visual literary production lies in its collective authorship:

these works emerge not from individual creators, but through collaborative groups or collectives. Consider cinematic productions, television works, animated features, and even radio dramas—all typically originate from a written screenplay. This textual foundation undergoes directorial reinterpretation, constituting a secondary creation phase where the director's overarching vision coalesces into narrative and aesthetic frameworks. Only then can the selection of actors, visual elements, and other semiotic substitutes commence, ultimately materializing the director's conceptual and artistic blueprint. Here, the screenplay serves merely as foundational substrate—while exceptional scripts may facilitate outstanding productions, the director's reinterpretation and the tertiary 创作 of semiotic encoding prove ultimately decisive. The audience encounters not the raw script, but rather its narrative and artistic actualization through codified performances that simultaneously embody textual content and directorial vision. Regarding the entire creation and production process of visual works, the director's role emerges as pivotal. As chief architect of the imagistic artwork, the director not only reconfigures the screenplay but also orchestrates the collective production body, exercising overarching authority over all semiotic reinterpretations. Thus, a director's creative vision, artistic caliber, reinterpretative prowess, and leadership over the collective production unit ultimately determine a work's success and quality. The crux lies herein: while external behavioral mechanisms and procedural aspects of visual literary production can be readily described, comprehensive and nuanced analysis of the creator's mental states, conceptual processes, psychological operations, and resultant behavioral patterns proves markedly more challenging. For the composition of imagistic literature constitutes an inherently more complex phenomenon than its textual counterpart.

In essence, the cognitive pathways of visual literary production are fundamentally multidimensional and interconnected—operating through both sequential and parallel circuits. The director must simultaneously engage with the screenplay (interpreting its content and constructing an envisioned narrative world), collaborate with actors (communicating creative concepts, storyscapes, and virtual representations), and coordinate with technical crews (including cinematography, lighting, and sound design). As semiotic conduits, performers interact not only with the screenplay's framework but necessarily with the director's vision, while also maintaining dynamic connections with other production elements. The production process of visual literature is undeniably a cognitive endeavor in its totality, yet its constituent stages may involve mechanistic actions—or even deliberate mechanical inaction—that only attain narrative logic and artistic significance through skillful editing and technical synthesis. Consequently, imagistic literary production constitutes both artistic creation and technical fabrication. Whether director or performer, each must simultaneously engage in conceptual ideation and artistic formation while meticulously addressing technical feasibility and refinement. This observation in no way overstates technology's determinative role in visual literary production. Ultimately, the value of imagistic literature resides in its spiritual exegesis and expression—the director's cognitive profundity and discursive capacity remain paramount, while performers' interpretive realization constitutes the definitive factor. Technical manipulations like editing serve merely as artistic auxiliaries. Thus, from screenplay through layered reinterpretations, visual literary production achieves multivalent semiotic transmutations between signifiers and signifieds—a fundamental ontological divergence from textual literary production.

III. Literary Dissemination

The contemporary era has witnessed historic transformations in literature's channels and modes of transmission. The primacy of print-based textual distribution has been fundamentally reconfigured, with cinema, television, broadcasting, and digital networks emerging as dominant literary conduits—particularly the internet, whose integration of digital intelligence, hypervelocity, massive bandwidth, and multimodal capacities (aural, visual, textual, performative) establishes it as literature's paramount exhibition platform. Noteworthy is how modern technology's multifunctional capacities have enabled film, television, radio, and digital networks to serve simultaneously as tools for literary creation, mediums for presenting and disseminating literary forms, and indeed the very ontological manifestations of literary art itself. As Shan Xiaoxi articulates: "Contemporary media have become the 'fifth essential element' in literary activity—supplementing the traditional four elements of world, author, work, and reader within the cultural context of modern communications."①

The communicative capacity of film, television, broadcasting, and digital networks is unprecedented in scale. The integration—indeed fusion—of these modern media with literature suggests not mere collusion, but rather media's intrinsic affinity for and indispensable relationship with literary art. Fundamentally, modern media remain technological and instrumental in nature; stripped of their technical parameters, they exist as empty vessels requiring the assimilation of cultural content to substantiate their inherent void. The crux lies in how modern media, empowered by cutting-edge technology, generate formidable magnetic fields that irresistibly attract both material and cognitive dimensions of human existence, transforming into inescapable habitats. Consequently, these media have metamorphosed from being supplicants demanding content to dominant suppliers. Literary artistry—with its aesthetic valence and allure—has become the coveted target of media's dual strategy: offering low-priced services while executing premium acquisitions. Yet this very transaction has engendered literature's pathological dependence on media platforms, progressively eroding its autonomy.

① Shan Xiaoxi, *Modern Media: The Fifth Element of Literary Activity*, Literary Gazette, March 29, 2007, p. 3.

The evolution of literary dissemination method has fundamentally rewritten literature's historical trajectory and contemporary landscape, while simultaneously transforming its essential forms and modes of existence. Primarily, it has redrafted the historical narrative of print-based textual literature, giving rise to a pluralistic ecosystem where multiple literary forms coexist and diverse consumption patterns flourish. Print-based textual literature long reigned as the canonical core of literary tradition and the dominant mode of societal literary consumption. Modern media, however, have enabled literature to discover new vessels and habitats—particularly through computers and digital networks, which allow literary works to be conceived, preserved, exhibited, and consumed in novel forms. Even traditional print literature now undergoes metamorphosis, adapting into films, television series, or digital formats for online dissemination, thereby transforming its ontological status and consumption paradigms. This media revolution has exponentially multiplied literature's existential and experiential possibilities.

Secondly, the production cycle has undergone significant compression, with dissemination accelerated and consumption intensified through heightened immediacy. The evolution of creative tools has demonstrably enhanced compositional efficiency—contemporary media platforms have effectively unleashed and amplified literature's productive capacities. This dual transformation manifests both in abbreviated creative cycles and exponentially accelerated circulation velocities. Beyond creators' inherent motivations for expedited distribution, media ecosystems fundamentally operate through perpetual novelty-seeking and trend-generation mechanisms to manufacture cultural capital. Their operational methodologies often constitute premature cultural extraction, where embryonic works—frequently underdeveloped—are forcibly channeled into distribution networks prior to aesthetic maturation①. Internet literature, by contrast, is both produced and circulated directly within digital networks, eliminating multiple traditional market intermediations. This very circumvention intensifies literature's temporal immediacy—new trends achieve instant prominence while existing phenomena cool with equal rapidity, resulting in heightened consumability at the expense of enduring cultural resonance.

Third, diversified consumption and increased demand coexist with a sluggish literary market, where buyer's and seller's markets remain unbalanced. Modern media have expanded literature's distribution channels, creating a unified grand marketplace for literary works. The contemporary literary market has witnessed exponential production growth, with thousands of full-length novels now published annually—not to mention countless novellas, short stories, and staggering quantities of cinematic and televised productions. While aggregate literary consumption demonstrates an upward

① Wu Shenggang, *On Cultural Fashion*, Journal of Shenzhen University (Humanities & Social Sciences Edition), no. 2, 2002.

trajectory, this demand becomes fragmented across proliferating media platforms where free access increasingly replaces paid acquisition. Compounded by literature's diminished permanence—where most works transform into disposable commodities—the erosion of collectors' purchasing incentives has rendered market stagnation inevitable.

Fourth, the market's multifaceted dynamics exert comprehensive influence on literary creation and production, triggering internal realignments that revolutionize value systems. Contemporary reality reveals waning regulatory control by dominant societal forces—particularly political authority—while market mechanisms increasingly assert and amplify their formative power over literature. Crucially, this market infrastructure owes its very existence to modern media platforms. Literature's internal reorganizations are ultimately dictated by external determinants—primarily the prevailing conditions and contingencies of today's literary marketplace. The market and its consumers' diversified demands now wield formidable influence as the primary conductors of literary production. Adapting to these market forces has become existential imperative for both literature and its creators—the self-imposed exile of aesthetic autonomy stands as indisputable reality. When authors recalibrate creative visions and literary conventions mutate according to market logics, traditional expectations about "what literature ought or ought not to be" become untenable. From serious/elite literature to popular/genre fiction, from digital narratives and fashionable arts to cinema/television productions—even controversial phenomena like corporeal writing or erotic fiction—all emerge as market-determined manifestations. An author's creative trajectory increasingly reflects not intentionality but market determinism. Crucially, this diversification may represent literature's irreversible evolutionary trajectory.

IV. Literary Value Assessment

From both macroscopic and microscopic perspectives, contemporary literature has undergone transformative shifts. This evolution compels us to confront a fundamental inquiry: Does literature that has undergone such significant transformations still constitute literature in its original conceptualization? More essentially, have the ontological essence and core values of literature itself been fundamentally reconfigured?

At the macroscopic level, literature's transformations manifest through territorial expansion and ecological recomposition, with market behaviors increasingly synchronizing with literary practices, and commercial frameworks merging with artistic paradigms. Microscopically, literature's former monolithic forms have yielded to pluralistic manifestations—propelled by market incentives, socioeconomic pressures, and systemic inducements that compel internal recalibrations. Survival adaptation has emerged as literature's indispensable strategic repertoire, forcing continuous metamorphosis of production and preservation methodologies through market negotiations.

These behavioral and practical shifts inevitably reconfigure literature's intrinsic quality and character.

These transformations, however, prove insufficient to demonstrate any fundamental alteration of literature's ontological essence or core values. Amidst the seismic shifts in literary paradigms and the metamorphosis of both its external manifestations and internal constitution, the most salient developments remain to be the evolution of conceptual frameworks about literature, and the quantitative variability in literary quality. The inflationary effect of media platforms and market deregulation have propelled literature into an era of contested hegemony, where diverse artistic forms involuntarily engage in omnidirectional competition for market dominance. This has yielded an unwritten multilateral compact—analogous to trade agreements—that mutually legitimizes all participants' market positions. Consequently, the traditional paradigm where sociopolitical power structures and institutional systems monopolized literary categorization has collapsed. Whether fiction, poetry, cinema, or digital narratives; elite literature or popular genres—none can legitimately claim privileged canonical status. The market has democratized literary ecosystems through three silent revolutions: equality among all forms, dissolution of hierarchical valuations, and institutionalization of pluralistic recognition.[①]

① Wu Shenggang, *On the Evolution of Literary Concepts in the New Era*, Journal of Xinyang Normal University (Philosophy and Social Sciences Edition), no. 1, 2007.

Yet the market positioning of various literary forms depends not solely on intrinsic merit, but predominantly on strategic market maneuvering. While the proliferation of emergent genres has quantitatively expanded literary output, the stimulation of production, circulation, and consumption cycles has spawned premature and malformed literary offspring. Qualitative breakthroughs remain wishful thinking, as the reality manifests in the gradual degradation of literature's average standards.

Quality stands as the paramount criterion for assessing literature's significance and efficacy, for it directly determines the actualization of literature's societal functions. As both an aesthetic mode of human existence and an embodiment of collective values, literature inherently possesses profound social utility. Within Chinese cultural traditions, the emphasis placed on literature's functional capacity surpasses even political and economic considerations—as encapsulated in the maxim "literature constitutes the foundation of statecraft." Such monumental expectations inevitably strain literature's expressive capacity. Undoubtedly, during exceptional historical conjunctures—the May Fourth Enlightenment or the Anti-Japanese War period, for instance—literature has demonstrated functional capacities far exceeding its inherent limitations. Yet we must recognize that literature remains fundamentally distinct from political science, ethics, sociology, and certainly economics. Under normative conditions, its efficacy operates strictly within its ontological parameters.

Contemporary literature exhibits pronounced dehistoricization tendencies, with intertextual ruptures and rebellious discontinuities constituting the core catalysts for its internal fission. Literature's rejection of historical consciousness has created fractures that resist immediate reconciliation. The fundamental challenge emerges: Can literature maintain historical continuity? More precisely, within globalization's paradigm and the Age of Images, can literature establish its distinct presence amidst materialistic expansion and epistemological instability? This interrogation tests literature's very ontological integrity. We maintain that literature can neither fully revert to past paradigms nor completely shed its ontological identity to undergo metaphysical transmutation. Although our era affords multiple transformative possibilities for literature, and though various developmental trajectories have been theoretically postulated, literature's inherent logic permits only one ultimate resolution: the return to its essential attributes.

To formulate realistic value assessments of contemporary literature, we must examine its actual efficacy and functional performance. While literature's consumptive aspects have intensified in modern society, its ultimate orientation remains spiritual rather than material—the psyche constitutes its primary marketplace. Frankly, literature's current impact on human consciousness warrants skepticism, though such doubts often harbor outdated frameworks. Having transitioned from historical to contemporary contexts, literature can no longer realistically be expected to function as salvific protagonist within belief systems. Yet regardless of historical or contemporary transformations, literature must never abandon self-restraint—its disciplinary principles demand unwavering adherence, and its humanistic essence must remain inviolate. We neither expect literature to cure all societal ills nor serve as messianic figure, but when indulging its ludic potential amidst modern carnivalesque excesses, it must simultaneously fulfill essential functions: intellectual enlightenment, aesthetic elevation, and ideological transcendence. Admittedly, within today's pluralistic value systems, literary worth necessarily diversifies—ecological variety precludes monolithic evaluation, requiring instead multidimensional perspectives and polycentric criteria for grounded assessments.

V. Literary Criticism and Appreciation

Given the current ecological landscape of literary territories, the principles, standards, and methodologies underpinning print-based textual criticism demand fundamental reconstitution. Conventional theoretical frameworks can no longer adequately address critical inquiries such as: the evaluative distinctions between verbal and visual expressivity; divergent lyrical modalities across textual and imagistic works; or the comparative narrative strategies and humanistic revelations in different media forms. Cinema possesses its unique cinematic qualities, television its distinctive televisual characteristics, while animation offers radically novel visual experiences. Internet literature, as an emergent form, has fundamentally subverted established literary hierarchies. The systemic overproduction stemming from proceduralization and mass replication has disrupted both internal literary structures and external cultural ecosystems. This necessitates—with both urgency and formidable difficulty—the construction of new evaluative principles, standards, and discursive frameworks capable of interpreting contemporary literary realities. Yet literature's inherent sense of ethical responsibility compels criticism to persevere against all odds—this very act of principled defiance shall imbue literature with renewed valor.

Therefore, literary criticism and appreciation must not succumb to the bewildering complexity of contemporary literature, nor become disoriented amidst its proliferating manifestations. Composure, sobriety, and analytical rigor must become the indispensable virtues of current critical practice. In this era of contested literary hegemony—where flattery, hyperbole, and sensationalism dominate discursive spaces—criticism must resist conformist currents and herd mentalities. The establishment of principled critical frameworks now constitutes nothing less than an intellectual imperative. To construct principles, standards, and discursive systems for literary criticism and appreciation with composure and rationality, we must meticulously examine contemporary literature's realities and fundamental patterns through scholarly rigor and humanistic perspective, striving to accurately grasp its essence. Vigilance remains crucial—amidst today's cacophonous and superficial climate, numerous pseudopropositions and specious theories proliferate, testing criticism's very capacity to distinguish truth from falsehood through its own critical faculties. Indeed, contemporary literature remains in dynamic flux—expecting criticism to immediately clarify all complexities amidst this proliferating diversity proves unrealistic. The viable path forward demands: resisting blind conformity, avoiding arbitrary judgments, and above all, eschewing unprincipled flattery. We must ground our approach in concrete textual engagements, commencing with meticulous case analyses to advance incrementally toward systemic comprehension.

The principles, standards, and discursive frameworks of print-based textual criticism retain their validity for traditional literature—yet even this paradigm undergoes historical transformation across material forms, conceptual paradigms, and value systems. The integration of contemporary realities necessarily enriches and develops print literature's essential constitution. Simultaneously, criticism's capacity to evaluate emerging forms like visual systems and digital literature constitutes theory's imperative historical adaptation to present contexts. While the characteristics and patterns evident in the historical development of visual systems have garnered some perceptual recognition, such understanding remains predominantly intuitive rather than systematically conceptualized. A comprehensive scholarly framework—encompassing the genesis, developmental trajectories, ontological modes, intrinsic structures, essential attributes, and spiritual significance of imagistic systems—has yet to be rigorously established. This necessitates methodical investigation to accurately discern their fundamental principles, thereby constructing evaluative criteria and discursive methodologies that align with both contemporary contexts and visual systems' inherent logic. Digital literature's rebellion against autonomous literary principles poses fundamental challenges to established theoretical frameworks. The urgent scholarly imperative lies in maintaining discursive authority and interpretive relevance within existing critical paradigms—while simultaneously addressing its defining characteristics: radical libertarianism (textual arbitrariness), hypertextuality, reality deconstruction, and trans-spatiotemporal communicative capacities. These phenomena demand theoretical reassessment through innovative evaluative and hermeneutic frameworks. Confronting emergent literary realities, theory must demonstrate renewed agency—grounded in meticulous analysis of contemporary practices and synthesis of multidisciplinary theoretical resources. This endeavor prioritizes systematic problem-mapping over premature conclusions, crucially incorporating literature's evolutionary trajectories as foundational theoretical horizons. The critical objectives emerge as, identifying conceptual nexus points between established theories and new constructions, expanding criticism's epistemological foundations, and establishing preliminary frameworks for alternative discursive systems.

Popular Culture: Mechanisms and Functions

I. The Connotation of Popular Culture

1. Defining Popular Culture

At its core, popular culture is a cultural form that circulates widely among the masses. Generally speaking, while the development of human culture may exhibit diverse manifestations diachronically, it predominantly follows a linear trajectory. Synchronically, however, it invariably presents itself as an expansive multiplicity of coexisting ecologies. Take contemporary Chinese culture as an example: in terms of its overall composition, it is a complex amalgamation of various cultural ecosystems. There exists elite culture or high art, which appeals only to the refined few, alongside popular culture and mass culture that permeate society. Alongside state-sanctioned mainstream culture, there are also ethnic and regional folk cultures from different nationalities and localities. These elements coexist within the same temporal and spatial framework, collectively forming the pluralistic ecology of contemporary Chinese culture. Popular culture is distinctly different from elite culture or high art. Its fundamental character and embedded cultural signification largely align with mass culture, constituting a consumerist and entertainment-oriented cultural type. Admittedly, under specific circumstances, we cannot deny the possibility of mainstream or elite culture gaining popularity—as seen during the "Cultural Revolution," when model operas and numerous red classics became widely circulated. Such popularity, however, was primarily the result of political intervention. It must be acknowledged that each era possesses its own distinct popular culture, and different ethnic groups, in principle, also exhibit their own variations. Although globalization has led to a convergence of cultural expressions worldwide, the ethnic imprints and characteristics of culture cannot be entirely erased—even within consumer culture. Various nations and ethnic groups have studied and defined popular culture within their own contextual frameworks, resulting in research that holds both universal applicability and localized particularities for examining contemporary Chinese popular culture. Investigating and assimilating foreign research—particularly from Western scholarly traditions—can broaden our analytical perspectives, serving as crucial corroboration and supplementation for our own inquiries into this subject.

2. Characteristics of Popular Culture

Popular culture exhibits distinct contemporaneous traits: ① Secularity. Emerging either from the grassroots of mass society or by catering to public demand, popular culture is inherently a product of secularization, intimately reflecting the raw fabric of everyday life. It is precisely this quality that renders it as unremarkable to the masses as eating or wearing clothes—neither rejected, evaded, nor shunned. One might argue that secularity constitutes the fundamental visage of popular culture. By dismantling the sacred and the canonical, it reverts to the mundane. This dissolution of boundaries fosters an existential identification between popular culture and the common populace, ensuring its unimpeded permeation into mainstream consciousness. ② Transgression. Typically, a nation's cultural landscape remains predominantly governed by elite and mainstream cultures. These dominant forms, bolstered by state-sanctioned prominence and institutional advantages, assert comprehensive territorial and demographic coverage. Under such cultural hegemony, alternative cultural expressions must negotiate their survival within the narrow interstices permitted by this monolithic order. To achieve societal permeation, popular culture frequently manifests stark antagonism toward elite and mainstream cultures. It aggressively ruptures established cultural values and aesthetic conventions, generating deliberate contrast effects that amplify its visibility. This strategic dissonance compels public attention and facilitates mass adoption. ③ Pervasiveness. Popular culture operates with unequivocal intent: to achieve maximum circulation. Like seasonal winds, most of its manifestations are never meant to endure through the ages—their very ability to captivate an era, however transient, constitutes their raison d'être. The duration of their existence or popularity ultimately proves secondary. ④ Ludic Essence. Fundamentally, human culture serves three primary functions: didactic, aesthetic, and recreational. The didactic leans toward orthodoxy, the aesthetic carries solemnity, while the recreational embraces levity. From the perspective of mass reception, lighthearted cultural forms encounter far fewer barriers to acceptance—unlike their didactic and aesthetic counterparts, which demand specific contexts and moments for engagement. Thus, the widespread dissemination and societal embrace of popular culture hinge upon its capacity to fulfill public desires, with the crucial mechanism being its generation of visceral pleasure and psychological gratification. Without this essential quality, the ubiquity of popular culture would remain unrealized. ⑤ Trend Dynamics. The ubiquity of popular culture is inextricably tied to innovation, avant-garde expression, and cyclical trends. It demands novelty not only in form but also in progressively transgressive content, making trend internalization its indispensable constituent. ⑥ Formalism. With inherently superficial and unequivocal content—devoid of profundity or richness—popular culture strategically prioritizes formal experimentation as its primary means of mass appeal. Eschewing substantive depth, it deliberately cultivates novelty in form, frequently elevating formal attributes above conceptual content, or more precisely, allowing form to eclipse substance.

II. The Formation Mechanism of Contemporary Chinese Popular Culture

It must be acknowledged that the generative mechanisms of different popular cultures share fundamental commonalities. However, in reality, every instance of popular culture emerges within specific historical circumstances and cultural contexts, each possessing its own unique particularities. Contemporary Chinese popular culture is born from the immediate sociocultural realities of present-day China; consequently, it undeniably bears the distinctive imprint of its temporal and spatial origins. What constitutes the historical landscape of contemporary, or more precisely, present-day China (primarily referring to the post-New Era period)? It is a China shaped by reform and opening-up, a China constructing a socialist market economy, a China striding toward modernization while integrating with—and projecting itself onto—the global stage. Above all, it is a China in the throes of social transformation. These defining characteristics undeniably form the historical determinants for the emergence of contemporary Chinese popular culture.

Social Structure and the Ecosystem of Contemporary Chinese Popular Culture. Since 1978, the comprehensive reforms triggered by the rural household contract responsibility system have permeated every facet of society. The restructuring of economic, political, and cultural institutions—alongside reforms in other social domains—has dismantled the planned economy system, gradually establishing a socialist market economy. As China engaged globally through dialogue and integration, its social fabric underwent profound transformations. The monolithic social structure was fundamentally reconfigured: work units ceased to be uniformly state-owned entities, and individuals were no longer solely defined by their institutional affiliations. A multi-layered, diversified social architecture emerged. Take the *danwei* (work unit) system as an example. Pre-reform China recognized only two types of institutional entities: state-owned and collectively-owned—both essentially public in nature. In present-day China, the composition of *danwei* and organizational entities has grown significantly more complex. Beyond state-owned and collectively-owned structures, private and individually-operated legal entities now constitute a substantial proportion, forming vital components of contemporary China's social architecture. This diversification extends even more profoundly to citizen identities. During the pre-reform era, citizenry was rigidly categorized into workers, peasants, merchants, students, and soldiers—with peasants belonging to rural collective economic organizations and all others being state-affiliated. The current social landscape has undergone fundamental transformations: most significantly, individuals have shed their immutable dependence on state institutions, gaining substantially expanded spheres for social mobility and personal development. This structural evolution inevitably exerts transformative effects on all social phenomena—an objective reality with far-reaching implications. Popular culture's emergence and sustenance in contemporary China are fundamentally rooted in the transformed social architecture. The expansion of social openness, democratic practices, and diversity (particularly through enlarged private spheres) alongside marketization has directly catalyzed pluralism in thought, ideology, and value systems—the very genesis of cultural multiplicity. Concurrently, these structural transformations have empowered individuals with greater autonomy in cultural reception and selection, creating the necessary ecosystem for the existence, dissemination, and circulation of polycultural expressions. Thus, absent this restructured social reality, the very existence of any contemporary Chinese popular cultural forms would remain inconceivable.

Social Psychology and the Developmental Trajectory of Contemporary Chinese Popular Culture. From a social psychological perspective, mass consciousness typically manifests two predominant tendencies: nostalgia and neophilia—the craving for novelty and change. While nostalgia predominantly characterizes middle-aged and elderly demographics, neophilia permeates all social strata with particular intensity among youth. This latter impulse invariably ascends to societal dominance, especially during periods of transformative change—a psychological orientation wholly congruent with the trajectory of human societal development. Human society progresses inexorably forward, with each evolutionary stride representing innovation and transcendence beyond established paradigms. In this fundamental sense, neophilia constitutes a primal driving force of societal advancement. Contemporary China, entrenched in continuous reform and transformation, has cultivated profound collective yearning—both for the crystallization of new social systems and the materialization of envisioned futures. Building upon entrenched reform momentum, the populace anticipates groundbreaking changes and novel phenomena, a demand that has transcended material necessity to dominate the spiritual marketplace. This transformative era necessitates the construction of fresh cultural paradigms and semiotic systems to articulate emerging ideological, psychological, and existential imperatives. Popular culture emerges as the ultimate synthesizer of these collective aspirations, packaging expressionist urges through universally accessible forms and aesthetics—thus becoming the definitive semiotic currency of transitional societies. A defining characteristic of popular culture—its transgressive novelty—emerges as a direct adaptation to mass psychological demands. The public's neophilic impulses and pluralistic aspirations have created an optimal ecosystem for the flourishing of contemporary Chinese popular culture.

3. Political Ecology and the Developmental Potential of Contemporary Chinese Popular Culture. A seminal outcome of China's reforms lies in institutional transformation and innovation—including the restructuring of its political systems. These changes have fundamentally reshaped the nation's political ecology, which now evolves along two primary trajectories: democratization and juridification.

Democratization here refers to the expanded development of socialist democracy amid economic reforms and the establishment of a socialist market economy. This process has necessitated structural political realignments—rational recalibrations of rights and obligations between the Party, the state, and civil society. The conceptual boundaries of state politics have become more clearly delineated, with democratic institutionalization progressing alongside depoliticized social spheres and expanded civil liberties. Juridification, conversely, manifests through the increasing legal codification of state political conduct. Administrative and managerial activities now fundamentally adhere to legal frameworks, with all state actions bound by jurisprudential constraints. Law has become the paramount measure governing state operations—this political standardization inevitably producing standardized state governance. The dual processes of political democratization and juridification have clarified rights-obligations matrices among societal actors, while rendering the domains, content, and parameters of state governance more precisely defined. This institutional precision eliminates ambiguities in administrative objectives and prevents arbitrary expansion of governmental purview. Consequently, political authority has reduced its intervention in social affairs—cultural forms now operate without arbitrary political interference, provided they comply with national policies and legal frameworks.

This transformed dynamic has significantly ameliorated the traditional dependency between cultural production and state political structures, establishing the fundamental political precondition for contemporary China's cultural ecosystem development. It must be acknowledged that the ameliorated political ecology in contemporary China has rendered the development of popular culture not merely possible, but structurally viable.

4. The Cultural Institutional Framework and Its Developmental Trajectory in Contemporary China. China's cultural system reforms, initiated in tandem with economic and political restructuring, have undergone pro-

gressive deepening. The fundamental achievement of cultural system reform lies in dismantling the monolithic state cultural apparatus. Primarily, cultural production has ceased to be a state monopoly—collectives, private entities, individuals, and even foreign organizations now participate as investors and operators. Even state-owned cultural institutions, particularly profit-oriented units, are undergoing corporatization.

This transformation has spawned diverse cultural entities: production companies, film studios, publishing houses, advertising agencies, entertainment venues, internet platforms, freelance writers, independent musicians, and producers—all proliferating like bamboo shoots after rain. A pluralistic cultural production ecosystem is thus crystallizing. Secondly, the censorship system for cultural products has undergone significant relaxation. The state no longer uniformly regulates all cultural output, instead implementing tiered management in accordance with legal standards. Concurrently, content review criteria have substantially expanded—while maintaining directional guidance, the policy now encourages pluralistic expression. Any product aligning with the "Two For" policy (*for the people, for socialism*) may enter public circulation, fostering a more permissive cultural environment. Thirdly, the distribution channels for cultural goods have been liberalized. State monopolies on cultural product operations and circulation have dissolved, with production and distribution rights increasingly vested in independent cultural entities. This expansion of autonomy for cultural producers and operators has markedly stimulated creative incentives, driving market-responsive cultural production.

The Structural Attributes and Capacities of Popular Culture. Despite its formal and generic diversity, popular culture exhibits shared intrinsic and extrinsic characteristics: content democratization, sensory-oriented tonality, formal simplification, and fashionable packaging. These features inherently mirror contemporary China's socioeconomic, political, and psychosocial realities, emerging as organic products of societal transformation. The post-reform era's institutional recognition of individual and collective agency has redefined Chinese society—no longer merely a national or ethnic construct, but fundamentally a human-centered one. This shift has catalyzed an inevitable transition from elite-dominated paradigms toward vernacular social structures. While mainstream values and elitist cultural paradigms continue to exert substantial influence over spiritual choices, individuals now exercise unprecedented autonomy—claiming private domains and sensory experiences that validate instinctual self-direction. This psychological shift fundamentally reorients China's collective emotional compass. Popular culture, with singular adaptability, has not merely responded to these sociopsychological currents but achieved rapid synchronization with the zeitgeist—its very existence predicated on this dynamic alignment. Undoubtedly, while popular culture may not consciously vie for dominance or territory against mainstream culture, it relentlessly devises strategies to carve out its own market niches and audiences. Consequently, it must cultivate distinct attributes, aesthetics, and forms—diverging fundamentally from both mainstream and elitist cultural paradigms to chart its unique path. Crucially, mainstream and elite cultures enjoy the liberty to prioritize their own paradigms, relatively unconstrained by societal factors, as they operate with institutional backing. Popular culture, however, exists at the mercy of market forces and audience preferences—it must cater to, even court, these contingencies, for its survival hinges entirely on their validation. Failure leaves it without institutional salvation. Thus, popular culture remains acutely attuned to audience reception and societal permeability. Its very existence depends on instantly captivating the public through accessible content, sensory-driven aesthetics, simplified forms, and trend-conscious packaging—achieving overnight ubiquity. This explains why its producers and distributors predominantly comprise private and independent cultural entrepreneurs. Their survival hinges on an intuitive grasp of mass sensibilities, coupled with the creative ingenuity to cultivate precisely those attributes that guarantee cultural permeation and collective embrace.

The Efficacy of Mass Media. It must be acknowledged that the widespread development of popular culture cannot overlook the contributions of mass media. Advances in modern technology have transformed mass media into a super-colossus, whose pervasive influence now reaches virtually every corner of China. An indisputable fact is that mass media has constructed a virtual society. Therefore, for popular culture to captivate audiences and permeate society, it must first conquer and dominate mass media. The high frequency, extensive coverage, live broadcasting, real-time transmission, integrated text and graphics, and animated combinations of modern mass media are unmatched by any other means of dissemination. In reality, popular culture's expansion has precisely leveraged the efficacy of mass media to achieve comprehensive societal penetration. This symbiosis, of course, serves distinct yet complementary purposes for both parties: popular culture utilizes mass media for its dissemination, while mass media employs popular culture to attract broader audiences and amplify its influence. Yet regarding popular culture's fundamental dependence on modern mass media, the latter effectively functions as its most capable agent and promoter.

Homogenization of Global Culture. Since the late 20th century, economic globalization and integration have become an irreversible trend, manifested through significantly enhanced economic interdependence among nations worldwide. For China specifically, the deepening of reform and opening-up policies—particularly after WTO accession—has undeniably strengthened its connections with the global community. This globalization and integration extend far beyond the economic sphere, with political systems, cultural domains, and other aspects of social life increasingly intensifying their ties with the world. Thus, within the tide of globalization, all national cultures inevitably become incorporated into this worldwide integration. First, the intensity and frequency of cultural exchanges among nations and ethnic groups have significantly increased. As culture serves as a vital manifestation of national power, every culture seeks to foster its growth and enhance cultural productivity through such intercultural interactions. Second, the scope of cultural dissemination has expanded dramatically. Facilitated by modern mass media and driven by the economic potential of cultural industries, the global promotion of diverse cultural traditions has become a prevailing phenomenon. Third, cultural interactivity has markedly intensified. The cultural activities of one nation now routinely influence those of another; the emergence of one cultural phenomenon often catalyzes parallel developments elsewhere. A culture's commercial success can achieve global ubiquity almost instantaneously—as exemplified by Hollywood's *Titanic*, which dominated worldwide box offices immediately following its American triumph. Fourth, cultural hegemony has gained new territories and markets. Given culture's intrinsic linkage with economic development, Western powers leverage their financial dominance to export cultural products—a process facilitated by unobstructed transmission channels that leave economically vulnerable nations with limited defenses. This constitutes a new form of cultural imperialism. While ethnic cultures retain their distinctive characteristics, global cultural convergence inevitably induces structural homogenization across nations. This gradual erosion of cultural particularities creates the necessary conditions for the emergence of universal popular culture.

III. The Function of Contemporary Chinese Popular Culture

The extensive presence and massive reception of popular culture undeniably attest to its significant impact on both societal development and contemporary cultural evolution.

1. The Necessity for Elite, Mainstream, and Ethnic Cultural Development. Contemporary Chinese popular culture undeniably emerges from the soil of China's ethnic traditions while simultaneously reflecting the realities of global cultural integration. We cannot wholly dismiss its national characteristics, yet must equally acknowledge its embodiment of globalization's modern and postmodern attributes. This cultural form inherently subverts traditions and dissolves ethnic particularities—an undeniable tendency that generates inevitable tensions with elite, mainstream, and ethnic cultures. Such friction fundamentally stems from their ontological incompatibilities. Nevertheless, in an era advocating cultural diversity and pluralism, no society can sustain itself solely through elite and mainstream cultures. The very existence of popular culture fulfills developmental necessities for these dominant forms. While even exemplary popular culture cannot be equated

with elite cultural production, prolonged sedimentation and refinement may facilitate such transformation. Fundamentally, all cultural typologies share identical ontological destinations. Popular culture at minimum injects vital democratic vitality and dynamic genetic material into the evolution of elite, mainstream, and ethnic cultural traditions.

2. The Role in China's Sociocultural Landscape. As a distinct cultural phenomenon and category in contemporary China, popular culture's enduring cultural impact remains challenging to assess, and the longevity of its specific manifestations within society is difficult to predict. Yet its sociocultural significance cannot be denied. In my observation, popular culture performs at least three vital functions: First, it generates cultural tides. Through its formidable momentum, popular culture creates waves and surges within the cultural sphere, cleansing the soul of societal culture and emerging as a dynamic current that propels cultural evolution. Second, it ignites cultural sentiment. Popular culture, saturated with emotional elements, disrupts cultural stagnation through its confessional, communal, and carnivalesque qualities—rekindling the affective dimensions of sociocultural development. Third, it accumulates ecological cultural capital. While popular culture may not achieve canonical status or secure permanent historical recognition, even its ephemeral manifestations—whether dominant for three or five years or mere days—constitute indispensable resources for China's cultural evolution.

3. The Influence on Mass Psychology. The impact of culture on audience mentality is objective, yet varies across different cultural categories. Popular culture primarily influences the public through its distinctive mass appeal and personalized perspectives, which generate tremendous persuasive power, enabling unconscious and involuntary psychological alignment. Having distanced itself from sanctity and sublimity, popular culture adopts mass consciousness and grassroots sensibilities as its vantage points. By pursuing individualized thinking and independent value systems, it readily penetrates the private spheres of the general public—this constitutes the fundamental reason for its rapid dissemination and the effortless assimilation of collective consciousness.

4. The Deconstruction of Political Power. We must acknowledge that popular culture unequivocally articulates its own stance while inevitably constructing its own form of power—without which its market dominance and pervasive influence would be unimaginable. Yet the fundamental question remains: what ideological positions does popular culture actually express? What kind of power does it construct? And what value judgments does it manifest? These inquiries lie at the heart of understanding popular culture's existential reality. Nevertheless, popular culture astutely establishes its value positions and constructs its power within the boundaries permitted by state laws and policies. While demonstrating rebellious and subversive tendencies toward cultural traditions, mainstream values, and social power structures, it neither poses fundamental threats nor challenges—let

alone forms essential opposition to dominant value systems and sociopolitical frameworks. In reality, popular culture adopts an intermediate stance: expressing middle-class perspectives, petit bourgeois sentiments, and cathartic releases of life's frustrations. These manifestations remain ethically neutral—neither superior nor inferior. Though popular culture may aggressively expand throughout society, state power systems find neither necessity nor justification for intervention. Thus, within the carnivalesque space successfully created by popular culture, political authority undergoes gradual softening.

5. The Mobilization and Catharsis of Social Psychology. Popular culture, saturated with emotional elements, undeniably possesses the capacity to provoke public sentiment through its pathos, satire, and social critique—its sudden popularity inevitably impacts societal stability. The competitive, tense, high-tempo, and crisis-laden nature of modern society has created a psychological state akin to "dark clouds looming over a beleaguered city." With many approaching their breaking points, while conforming to reality, people simultaneously harbor rebellious sentiments. The widespread appeal of popular culture—which emerges from these psychological depths and reflects such rebellious impulses—undeniably mobilizes this collective counter-cultural mentality. However, the phenomenon invariably presents another dimension. As entertainment and carnivalesque revelry constitute defining features of popular culture, its primary function lies in synchronizing masses to its rhythms and sensations—immersing participants in its

manufactured ambiance while subconsciously discouraging critical thought. Consequently, this very capacity for thought-leveling and self-effacement alleviates modern anxieties. The collective catharsis engineered by popular culture unexpectedly generates essential social cohesion and adhesive forces.

The dynamism of popular culture lies precisely in its "liberalization" (including freedom in both content and form) and marketization. By "liberalization," we mean its relative freedom from institutional constraints and its non-adherence to the self-disciplinary principles of mainstream (serious) culture. By "marketization," we refer to its predominant obedience to the dictates of economic market forces—forces which themselves possess inherent blind spots. Therefore, complete laissez-faire toward popular culture is untenable, yet wholesale institutional co-option would inevitably sap its vitality. Moderate guidance and regulation thus present a profoundly challenging dilemma.

Popular culture constitutes both a cultural and social phenomenon—a CT scan revealing societal realities and a mirror reflecting social conditions. As a dynamic force at the forefront of contemporary Chinese society, it provides critical insights when examined through the lenses of mass psychology, social structures, and cultural logic. Understanding its genesis, evolution, functions, transformations, and ultimate trajectories carries threefold significance: (1) facilitating dual perceptual and rational comprehension of modern Chinese society; (2) advancing cultural development; and (3) through proper cultural guidance, fostering healthier cultural ecosystems that contribute harmonious elements to social construction, thereby facilitating the establishment of a harmonious society.

Postscript

Contemporary society distinctly exhibits a hybridity of modern and postmodern characteristics. On one hand, economic globalization continues to deepen, with China experiencing rapid development through its integration into this global framework—the modernization level of its coastal regions now rivals that of Western nations. On the other hand, vast inland and central-western regions remain mid-journey in their modernization trajectories. As Xi Jinping articulated in the 19th CPC National Congress report: "The principal contradiction in Chinese society has evolved into one between unbalanced and inadequate development and the people's ever-growing needs for a better life." This imbalance constitutes a defining characteristic of contemporary China. This imbalance manifests prominently in the spiritual realm through dual dimensions: First, the disparity between material and spiritual development persists. While most citizens have transitioned from basic subsistence to moderate prosperity, their spiritual enrichment fails to keep pace—evidenced by China's reading gap with developed nations, alongside prevalent phenomena like eroded faith, moral decline, and cultural stagnation. Second, internal imbalances within the spiritual domain emerge: refined, pure, and sacred cultural products remain undersupplied, whereas fragmented and vulgarized spiritual consumption proliferates excessively. What exists manifests its own rationale. Without delving into philosophical validation of present realities, we must acknowledge their inevitable refraction through cultural and literary forms—establishing intertextuality with contemporary social conditions.

Chinese literature has undoubtedly evolved alongside the nation's progress, yet whether it truly fulfills public needs, keeps pace with national development, or provides substantial societal support remains a complex question. Notably, Mo Yan's record-breaking Nobel Prize win drew global attention to Chinese literature. As emphasized in Si Jinping' speeches at the Forum on Literature and Art, cultural works play a pivotal role in articulating China's narratives and reshaping its spiritual identity during this historic march toward the Chinese Dream of national rejuvenation. We can confidently assert that national rejuvenation and modernization demand cultural prosperity and revival—requiring literary and artistic works to articulate the renaissance narrative with greater brilliance. Cultural confidence necessitates cultivation through more exemplary classics, for a modern powerhouse requires not only economic might but also cultural soft power. Thus, enhancing cultural productivity and elevating creative quality constitute the paramount responsibility of contemporary cultural practitioners.

"Literary criticism serves as both a mirror and a curative remedy for artistic creation—a vital force that guides creative practice, fosters masterworks, elevates aesthetic discernment, and steers cultural trends." Authentic criticism must maintain close proximity to reality, penetrating both texts and phenomena to decode their signifiers and signifieds, thereby elucidating embedded meanings and diagnosing contemporary symptoms, all while striving for substantive critical impact. As university scholars specializing in literary education within Chinese studies, our mandate is threefold: to guide students in understanding literature, embracing literature, and creating literature. This necessitates immersion in literature's authentic universe—comprehending its "past and present incarnations" and perceiving its essential nature. Such endeavors fundamentally require commencing with textual analysis and concrete phenomena, thereby establishing an unshakable foundation for both pedagogical and scholarly pursuits. In recent years, adhering strictly to this principle, I have endeavored to conduct textual and contextual analyses, imparting such interpretive methodologies to students to cultivate their pathways and techniques for literary comprehension.

This anthology presents selected contemporary textual analyses and critical commentaries, including: literary critiques addressing salient social issues, investigations of Henan's cultural and literary texts/phenomena, and examinations of current cultural specimens. These works collectively reflect my humble perspectives on modern literature and cultural discourse—likely superficial—and I earnestly welcome scholarly critique and correction.

Wu Shenggang

July 16, 2018

At the northern foothills of Xian Mountain

www.ingramcontent.com/pod-product-compliance
Lightning Source LLC
LaVergne TN
LVHW010633110826
845149LV00014B/2840

* 9 7 8 1 9 6 5 8 9 0 8 7 5 *